Tina's Story

Urban Fiction Gone Viral

By

Tina Story

Connect with Me:

Snap Chat: tinas_story

Instagram: readtinasstory

Twitter: tinasstorygroup

Tina's Story Presents

P.O. Box 24029

Cincinnati, OH 45224

www.tinasstory.com

ISBN: 9780692622988

Printed in the United States of America

For my family

&

Everyone in on my Facebook and Instagram pages who supported me!

This is my first book and a major accomplishment for me!!!

Chapter 1

"What are you going to do to me?" Tessa sobbed.

"Whatever the fuck I want!" Mila yelled, taking a long, slow, drag of her joint.

"Bad bitches always get their way. You tried to shade me, and now look at you!"

Mila was known for being a ruthless bitch. Many didn't respect her gangster. They believed she fucked her way to the top.

Mila had a smooth cinnamon complexion and dainty features. Her hair was halfway down her back and it stayed styled to perfection. If it wasn't real, then she damn sure had everyone fooled. The outfits she wore cost more than a stack, not including the diamonds on her ears, neck and wrists. The cherry on top was her round ass and wide hips. She was a brick house and she knew it. Arrogance corroded her mind and had her thinking that she was untouchable.

Mila's heels clicked loudly on the concrete of the basement floor as she walked circles around her prey. "I am not one to be played with!" she said.

Tessa had known of Mila and hoped to never meet her. She looked down at her hands, which were bound with duct tape. Her heart was beating fast and she could barely keep her eyes opened.

"Please don't kill me!" Tessa pleaded, hoping to convince Mila to let her go. "I will never see him again.

Dred told me that you two were over! I would never disrespect you!"

Tessa groveled and begged Mila to let her go. Little did she know, she was dead the moment she was stuffed into the trunk of that all black Lincoln.

Mila dropped her joint on the ground and stepped on it with her five-thousand dollar red bottoms. Her heart was so cold that she never thought twice about the next words coming out of her mouth.

"Kill that bitch!" Mila said calmly, walking up the steps. She never looked back while her goons lit Tessa's body full of bullets.

Mila shut the basement door and reached into her Louie bag for her iPhone. Even that was stylish, with a custom designed case that cost more than the phone it held. She keyed in her man's, Dred's, telephone number.

He didn't yet know that she kidnapped and murdered one of his side pieces. It was the second time this year, and you would think these hoes would have learned by now that he was off limits.

"Hello?" Dred answered, in his deep and sexy voice.

"Bae, let's go out tonight and have some fun!" Mila said, using her softest and most seductive voice.

"I got business to handle tonight. Let's do it this weekend Babe. I will see you when I get home tonight." he said.

Mila was disappointed in him. She knew what his actual plans were tonight. She smirked to herself when she thought about him finding out Tessa was dearly departed.

With an attitude, she sucked her teeth and said, "Okay," before she promptly hung up.

Across town Dred was calling Tessa's phone and getting no answer. He was beginning to get worried because he knew Mila was a vengeful bitch. He had been trying to figure out a way to break it off with her. Dred realized what type of person she was. Although it was good for business, it was not what he wanted out of a wifey. He thought he was going to leave her and be single for a while.

Dred was 6'2" and 220 pounds of chocolate sexiness. He had dreads that hung down to his shoulder blades, not the raggedy unkempt kind, but the well taken care of, fragrant type. His name was David, but most people just called him Dred. He was more handsome than you could even imagine. His full lips were complemented by the whitest smile. Everywhere he went he was approached by women and groupies alike. He was a well-known hustler, a local celebrity. If you ended up in his bed, you were sure to have the night of your life.

Mila hopped in her ride and turned the music on blast. Music was the only thing that could quiet the anger brewing in her heart. She was ungrateful, spoiled and detached from reality. Dred's money had gone to her head, and it was the only thing she cared about besides herself. Mila didn't love Dred honestly. Mila only wanted him for money, status and his mean dick game.

It didn't matter that she was six months pregnant by Dred. She knew that she didn't have enough love for a child. She reasoned that nannies would raise it and she would just be a face in the family pictures. Yesterday she noticed the first stretch mark on her stomach and she spent the whole day angry. Mila grew bitter over how her body would look after she pushed this baby out.

Dred wanted to shop for baby clothes and supplies for his unborn baby girl but Mila, on the other hand, only checked into the procedures she would need to get her body back to normal. Everyone close to her knew that being pregnant was the only way for her to keep Dred in her life. Even she noticed that he no longer looked at her the same way he once did. After he realized that she was an empty shell her beauty couldn't keep him loyal. He started to cheat on her with random women.

Mila slid in and out of traffic on her way home, trying to catch Dred before he left. She almost ran an elderly lady off the road, and laughed hysterically as she passed by and saw the look of horror on the woman's face.

Dred was still parked in the driveway making calls when she pulled in next to him.

Damn, he thought, *ain't nobody got time for this drama. Next time I need to make sure a bitch got some damn sense before I wife her.*

Mila hopped in her ride and turned the music on blast. Music was the only thing that could quiet the anger brewing in her heart. She was ungrateful, spoiled and detached from reality. Dred's money had gone to her head, and it was the only thing she cared about besides herself. Mila didn't love Dred honestly. Mila only wanted him for money, status and his mean dick game.

It didn't matter that she was six months pregnant by Dred. She knew that she didn't have enough love for a child. She reasoned that nannies would raise it and she would just be a face in the family pictures. Yesterday she noticed the first stretch mark on her stomach and she spent the whole day angry. Mila grew bitter over how her body would look after she pushed this baby out.

Dred wanted to shop for baby clothes and supplies for his unborn baby girl but Mila, on the other hand, only checked into the procedures she would need to get her body back to normal. Everyone close to her knew that being pregnant was the only way for her to keep Dred in her life. Even she noticed that he no longer looked at her the same way he once did. After he realized that she was an empty shell her beauty couldn't keep him loyal. He started to cheat on her with random women.

Mila slid in and out of traffic on her way home, trying to catch Dred before he left. She almost ran an elderly lady off the road, and laughed hysterically as she passed by and saw the look of horror on the woman's face.

Dred was still parked in the driveway making calls when she pulled in next to him.

Damn, he thought, *ain't nobody got time for this drama. Next time I need to make sure a bitch got some damn sense before I wife her.*

Chapter 2

"Hey, this is your sister. Pick up the got dang phone! Where are you? We are so worried about you! CALL ME!" said Tina, slamming her phone on the table. She hadn't heard from her sister in five days.

This was not like her at all. Tina could feel in the pit of her stomach that her sister was in danger. Something was wrong. She had never gone this long without talking to her. Tina went to the police and reported Tessa missing on Tuesday. It was now Friday, and no one had a clue where she was.

Tina felt it was time for her to put her ear to the street. She knew her sister had been fucking with that nigga Dred.

Tina told her time after time that he was a dangerous man. The word in the hood was Dred's girl, Mila, was one psycho bitch. Tina thought, *if she fucked with my sister, I'm coming for her ass.*

Tina could barely compose herself to get ready for work. She was a stripper at a gentlemen's club in downtown Cincinnati. She would use her fat ass to get information on this Mila bitch.

At the light she loaded a gun she kept in her glove box and took a deep breath. She did not want to use it, but for some reason she felt that she would have to that night. She could not go another day without finding Tessa. "Hey, this is your sister. Pick up the got dang phone! Where are you? We are so worried about you! CALL ME!" said Tina, slamming her phone on the table. She hadn't heard from her sister in five days.

This was not like her at all. Tina could feel in the pit of her stomach that her sister was in danger. Something was wrong. She had never gone this long without talking to her. Tina went to the police and reported Tessa missing on Tuesday. It was now Friday, and no one had a clue where she was.

Tina felt it was time for her to put her ear to the street. She knew her sister had been fucking with that nigga Dred.

Tina told her time after time that he was a dangerous man. The word in the hood was Dred's girl, Mila, was one psycho bitch. Tina thought, *If she fucked with my sister, I'm coming for her ass.*

Tina could barely compose herself to get ready for work. She was a stripper at a gentlemen's club in downtown Cincinnati. She would use her fat ass to get information on this Mila bitch.

At the light she loaded a gun she kept in her glove box and took a deep breath. She did not want to use it, but for some reason she felt that she would have to that night. She could not go another day without finding Tessa.

After Tina got dressed she looked at herself in the mirror and nodded with approval.

She had a black La Pearla bra and panty set with thigh high fishnet stockings. Tonight she was going to keep it simple and let her body talk for itself.

Tina placed her hand on the door knob and took a deep breath as she turned it. The long hallway leading to the stage was dim, and with each step she took she felt closer to finding her sister.

"Somebody knows something," she muttered to herself, walking through the red satin curtains leading to the club. As soon as she stepped her six inch Monolo Blanik into the room she began twerking like there was no tomorrow. There was a feature girl dancing on the stage, but Tina was clearly stealing her shine. Soon half the room was looking at her rolling her hips and swinging her ass from side to side.

Tina made eye contact with the men. They thought she was being seductive, but for Tina it was game time and she was scanning the room for anyone connected to Dred.

She strutted her way to the V.I.P., ignoring the men as they were drooling over her and asking for private dances. Tina stopped at the stairs of the V.I.P. area. Her nerves were starting to get to her. *What if Carlos didn't show up tonight? What if her sister wasn't really missing and she just ran off for a breather?* The last thought she was able to immediately toss out the window. Tessa was very predictable, and she never kept a secret from Tina.

"There is no way she would sky up and not tell me," she exclaimed to herself. The bitter reality hit her with the strongest force. *Something is definitely wrong!*

With that thought she looked up and immediately made eye contact with non-other than Carlos. Tina smiled at him as thoughts of mayhem danced around her head. *I will fuck Dred's whole crew up if my sister don't fucking turn up safe.* She walked seductively over to Carlos and stopped within inches of his face.

"Hey baby, you are so damn fine," she whispered into his ear, knowing her voice would mesmerize him.

"No, that's you Babe. Let me see what you working with!" Carlos replied, anxious to finally be this close to Tina.

He never stopped to wonder why she never seemed so into him before. He felt like a Boss with her coming straight to him. He had been watching her from the moment she walked into the room. She was the baddest female in here. It had even crossed his mind that maybe he could wife this bitch and change her life.

Tina pushed Carlos back into his seat forcefully. She turned around and started to move slowly, winding her hips to the rhythm and putting her ass on his face.

Tina looked over her shoulder and mouthed, "You want to come home with me, baby?"

Little did he know that by the end of the night he would not be thinking about saving Tina, he would need someone to save his ass.

Chapter 3

Tina wrapped her arm around Carlos as he staggered towards his cherry red Lexus. The parking lot was still thick, and the cool air breezed through her hair. It was needed after leaving that hot ass place.

A black car recklessly turned into the parking lot as they were half way across the lot. The car came to a screeching halt in front of Tina and Carlos. The black tinted window came down slowly.

"Oh shit, Mila! What's up queen?" Carlos slurred.

"Get yo ass home nigga. Aye yo, Dred in there?" Mila asked, rolling her eyes.

"Ummm," Carlos hesitated. He knew Mila well.

"Bye Nigga. I'll take that as a 'yes!'" Mila smacked.

Mila sped off and Tina was on fire! *Yea, this bitch thinks she way up. Let shit be off with my sister,* Tina thought. She felt the need to get this nigga back to the crib more than ever. Before they left she stopped by her locker and the dressing room and picked up her back pack, A.K.A., kidnap kit. She thought, *Sis I will find you!*

Mila sat in her car outside of the club rolling a joint as she watched Tina and Carlos pull out of the parking lot. *Damn she look familiar,* she thought. *Where have I seen this bitch?*

She blew one, thinking about her relationship with Dred. Mila thought back to the first time she tried to murk Dred ass.

She made him sushi rolls for dinner. Mila laughed at her own joke. *Like really, that shit was poison rolls.* Dred never liked her food, and he knew she couldn't cook. He put his plate under the table and let their dog, Curtains, eat that shit. She would never forget them going to bed that night and how she planned out her reaction to his death. Bright and early she arose to Dred still breathing. *WHAT THE FUCK!* Mila ran down the stairs to get a drink when she noticed the dog was dead on the kitchen floor.

"Baby," Dred called.

"Oh shit, oh shit!" Mila chanted, stuffing the dog into a trash bag, and running out the side door.

Looking back, she thought it was hilarious. She was too cold to even show love for a pet they raised for years.

Mila sat in her car outside of the club rolling a joint as she watched Tina and Carlos pull out of the parking lot. *Damn she look familiar*, she thought. *Where have I seen this bitch?*

She blew one, thinking about her relationship with Dred. Mila thought back to the first time she tried to murk Dred ass.

She made him sushi rolls for dinner. Mila laughed at her own joke. *Like really, that shit was poison rolls.* Dred never liked her food, and he knew she couldn't cook. He put his plate under the table and let their dog, Curtains, eat that shit. She would never forget them going to bed that night and how she planned out her reaction to his death. Bright and early she arose to Dred still breathing. *WHAT THE FUCK!* Mila ran down the stairs to get a drink when she noticed the dog was dead on the kitchen floor.

"Baby," Dred called.

"Oh shit, oh shit!" Mila chanted, stuffing the dog into a trash bag, and running out the side door.

Looking back, she thought it was hilarious. She was too cold to even show love for a pet they raised for years.

***

Dred walked his sexy ass towards Mila's car. *Damn, why the fuck she here?* He went out in hopes to stop by Tessa's house afterwards. *Why she ain't returning my phone calls?*

Tessa told Dred that she was unhappy with his lifestyle and wanted more out of life. He could respect it, though, because he did too. He had begun to think she was done with him. The funniest part was he could not figure out why he cared so much.

Damn, I'm slipping, he thought, *I'm really feeling her ass. I'm having her*, he resolved. He would put a hood A.P.B. out for her ass if she did not answer her door.

Each step toward Mila's car drained more and more of his energy. *Fuck that*, he thought, making a B line for his own whip.

"Hey Bae!!!"Mila yelled, getting out the car.

Damn, he thought. He was the master of ignoring a mother fucker. He pretended not to hear her as he pressed toward his car.

Mila, unwilling to look desperate, got back in her car, pissed!

"It's O.K. babe. I'll see you tonight. I'm ready to take the throne. You won't see the fucking light of day!" she promised.

As Dred caught a glimpse of Mila looking pissed off, he thought, *she done. She gotta get the fuck out!!*

Chapter 4

Tina walked out of the bathroom with the nine in her waist. In the kitchen Carlos was on a call. She began to walk slowly so she could listen in on his conversation.

"What... Bro, sure. Come through. My house is yours. Mi casa, su casa, nigga!" Carlos said.

Damn, what the hell! She thought. Tina slowly slid her piece back into her bag.

"Hey sexy. My nigga Dred need to stay the night. His female tripping." he said.

Damn, is this good news or bad news? Can I take both these niggas? She thought. Dred was definitely the one that was the best source.

Hell yea, she thought, *let his ass come on*.

Carlos looked Tina over, *damn, for real, she my fucking type*! He watched Tina as she bent over and set her bags down, her round ass cheeks spreading apart.

"Can I have a tour of the place?" she asked.

"Yeah grab yo drink, let's start upstairs," Carlos said, *looking fine as hell*.

"Na, I wanna start at the bottom and move up," Tina said.

"Hell nah. I don't feel like going down there right now. Who starts a tour in the basement?"

"Come on babe, I know there are a wine cellar and a pool table down in that bitch!" She said, rubbing her breasts on his arm.

She knew his team was notorious for a basement beat down. It was a long shot, but shit, she was desperate. The blade she had in her bra was subject to disrespect his neck if he made one fowl move.

"Ok, let's go downstairs then." he said, giving in.

As they walked down stairs, Tina's heart started to beat fast. *Look at this big ass house... What are they doing taking that cash? What if this nigga Dred so caked out he flew her to a spa*, she thought over and over again? *Hell no, she would take me.* Inside, it was a battle.

As they walked down the steps, Carlos phone began to ring again. *Damn*, she thought, *this nigga got the hotline bling.*

"Don't answer that," she said, hanging off his arm.

"One second, sexy. I got to, it's family." he said.

Trying to be nosy, Tina continued to hang on to his shoulder as he started his conversation.

"Los! Where Dred! He wit you?" Mila asked.

"Nah, he not with me," he laughed. *She starting to get weird*, he thought.

"Well, at least I know that nigga not with that Tessa bitch. Thanks for handling that for me." Mila sang, happy that hoe was dead.

It took everything for Tina to compose herself. Venom shot through her veins. *Is she dead?*

Tina wanted to scream, and she wanted to kill Los right then and there!

Los could feel Tina's grip tighten on his shoulder. *She must be ready for a nigga to lay the pipe. She all over me. She feel these muscles. Man, I'm that nigga!*

Tessa, my sis, my everything, she thought, fighting back tears. *All three of them have less than 24 hours to live. I wanna know where her body at!* she thought, angrily.

Tina's mind was racing and her years of stripping at that moment started to come in handy. She was about to put on the performance of a lifetime.

Boom! Boom! Boom!

"Damn, that's my boy at the door. We will finish this tour later. Babe, this will all be yours one day anyway!" he said, half joking, half thinking maybe.

Tina forced a smile on her face, "You might be right about that!" she said playfully.

Tina met Dred before and she wondered if he would recognize her. As much as she favored Tessa, she still had her own look and her own style. Tessa was the good girl out of the two, and her trusting ways kept Tina getting her out of shit, though.

When the door opened Dred looked at Los and this fine ass female he had standing in the shadows behind him. He could not see her face, but he thought there was no way she could be ugly with a shape like that. Dred closed the front door behind him as he started to complain about Mila.

No one noticed Tina sneak over to her bag. They had started talking shit to each other on the way to the kitchen.

"Put your FUCKING hands in the air!" she yelled.

Los and Dred turned around to find Tina with tears streaming down her face.

"Where the FUCK is she?!!!!!" Tina demanded.

"Ahh shit!! What the fuck you doing? YOU KNOW WHO YOU FUCKING WITH?!!!" Los screamed.

Dred immediately recognized Tina, and just like that, his smart ass pieced together a fucking jigsaw puzzle in his mind. Tessa, Tina.... MILA!!!!

"Shut the fuck up you asshole! You think I really fucking want you? I don't want you! I'm here to find out what the fuck happened to my sister, BITCH!" she screamed.

"Tina, I been looking for her. I JUST LEFT HER HOUSE!" Dred breathed.

Dred looked at Carlos, "Did you have something to do with this nigga? Who the fuck you take your orders from now? I did NOT give orders to MERK anybody! Where she at dog? She dead? Is she dead?!" Dred questioned.

Mila was ruthless, but Dred was a straight up fucking killer! He was what some niggas called a killer with a heart, a gentleman's gentleman. A high class ass no joke ass nigga.

Carlos let out a deep breath before he spoke and thought, *Good thing I kept her ass alive.*

Chapter 5

Five days ago.....

Tessa screamed with all her heart as the men began to open fire on her. She heard the bullet's hitting the wall behind her. Her heart beat hastened as her life flashed before her eyes. She was terrified of taking her last breath. The fear of knowing that it was her time to die gripped her. She began to pray with everything in her.

She was beaten, weak and a little disoriented. Before she knew it the bullet's stopped. *Am I dead?* She asked herself. *Wait, I'm still here. I'm still here*, she sobbed.

"Hey Bitch, hold up your head. We going to have a little fun with you first." said one of the men.

She screamed and fought as they began to untie her from the chair.

"Ohhh wee, look at this bitch! I been wanting this. I been watching you with Dred!" said another man.

"Get her ass in the trunk. I'm taking her home!" Los laughed.

His boys grumbled. They wanted to have some fun with her.

"Nah, fuck that. This *my* shit now!" said Carlos wanna be Dred ass.

Tessa was gagged and hog tied in the back of Carlos' all black, Lincoln truck. They were professionals. They tied her down so tight she could barely move.

All she could do was think about how she regretted the day she first met Dred. Tessa fell for him, no doubt. Besides his street life, he was everything she ever wanted. Now her love for him was turning into hate, and no dick was worth this.

She thought about her sister, Tina. She didn't know if she would ever see her again.

True, she was still alive, but for how long, she didn't know. Her stomach did flips as she felt the car slow to a halt. The trunk opened and she looked at the four niggas standing above her. The worst part about it was she knew all of them.

They were Dred's workers and his right hand man, Los.

Los grabbed her out of the trunk and threw her over his shoulder like a rag doll.

He smacked her on her ass and said, "Welcome home!!!"

Tessa tried to make out her location, but it was very dark outside. This was her worst nightmare come true, and as he carried her through those double doors, she cried and thought, *Will, I make it out alive?*

Tessa could not kick or punch. She could only squirm as his boys helped him carry her down the stairs. She continued to pay attention to her surroundings, and the house was so huge. Once they got into the basement, she saw Los bend over and move the rug on the floor.

"Oh, fuck no!" she said, trying to break out. The gag was so tight on her mouth her lips felt numb.

Under the carpet was a door. As he opened the door she got a quick glimpse inside. It was a room the size of an upright coffin.

Her skin crawled. This room scared her more than death did. She was powerless. As they began to lower her into the small room, she fainted.

"Hell yea! That's my hiding spot just in case shit pop off, ya dig!" Carlos laughed, closing the door and replacing the carpet.

"I knew that she would come in handy one day." he said.

They all laughed and joked their way up the stairs – no remorse, no sympathy and no love.

Chapter 6

Dred reached into his pocket so fast that Tina had no time to react.

Before they knew it he had his gun at Los' temple. See, he was starting to love Tessa and he knew she did not deserve whatever was happening to her. But even more than that, the pure disrespect Carlos showed him had his mind blown.

"You don't touch what's mine nigga. Where the FUCK is she!? he demanded.

"Mila!" Los stuttered, "It was her, she made me do it!"

"WHERE IS SHE!?" Tina screamed. Tina knew Mila was behind this shit, that bitch is certified nuts. Revenge is mine!

Los hung his head and muttered, "Downstairs!"

"WHAT DA FUCK!!!" Dred shouted, digging the nozzle into his forehead.

"DOWNSTAIRS!" Los screamed. He was trembling. The night took a turn for the worst and he knew he was dead. There was no way Dred would forgive this.

Tina bawled. She had to compose herself, but her mind was spinning.

At the same time, both Tina and Dred lost their cool and opened fire on Carlos' lame ass. The bullet's riddled his body. His ass was dead before he even hit the floor.

"I know his hiding spot, come on." Dred said, rushing toward the basement, grabbing Tina's hand.

Tina cried and ran down the stairs right behind Dred. With her head still pounding, ears ringing, she was starting to think she was going into shock.

"Tessa!" she screamed, "Can you hear me?"

Dred ran over to the black carpet in the far left corner of the massive basement. He hurriedly ripped the carpet off the floor, uncovering the black square trapped door.

Tina immediately fell to the floor, grabbed the handle and threw the door open.

Once she saw what was inside, Tina let out the most gut wrenching scream, "AAAAAAAAAHHHHHHH!!!!"

In the small room Tessa was crouched down in the corner with a bowl of water next to her like a common dog. She was beaten, bloody and naked. She could barely lift her head. Her long, natural hair covered her face. Her breathing was labored and the room smelled of piss.

"Call 911!" Tina screamed.

Dred reached his massive arms into to the hole and pulled Tessa out with ease.

"What the fuck? What the Fuck? WHAT THE FUCK?!!" Tina yelled.

"We can't call the police, remember?" Dred said calmly.

Tessa was completely passed out. Tina held her and cried in pain and for joy. At least she was alive. The more she thought about it, the stronger she got.

At least she was alive.

Dred got on his phone, "Yayo, get the chopper over to Los crib. Now, Code 19 nigga. Get Doc ready!"

Dred scooped Tessa out of Tina's arms and held her like a baby.

"Let's head upstairs. I got help coming." The wind whipped the trees as the noisy ass chopper landed in the grass outside of Los' house.

The wait felt like hours as Tina questioned Dred.

"So, I believe that you had nothing to do with this, but this shit came from your camp. Your girl Mila, you know she dead, right? You KNOW on sight her ass dead, right?" she said.

Tina's beautiful eyes filled to their capacity with tears. She wrapped the comforter tight around Tessa's neck. They sat on the back patio to wait. Tina could not stand to be in that house for another minute.

"You can't kill her." Dred said.

"I CAN and I WILL!" Tina yelled. She was slighted by his last comment. It took her back, *where is he taking us?* she thought.

"She's Pregnant." Dred said quietly, sounding troubled, but composed. "After my daughter is delivered, do whatever you want to her. I can't let you kill my daughter." Dred paused. "Trust me. I don't have a need to lie to you... I hate her, and if I don't get rid of her soon, she will be my downfall."

They were just finishing that conversation when they spotted the helicopter. Tessa was loaded in first, and then Dred and Tina climbed in after her.

They were in the city in no time. The helicopter landed on the top of the penthouse floor in one of the most sought after buildings in downtown Cincinnati.

"This is my doctor," Dred said to Tina. He spoke through the head phones in the chopper. He continued, "She will be fine."

Chapter 7

Tessa opened her eyes to see a bright light around her. *Is this heaven?* she thought. As her eyes began to focus she could see the sunlight streaming in through the windows in the oversized bedroom.

She had no clue where she was. There was an IV in her arm and a heart rate monitor next to her. Finally, Tessa's eyes settled on to her sister.

One moment she was in the dark in that room, and the next she is here with her sister. "What the fuck just happened?" Tessa asked.

***

Mila could not believe Dred did not come home last night. She sat back and thought that maybe she shouldn't kill him, and maybe they could work it out. Dred not coming home last night made her feel some type of way.

Maybe I should have this baby first, she thought.

"Naaaa, this nigga gotta GO!" She said. "I am going to put a bullet to his head or should I try to....."

Outside Mila's room, in the hallway, the maid heard every word she said. She quietly shuffled to the closet and got her coat and keys. Once she was downstairs she ran out of the house and straight to her car.

The maid closed her car door and took deep breath, then exhaled, "I fucking QUIT!"

***

Dr. Bruce was a fine ass middle-aged doctor. He kind of put you in the mind of Richard Gere in the movie *Pretty Woman*. He was a private doctor to the richest people in the city. Dred used his services often.

The doctor's Penthouse was set up like a small hospital with the best technology money could buy.

"She's traumatized and dehydrated, but she will be fine. I need to keep her for observation for at least 24 hours."

Dred thanked the doctor for his help while handing him an envelope full of crisp one hundred dollar bills.

"Take good care of her Doc, I love her." Dred said seriously to him.

Dred opened Tessa's room door to find her and Tina hugging and crying.

That's real love, he thought. He wished he had that kind of love in his life. Hopefully, one day, Tessa would be that for him.

He stood by the door and let the sisters have their moment.

When Tessa saw Dred she felt a wave of different emotions. She was angry, yet happy. She did not know how to react to him.

As he came closer she could smell his cologne. Tessa felt a warm wave of anticipation sweep over her body with each step he took.

Damn, she thought, *I still want him.* Should she blame him for Mila? Could she?

Dred shushed her as she started to speak.

"Not right now, just rest. I need to go change clothes. Finish up with Tina. I will be right back." He said, putting his hand on her cheek. "You don't have to respond right now, but I love you and everything is going to change. I promise." He kissed her battered and swollen face.

He tried to keep his composure. Although he would not be merking Mila just yet, he planned to find out who in his crew was taking her orders. Who in the fuck was keeping secrets? There would be a crime wave today, bodies were going to drop. That, he knew for sure.

As he closed the door behind him, Tina was right on his ass.

"What do you plan to do?" She asked. "I want parts! I saw the look in your eye."

"Nah, stay here with her," Dred said in his usual calm demeanor.

"She is tired. She is almost dozing off. She will be safe here." Tina responded.

"Naaa-" He said.

Tina cut him off mid rejection. "Right now who can you trust besides me? No FUCKING body! Now let's change clothes and find the other three niggas my sister just told me about."

Chapter 8

Dred was smooth, calculating and charming. He was forming a plan in his head to set all this shit straight.

In the passenger seat of his crispy ass black Audi Tina was thinking of her own Master Plan. *This nigga talking about don't kill her ass. Ion know, the jury's still out on that. She deserves it. Ion know how to feel about her ass. Somebody need to get her wack ass off the streets A.S.A.P.*

Tina had an intense look on her face. Dred could tell she was still deep in thought.

Tina looked at the clouds and the sun hit her face. She was alive. The thought hit her so hard she almost said it out loud. She could handle her business with a clear mind. She had been stripping for that long money, but for real, she was polished and she was built to be a part of Dred's team.

Shit, if he gonna be with my sister, there is nothing wrong with a female chief of staff, Tina thought, chuckling to herself.

The first hit would be an easy one, Dred thought. He knew exactly where to find Printer's fat ass. As they cruised the street he decided to share part one of his plan with Tina.

"Alright T, this nigga don't get the easy way out. Straight gruesome for his ass. I own a building around the corner from the Chicken Spot. Imma drop you off there. Imma go get this nigga and bring him there. You wait inside with the strap. Point that shit at the door until we get there," Dred explained.

"That's it? Cool, but the next one dies my way." Tina snapped.

He dropped her off at the spot and she was shocked as hell when she walked inside. This was a dope ass contemporary designed ass apartment in the middle of the fucking hood. There were black leather couches and two flat screens on one wall, with expensive ass rugs and black out curtains.

"Damn, this the shit… This nigga got that Oprah money." Tina said.

The feature of the apartment that stood out the most was the big ass fish tank that spanned a wall and divided the two rooms.

"Damn, that's dope!" She said. *Who decorated this shit? Dizzam*, she thought. Tina sat on the couch and made herself comfortable as she pointed her strap at the door just as she instructed.

A few minutes later she saw the door knob turn and in walked this big fat greasy ass lamp shade head ass nigga, with Dred close behind him.

As Printer stumbled in the room he said, "Damn Dred, you got a new guard dog?" He laughed.

Oh, this big ugly ass nigga touched my sister. Ugh, got damn I would not even dance on him at the club. Dude straight shitty. She started to see red, and before she knew it her finger was gripping the trigger just a little tighter.

Dred said to Printer, "What's up my nigga? Have a seat. Let me get you a drink. You thirsty?"

Dred's white ass smile was on fleek. He and Tina started to grin. This nigga was a walking inside joke.

Printer replied, "Yeah, I'll take a drink Boss!"

He was excited, thinking Dred had good news for him. *Yeah, looks like yo boy getting promoted!! I could use the extra paper.*

Dred handed him a drink and watched as he took it back whole.

Dred raised his eye brows and said, "Damn."

Just that quickly Printer fell off his chair and onto the floor.

"Dred, man I can't feel my legs, call 911!" said Printer.

Tina started to clap, "Nigga, that shit was brilliant. You froze his ass in his body. Oh, this some movie shit."

Before Printer knew it he could not even talk anymore. He was left only with his thoughts, hearing and sight. He began to try and piece together what was up.

Tina bent over and whispered to Printer, "You know ole girl you put in the hole in the basement? That was my sister!!!"

She kicked him dead in his face and he didn't even flinch. She grew angrier that this nigga could not feel his body.

"Dred man, I am starting to think you fucked this up. How am I gonna beat his ass if he numb?" Tina snapped.

"This is my turn, remember? This how I do shit, watch and learn." He laughed.

He went to the bathroom and filled the tub up with water.

"Help me roll his ass back there," He asked Tina, walking back into the living room.

"This big burly ass nigga? You tryna make me throw my back out?" Tina joked.

As they rolled him, laughed and talked shit to Printer, Tina wanted him to know that he was about to get fucked up.

Tina watched as Dred ran over to the massive fish tank. With his net he began to remove certain fish and throw them into a bucket that he got from under the sink.

"What the FUCK? What are thooooossseee?" Tina yelled.

"Piranhas!" Dred said, and then he stuck out his tongue, mocking Tina.

"Got emmmmmmm!!!" she said.

They put his ass in the tub filled with Piranhas and rolled a joint as they began to eat Printer ass alive.

"Dammmn," Tina said. "That was some Saw type shit. Oh yea, you officially my brother now! Let's get the fuck out of here, this shit is gross!"

Tina hopped in the ride with a big ass Kool-aide smile.

"OK, who next? I need details on dude." she said.

"Fooley," Dred said. "He been with me for years, but after this I can't trust his ass no more. He is a little higher up the ranks than Printer"

"Fooley?!!!" Tina exclaimed. "WHAAAA, hold up, I know this dude from my job… He stay in the strip joints."

And he fine as hell too, she thought. *Dude obviously got ends too, he fly as shit.*

"So, what's up your sleeve Miss Lady?" Dred said, looking over at Tina grinning.

"Take me to my Crib, I need to get changed!" Tina said, feeling excited.

Dred waited in the car listening to music as Tina ran inside for a quick change. When she walked back out the house she had a clean ass white crop top and fitted black circle skirt. Her hair was pulled back into a sleek genie pony tail with a perfect face beat!

Her Zanotti Guiseppe Cruel heeled sandals hugged her feet and made her look like a certified diamond!

"Damn, what the fuck she up to!" Dred said.

"Alright, you got his location yet bro?" Tina said, sliding into the passenger seat.

"Yea, this nigga at the fucking underground swinger spot." Dred said coolly. "This nigga a straight horn dog."

As those words left his lips he wondered if Fooley ever touched Tessa. The thought had him shaken. He almost wanted to save him for last. Tina was already in character, so he decided to stay on course.

"That I know, and that's why I am going to be the bait." Tina winked.

"Alright, let's get something to eat first. It's 5:30 and I haven't even had lunch yet." Dred said.

After they left from getting a bite to eat they headed in Foley's direction. They pulled up to the spot and Dred let the valet park his car.

"W.T.F. Since when do the sex party got Valet?" Tina asked.

"This spot exclusive, not just anyone can walk they raggedy ass up in here." said Dred.

When she stepped foot into the foyer she could not believe her eyes. She was used to the scene, but not on a million-dollar level.

"Well, looky here!" Fooley said as he approached Dred from the back.

"What up family," Dred said very lowly.

He was not a fake type of nigga. He would have to use discipline to keep this fake ass smile on his face.

"Hiiiiii!" Tina said, singing in Fooley's ear. Her breath smelled like fruit as she purposely blew on his neck.

"Damn!" he said under his breath.

"This you, Dred?" Fooley asked.

"Nah, this a business partner of mine," Dred said, knowing that it would increase Tina's beauty in Fooley's eyes.

"Hey, come here, let's talk," Fooley said, grabbing Tina by her waist.

"Catch you later D. I'll meet you at the spot," Tina said.

Dred had no clue what fucking spot she was talking about. The one they just left, maybe? *I am gonna have to follow her ass around here. She sharp, but she new to this shit.*

When Tina and Fooley found a seat they began flirting heavily. He tried to put his hand under her skirt.

"No, not in here. This too out there for me. If you want these goodies, let's go somewhere else more private. I'm wild though, so it's still gonna be mad exciting!" she said.

"Oh, you wild baby?" Fooley asked. "What you have in mind?"

"I always wanted to fuck at the Look Out Park, you know they call it Lover's Lane," Tina said in her sweetest "give me what I want" voice.

Fooley looked like a fucking model. He was damn near perfect, but not as handsome as Dred, though. He reminded Tina of Tyrese's sexy ass. That shit was pointless to her now. Stick a fork in this nigga, he done!

Tina stood up and purposely dropped her purse so she could bend over in his face.

"Damn, I'm game, let's go." he said.

Dred was watching from the other side of the room. He ran to the valet and asked for his car when he saw them heading toward the door. Since he was the top nigga there his shit was sitting right up front. He sat in the whip waiting to follow where ever they went.

His phoned beeped and it was a text from Tina that said:

Lovers Lane

Hell yeah, Dred thought. *She on point.* He sped off in the direction of "Look Out Park."

As Tina gave her sexiest walk toward Fooley's car she could feel the anger brewing within her.

Her mind shot back to her sister in that fucking pit!

"Fucking BITCH!" she said under her breath.

"What?" Fooley asked.

"Nothing I just saw somebody I think I know," Tina lied. She pulled her purse close to her as she got into his car.

They had small talk on the way to the park. He was so fucking aggressive. He kept grabbing her breasts and legs. She was disgusted.

On their way to Los' crib they had stopped by one of Dred's ducked off properties so he could change. He wanted to go check on Tessa after this.

"See, I am always prepared, nigga. I was the best Girl Scout in my troop!" said Tina, pulling gloves out of her backpack.

"I said I am not touching this nigga," Dred laughed, grabbing some extra rope out of the back seat.

Fooley was in shock. "This is a Dred hit! I am fucking dead," he said. Just as he had that thought, he and Dred locked eyes. Dred showed his fresh white smile and winked as he tied the extra rope to Fooley's already tied arms.

"Yo, what you doing?" Tina asked.

"I am going to drag his ass!" Dred said, grinning.

She looked at Fooley, smiling hard. PAYBACK TIME! Fooley couldn't talk. He could only look and mumble. The gag was tied super tight in his mouth. Dred tied him up in the same method he taught Fooley back in the day. He knew that if he struggled it would only make the ropes tighter.

"AHHHHAHHHH Bro!! You the da shit!!!" she said, hitting the Quan.

She stuck her tongue out at Fooley as they began to pull the rope and drag his ass towards the house. They pulled him passed Los' dead body, down into the basement, all the way over to the black trap door. This was the same small room where Tessa spent her days while she was missing.

Tina held the pistol to Fooley head while Dred began cutting the ropes to untie him.

"Don't move, nigga!" Tina yelled. "You put my sister in this bitch!! You put my FUCKING SISTER IN THIS GOT DAMN HOLE!!!"

Tina's blood was boiling; she was losing her cool. The more she saw that fucking hole the more enraged she became.

POWWW!

"Aw, hell nah!!" Dred yelled, covering his ears.

Fooley screamed in pain as he felt the hot slug hit his leg.

Tina felt a release as she shot him.

"Aw hell nah, MY FIT. T, this was custom." Dred said calmly. He was light weight pissed, but as he looked at the pit he knew why she reacted like that. He knew he could not be mad at her. He respected the love she had for Tessa. He knew she was a loyal, down ass bitch.

"Fuck it, throw his ass in there." Dred said.

They both tossed him in the hole as he screamed in pain. They closed the door on his ass and locked it.

"What now?" Dred asked.

"That's it, he gonna die in that bitch!" Tina said.

"Cold fucking blooded!" Dred said, smiling to himself.

They put the carpet back over the door and headed back upstairs.

"Alright, where the third nigga at? We gonna tag team his ass," Tina sung, opening Los' refrigerator.

"Third one is going to be a little more complicated," Dred said, walking into the kitchen.

"We unstoppable, FUCK that! This nigga going down, down, baby, BOOM boom, baby cocked, ready to let it go," Tina sung, fucking up Nelly's song.

"He's Souped's best friend," Dred said, staring off into space.

"Who is Souped?" Tina asked. She could tell Dred was serious.

"My brother." he responded.

Dred and Tina bobbed their heads in the studio as Souped slayed the hook to his newest street anthem.

"Cruzing through the streets fresh all the time, bad ass bitches with my dick on they mind. They crave a nigga like me, Ion gotta beat. My dick stay serviced by a muthafuckin freak!

"Get low or Get lost Bih, owww, Get low or Get lost, I ain't got the time unless she a dime, Nigga like me keep that pocketbook fine, Get low or get lost!" Souped rapped into the Mic.

"Damn, I can't believe Souped is his brother," Tina said under her breath. When he first said his name she was so caught up in anger that it took her a second to recognize his name.

Souped was sexy as fuck. 6'2" like Dred, same built, wide ass sexy back. He had a fade so crispy it looked like the barber just cut him a few minutes ago.

"Got damn!" Tina said. This nigga will make a bitch bust one. "Aye, I need a double date A.S.A.P." she said.

"I am getting ready to holla at him about this shit. He's been his boy for a while, so I really can't call how he will react. We don't like disloyal niggas, though, and ultimately this shit ain't up for debate," Dred said, always smooth, always in control.

Souped saw his bro and immediately came out of the booth. That was his ace boon. If it were not for Dred, he wouldn't know how his life would have turned out.

"Bro, let me talk to you in private for a second," Dred said as Souped approached him.

Oh fuck, Souped thought when he caught a glimpse of Tina.

"Alright bro, this you?" he asked.

"Nah, this my new right hand," Dred said.

When Tina and Souped shook hands she felt a spark shoot through her whole body. When they locked eyes she knew right then and there he felt that shit too.

Damn, Tina thought. *What's a girl to do?*

Souped flashed the brightest, sexiest smile he could muster. He thought something was really different about that girl.

Chapter 9

Mila circled the parking lot slowly looking for the hottest whip in the parking lot.

She knew for damn sure he would not be in a fucking minivan.

"What the fuck? These dusty cars, ughhh!" Mila said, pushing her hair out of her face.

BUZZZ BUZZZZZZ.

Mila grabbed her cell phone, thinking it was Dred. Her screen flashed the name "Bear."

What the fuck this nigga want?

"Hello!" Mila snapped.

"Aye, I'm at Los' Crib he dead!!!!" Bear said, trembling in his fucking boots.

"Why the fuck you calling me? Call Dred. As a matter of fact, I'll call him my damn self!!" She said as she began to hang up.

"Wait, there's more… You know that bitch that you had in the basement? We didn't kill her!" Bear said. He rehearsed this conversation five times before he called her.

"What you mean?" Mila screamed like a maniac.

"We took her to Los' house to have some more fun, and she was in the pit he always bragging about in his basement. I just went to check on her and she's missing."

"She's WHAT?!!" Mila scream. "You fucking idiots!"

"Fooley was in the pit!" he whispered.

"SPEAK YO ASS UP!!! WHAT!!??" Mila said, putting her car in reverse.

"She nowhere to be found. Fooley in the fucking pit. He shot but he still alive. Should I call Doc?!!?" he responded.

"No! DON'T DO SHIT UNTIL I GET THERE! You hear me you FUCKTARD!!!" Mila screamed. The kids at the bus stop all looked in her direction. The light changed and she sped off to Los' house.

"Put Fooley on the phone, ASAP." Mila growled.

"I can't, he passed out. I don't know what the fuck happened!" Bear yelled.

Mila Pulled up outside of Los' house and called Doc. "I wanna know what the fuck happened," she said.

"Doc, my cousin just got shot. I am bringing him to you now!" she said on the phone.

Mila thought, *good thing there is a fucking Doctor on payroll*, and she ended the call.

"Bear!" she yelled as she was getting out of her ride.

He came running to the door.

"Get Fooley in the car now!!! I wanna be there when he wakes up. We taking his ass to Doc," she said, hurriedly.

"What about Los body?" he asked.

"We can handle that in the morning. Come THE FUCK onnnnn!"

Bear hauled Fooley's bloody body in the car. He looked bad, but his heart was still beating. He closed the back door and grabbed the handle to get in the passenger side.

"Naaah nigga, you stay here till I sort this shit out!!" Mila said, being mean as fuck. He wondered how such a bad bitch on the outside could be straight nuts like that.

Bear turned to walk back into the house. He ain't say shit. He knew better than to argue with Mila.

As soon as Mila saw Bear's back, she pulled out her pistol and shot Bear point blank through the open window in the back of his head. His body hit the ground like a sack of potatoes.

She cackled as she sped off to Doc's Penthouse.

"What the fuck you MEAN 'kill him, Bear though?' Come on now, that's like family to me!" Souped said. He is Dred's younger brother and fucking rap superstar.

"No nigga, I'm like family to you. You got to see that nigga for what he is! We came here just to let you know we gotta merk him" Dred shot back. "Have I ever steered you wrong? I know what the fuck I'm talking about. It's not just this shit he pulled! This nigga been doing dumb shit, he just never stepped on my toes before!"

"24 hours, man. Give it 24 hours!" Souped asked, "for me nigga, your brother."

"I will give it 24 hours, that's it," Dred said, walking out of the room.

Souped thought how much he was feeling shorty in the studio. *Fuck that*, he said thought, *my nigga in danger. I need to get this nigga a new I.D. and get him out of the city fast as fuck.*

"Alright D, I gotta go find this nigga!" Souped said, grabbing his coat and rushing down the stairs where his driver parked outside. He paid his driver extra to stay parked right up front everywhere he went. The haters in the city were at an all-time high and sometimes the studio could be the most dangerous place to be.

As he got into the backseat Tina's pretty smile flashed in his mind. He pulled out his phone and texted Dred:

What's ole girl you wit number?

He told the driver to head to Bear's crib. He thought this nigga would be there.

Souped pulled up outside of Bear's crib, feeling light weight sick. *Why the fuck you cross Dred my nigga? I told his ass he better be all in before he joined up with him. What the fuck did he do? Dred was one of the coolest, fairest street niggas out here*, he thought, knocking on the door.

He wasn't surprised, for real, when no one answered the door. He tried his phone, but it was dead. It kept going straight to voicemail. He's been hanging with Los lately. He called Los' phone too, and got no answer.

"They probably together," he said, heading to his car.

"Homie take me to Los' Crib," he told the driver.

Souped looked out the window behind the tinted windows of the all black Cadillac Truck.

As his driver turned into Los' U-shaped driveway, Souped could see a man lying on the ground.

"Huh, What the FUCK?!!" he exclaimed.

As he got out of his car he let out a loud ass wail, falling to his knees on the pavement when he realized it was Bear. *What happened to you my nigga?* he thought.

Souped knew off top it was not Dred. His brother had never once lied to him, EVER. Something was going down and he had no fucking clue what it was.

He wiped the tears off of his face as he called Dred.

Mila pulled into the underground parking lot right next to Doc's private elevator, which led straight up to the top floor.

Chapter 10

Mila called Doc to send an order down to get Fooley out of her car.

She did not know if he was going to make it. Her back seat was bloody as fuck.

This nigga gonna pay to clean my car if he makes it. Dumb ass, she thought. She actually kind of liked Fooley's ass, and plus, he owed her money.

The elevator doors opened, and Mila stepped on and held the door as two men dressed in all black put Fooley on a stretcher.

While they lifted him he opened his eyes a little and started to moan, "The clown... The clown..."

"Who did this shit to you?" Mila asked, but Fooley had no more strength, and he passed out again on the stretcher.

One of the men said he's losing blood and they should hurry and get him upstairs.

They all got off the elevator, and Mila was irritated as fuck. She held her nose the whole time. *This nigga smell like fucking diapers. Oh fuck,* she thought. *What am I going to do with a baby?*

They rushed him off to surgery and told Mila to wait in the lobby.

"Well, how long this gonna take?" she asked the nurses.

"Dr. Bruce is on his way here. He was at home. We are going to prep him, but it could be hours." One nurse said.

Fuck it. I am gonna step out for a second, then I will come right back, she thought.

As Mila got off the elevator in the parking lot she saw Dred's car headed her way.

At the same time, Tina saw Mila coming out of the elevator and held her chest. *What the fuck!!* she thought. Tina reached in her purse for her pistol.

"Tessa!" She breathed, "Stop the FUCKING car Dred."

"NO! Don't shoot. My seed!! That's my daughter in her!" Dred said with more emotion than he had shown all night.

Mila started running towards the car as Dred swung past her, nearly hitting her.

Mila ran as fast as she could, then hopped in her car and sped off behind them.

In Dred's car Tina was in the front seat with her gun pointing toward the back window.

POW! POWW! POW!

The shots rang out as Tina, in a rage, starting bussing at Mila.

"Oh, word!!? Who the fuck is this Bitch?" Mila was confused as fuck. The first shot broke her whole front window. Mila covered her face as best she could, but a couple of shards still hit her in the face.

The next shot whizzed so close to her face that she felt the wind blow as a lock of her hair fell on her lap. Her strap was in the glove box, but she could not reach it. She knew she would not win this one. She threw her car in reverse and start swerving to a higher level. If she could just get to Level 2, there would be another exit that let off on to a different street.

Meanwhile, Dred stopped his car and grabbed Tina's hands. He was pissed and worried about his baby. Even though he hated Mila, this child was not her.

"T!!" he screamed in her ear, "calm down!"

Tina was crying and screaming.

"Let me go. I got to see her!" Tina drew her gun as she ran to the elevator, not sure if Mila was still around somewhere.

Tina thought, *Mila's dead, I cannot wait another day. That BITCH IS DEAD!*

The elevator dinged and Tina turned around and let off two shots in the direction that Mila headed, out of pure anger.

Her heart was pounding. She could not bear to lose her twice in one day! "Why did I leave her here?" she said, over and over again.

When she got off of the elevator, she burst into Tessa's room, only to see her lying in her bed reading a book.

"Sis!" Tessa shouted happily. "Where's Dred?"

Downstairs in the parking lot Dred was frozen in his car. He called upstairs to check on Tessa and found that she had not been harmed.

He also found out from the nurse that Teddy Berton, A.K.A. Fooley, was in the operating room and his surgery would be going on for three more hours.

Out of nowhere Mila started to blow his phone up. He had tried to check on his daughter first but when he called her phone it was just dead.

"Who the fuck was that in your car!!" Mila screamed as soon as he picked up.

"Did you get hit?" he said, calmly, but pissed.

"NO, BUT...." she responded.

As soon as she said "no" he hung up the phone and blocked her number.

He pulled into a parking space and got a big white envelope out of the glove box. In a hurry, he jogged over to the elevator.

While he waited he called his pilot arranging for his helicopter to come pick him, Tessa and Tina up from the hospital. It was not safe here anymore.

As soon as he got off the elevator he asked the first nurse what room Teddy Berton's surgery was in and the nurse blushed. Everyone knew Dred there, he was V.I.P. The nurse got up and told him that she would walk him there.

"Alright, thanks!" he said.

He opened up the door to the O. R., "DOC, hold up, come here a second."

***

Souped was on the highway headed to meet Dred, and wondering what the hell was going on.

Dred kept it short with him. All he knew so far was that Dred was about to get on his chopper and head to his house.

Souped sat stone faced as he thought about Bear. He was not blood, but he was just as important to him. They used to play ball together as kids. *He was a goofy nigga, but he always had my back,* Souped thought.

Souped tapped on the custom divider, "Yo, speed this shit up!" he commanded.

This is a fucked up ass ride, he thought as he heard Bear's body in the back hitting the wall.

Shit, he thought, *I am going to have to buy a whole new whip. It's cool, but ain't no fucking way I was gonna leave him out there on the concrete like that.*

He did a little more maintenance before he left Los' house. He went into Los' house to see what the fuck else was up. When he saw Los dead on the floor in the hallway he drew his gun and searched the whole fucking house, daring a nigga to step to him.

He never found anyone else but he did get Los' keys so he could lock the house up. He kicked the fuck out of Los' body as he walked toward the door. He never liked that lame ass fool anyway. He wished he would find the nigga that killed Bear. *Just wait until I pieced this shit together,* he thought, *they ass flat-lined.*

Once Souped got to his crib he was a little less tense. He knew he had balls of steel to ride around with a fucking dead body in the back.

Just like clockwork the chopper was landing in his back yard. Souped ran inside and walked through the house to the back patio. As they landed, he saw that Dred had people with him. *Are those females?*

Five seconds later, Souped and Tina locked eyes through the window. *Who is she? Something about this girl, man...*

"*Fuck!* Tina thought, *he so fine.*

"This has been a hell of a night," she said.

She looked over at her beautiful sister, Tessa. The most indescribable feeling swept over her. *That's my bitch, man!*

She looked over at Dred and gave him the thumbs up. *He a real stand up dude,* she thought, getting ready to exit the chopper.

"He was really riding for his baby that ain't even born yet. Niggas don't be on that shit these days. My sister is one lucky ass chick," she said, smiling at them.

Tina got off the chopper behind them as the wind whipped her pony tail around. The noise from the engine started to die down. She ran up to Dred and Tessa walking arm and arm and hugged them both.

"I love you," she said to Tessa. "I am starting to love your big head ass too," she said to Dred, slapping him playfully on the back of his head.

Souped looked at them getting off the and started to relax. *He must really be down for them. Alright, they gotta be cool ass peoples.* He checked Tina out harder this time. *Got damn look at that pretty ass face, look at that fucking body! I don't even know her name yet.*

Dred saw his brother standing on the porch. He could read him. He knew he had to be hurting. *Damn, look how he checking T out.*

Once they got in the house they all sat around Souped's table in his huge ass dining room. Dred, Tessa and Tina came together filling him in on everything that happened. As he soaked up all of the details he started to respect Tessa and Tina even more.

"So y'all think Mila killed Bear," Souped said.

"Hell naaah. Fuck that, I know she did," Tina said.

"Dred, Bro, she gotta go," Souped said. "We gotta get her off the streets… You know what the fuck she is capable of. She crazy as fuck! She kidnapping people and shit."

Tessa started rubbing her eyes.

Dred put his arm on her shoulder and said, "Aight, you tired? You wanna go lay down?"

"Yes," Tessa said, feeling drained. She just had the longest week of her life. She would wait until tomorrow to tell her sister what happened to her at Los' house in full. She did not want Tina go to bed with that on her heart.

Dred got up and grabbed Tessa out of the chair. He picked her up in his arms while she held his neck. I'll be right back," he said. "Let me go lay her down."

Tina and Souped were in a room alone together for the first time since meeting. They both had the same thing on their mind, Mila.

"So," Tina started, "what we gonna do about this bitch?"

"I am thinking take a page out of her book." Souped said. "We need to kidnap her ass and hold her until she drop that baby. She can't be out there loose like that."

"Shit, let's do it" Tina said standing up. "Get yo keys, nigga."

"Shit, that's a long drive, let's fly there." he said.

"I'm down!" Tina laughed. "Where you think she at?"

"Ion know yet, but the streets do!" he said, grabbing his phone. He let her walk ahead of him so he could watch her sexy ass.

Damn, so our first date is to go do a fucking kidnapping together, he thought, laughing to himself.

****

Mila was at the home she shared with Dred, and she was pissed off. She had five of Dred's niggas over, discussing with them how she could put them on to make more money.

"So, what's up, why we here?" one of the niggas said.

"You getting ready to find out. If anyone got problems merking a female get the fuck up and walk out right now!" Mila snapped.

No one moved. *Good,* Mila thought.

"Now, here is the plan!" she continued.

Chapter 11

Dred heard the engine of the chopper revved up in Souped's backyard. He walked over to the window to see what was up.

"Man, what they doooinng!" he said.

Souped and Tina were outside walking toward the chopper, kicking it hard.

He laughed out loud, *what's up with them?* If his brother was feeling Tina, then he thought that was dope. He reminded himself to have a talk with him though. *Lil bro a star out here, and I don't want him to hurt her. She family now.*

"Ahh haaa haa!" Dred chuckled loud as fuck, which disturbed Tessa.

That's a sexy ass laugh, Tessa said, hugging her pillow tighter.

He could not help it. Tina ass was out on the back lawn hitting the damn Quan to the chopper.

"She a fool," he said.

Speaking of fool... he thought.

That nigga got the Doc special. It cost him 75k large but it was worth it. He thought about how he put on those damn scrubs.

In the helicopter Tina was talking to Souped, and she had his undivided attention. It was like she was the star of the two.

"Yeah, Dred crazy!!!" she continued. "He put on the damn scrubs and stood over Fooley on the operating table," she said, laughing her ass off.

"He made them wake that nigga up in the middle of the damn surgery. He over in Fooley's face like... TH THH" she stammered in gut busting laughter. "The DOCTOR'S IN!! HOLDING THE SCALPEL UP AND EVERYTHING!

"He merked his ass slowly right then and there. This nigga Fooley was screaming the whole time," she continued. "Dred was like, 'Die like a man, nigga!'" she said in her best Dred impression.

Dred stood in the window as the chopper took off. *Shit, they probably going to hang out.* He was tired, and he went to go lay down with Tessa.

Buzz! Buzzzz!

Dred checked his phone. It was a message from Souped.

BRB, WE GOING TO SNATCH MILA

As Dred laced up his shoes he thought about how Mila was fucking shit up.

Who else fuck with her that long way? he thought, asking himself. *I can't believe she having my baby. It should have been Tessa, but oh well*, he decided. *I can't take that shit back now.*

"What the fuck else she been doing on the low?" he questioned. "This bitch doesn't deserve to be trusted. Why the fuck am I trusting her?"

"Doc, I know it's late and I'm tired as fuck too man..... Tessa, yes she good," Dred spoke into the receiver. "Can you do a DNA test while the baby in the womb? Is that possible? She's 6 months... HELL YEA!!! THANKS DOC, IMMA NEED YOU TOMMORROW," Dred said, hype as fuck!

He hung up quickly and dialed Souped's number, but got no answer. *He probably can't even hear that shit in that loud ass chopper.*

"Damn," he said, turning around to kiss Tessa on her forehead. *My baby need protection,* he thought. Since something was up in his crew, he decided to call up another nigga with principles, Ol' School Joe.

Tina and Souped stopped by Tina's crib so she could change. She needed some new sporty shit to wear.

They landed the chopper and had another car waiting to pick them up. In the back seat they relaxed for a second, smoking a blunt and listening to music. *He real chill,* Tina thought.

BZZZ! BZZZZ!

"DAMMMMN," Souped jumped to the edge of his seat. In the last ten minutes he had received fifty-seven missed calls and twenty-four text messages. This was his private line, only a select few had this number.

"What the hell is going on?" he said to Tina while he opened the first text:

THE WISE MAN WALKS ALONE

"What it say?" Tina asked. "Let me see?"

She took a look at the message. "What the fuck that mean?" Tina asked.

"Something big as fuck going down, RIGHT NOW!! This shit means it's a big ass snake in Dred's fucking grass." he said.

***

"Damn!" said Dred. He was across town on the side of the bed next to Tessa reading the same message.

He was calm. He was cool. At that moment he knew for sure what his whole relationship with Mila had been about.

Money and Power.

Mila never loved him because it is not in her to love. Her fucked up childhood stole her love. He gave Mila the benefit of the doubt for years... A fucked up childhood does not always turn you bad. Some people get stronger and better.

Mila could have had all the money and respect she wanted had she stayed the girl he met. *She would have had something even more valuable,* he thought. *This bitch was too blind to see that the woman of the top nigga, if his love is true, is NUMBER FUCKING ONE ANYWAY. You control the Top nigga heart...* His thoughts trailed off. *Fuck Her!!!*

He called the nigga in his crew who just tipped him off.

***

Mila stared at her new team.

"As a token of my appreciation I have a little gift for everyone." she said.

She passed to each of the five bosses a leather bag filled with unmarked twenty and one hundred dollar bills totaling fifty-thousand dollars.

Rocko looked in the bag like, "this ain't shit." *My outfit and pinky ring more than this.* His phone began to ring, "I'll be right back. I gotta take this call," he said.

Tina rushed out of her crib with some custom rainbow Jordan's and an all-black Nike track suit. That shit was hugging her curves.

She had been natural for seven years, so she decided to rock her long textured hair. When she got back in the car, Souped's dick almost got hard.

"Damn, you smell good den a muthafucka," Souped said.

"Nigga, I got some of that blueberry yumm in my backpack!" Tina said. It had been a long ass day but being around Souped energized her. She did not want the night to be over yet.

"Oh, word? Roll that shit up then!" Souped said playfully, trying not to stare at her too long.

Tina reached into her backpack for the Mason jar with her weed in it. She got the Rellos out of her side pocket.

Oh Mmm Geee, she said slowly. *Is his dick hard? Is that his long ass thick ass dick? Nah, that ain't dick... That gotta be something else.* Her conscious said, *bitch, you tripping. That is damn sholl dick.*

Souped looked at her pretty ass hair. He wanted to touch that shit so badly. *What? She's staring at my dick.*

Souped shifted his body a little so she could get a better view of his print. *Shit, she might as well know what she in store for.*

****

"Can that call wait until after our meeting!" Mila snapped at Rocko as he headed towards the door.

A few faces in the room looked at her like, *huh?* These were smart niggas! She thinks she is fucking running shit already. *Aye, this bitch is straight bananaaaasss,* Rocko thought, *I know crazy when I see that shit.*

"As a matter of fact, you right. This can wait. Let me hear what the full plan is." Rocko said.

Rocko accepted Dred's call and put the phone face down on the table. He was hoping Dred could hear every word she was about to say.

While Tina looked at Souped out the corner of her eye, she saw a flash.

"Ahhhh! They SHOOTING!!" she screamed, covering her head and ducking down to grab her pistol.

Souped busted out laughing, "They shooting pictures. That's the fucking paparazzi."

"Hold ya head up, mama, and roll down the window so they can get a good picture!" he said.

"Whaaaaaaat!" Tina said, uncovering her head, "For real!?"

She looked over at it, and there was a car full of people with cameras driving in pace with their car taking pictures from the back window.

"Alright, y'all got y'all pic, now fall back!" he said to the photographers.

Tina was floored. She almost forgot this nigga was famous.

"Ohhhhh shiiit," Tina screamed. "That was live as fuck!"

"Go ahead and say it shawty!" Souped said, smacking her leg.

"Aahhhh, I'm going fucking viral!" Tina screamed, *Damn, did he just lay claim to me? I ain't never seen this nigga booed up in the blogs.* At that moment all she could think of was his sexy ass lips and how bad she wanted to kiss him.

"Souped, I can't hold back no more!" Tina said softly

"Don't then!" he said, pulling her close.

"In the car?" Tina whispered.

"Yeah," he said, kissing her.

"Right now?" Tina breathed.

"Yes," he said, kissing her again.

"What about the driver?" Tina said.

"FUCK HIM!" he said.

Tina could not believe that her and Souped were kissing. His lips were soft and his mouth smelled and tasted of mint.

"Damn daddy, you yummy," Tina moaned as her lips touched his.

"Oh really," he said, gripping her ass hard with both hands as he completely controlled her body. Still fully clothed, he began to rub his dick print against her pussy print.

Tina forgot there was a driver. She was in his world now. She felt a craving for him, right now in this moment, more than she ever had for any man in her entire life.

Souped liked the space and roominess of the Cadillac Escapade truck. He had three of them. He stretched his legs out as Tina began to grind slowly in circles on his lap. He stretched his arms and used his hands, grabbing her breasts and massaging them.

"Let me see these pretty ass titties," he said, passionately raising her shirt up. He caressed both of her nipples. Tina leaned her head back in pleasure. The sheer sight of this man was enough to drive a woman crazy.

He flashed his white smile at her. "Take this shit off," he said, not even really giving her a chance to do it herself.

He thought, *if she had a change of clothes I would rip this shit off.* "Damn, look at that fat ass," he said. He put his hands at his side and just relaxed in the seat as he watched her reveal the body he wanted to see all night.

When she bent over to pull her pants down she was facing the front seat. She sat on his lap like he was a chair. She had on sheer black panties.

"Damn," he thought. His dick wanted to be freed from his pants. It was throbbing and at its full potential. He hoped that she would be able to take his entire dick.

She lifted her ass up to take off the panties next, and he caught a glimpse of that pussy print from the back. Almost on instinct, he spread both her fat ass cheeks apart and put his sexy ass mouth directly on her clit.

He sucked it in a pulsating motion. His soft lips covered her whole clit. He kept thinking, *Damn, this pussy tastes so sweet!*

Tina was getting the best head of her life! Just based on the nigga it was coming from made it ten times better.

"Eat this fat pussy," she moaned, looking back.

Her round, firm ass covered his whole face and he loved it.

Tina could feel her nut building hard. It was like a tornado in her pussy.

"Man, turn the fuck around and sit that wet pussy on this dick," he commanded as he came up for air.

He pulled his pants down and his fat chocolate dick popped out and landed on his leg like it weighed 20 pounds.

"WWWHAAAA THAAAA FUCCCCCKK!" she exclaimed.

Tina saw that dick like, "Look at that big pretty muthafucka!"

Tina straddled Souped as soon as he got those pants to his knees. She held her breath as he began to slap his dick on her clit. She let out the most orgasmic moan he had ever heard.

She thought, *damn.* Laughing, *where that moan come from?* She was in the zone.

Souped had his own rolled joint behind his ear. He pulled it out and lit that shit up as Tina grabbed his dick and slowly slid it into her dripping wet pussy.

She could feel his dick touching every side of her pussy as she took each inch in. Once she got it all in, Souped adjusted his body so that his dick head was pressed up against her G spot.

"I know exactly where it's at," he whispered to her.

Souped could not take his eyes off of her. *She got some sexy ass fuck faces*, he thought. His dick could not get any harder. Her pussy fit like a glove, like that shit was meant to hold his dick. He took a strong hit of the weed and grabbed her neck, putting his lips on hers. They kissed passionately while the smoke from the Kush surrounded them.

"Don't move. Just feel this dick for a second. Just feel this dick," he moaned in her mouth, holding her hips in place.

"Ahhhhahhhhhahh," she moaned. The combination of his voice and kisses sent her reeling over the edge.

Souped could feel every throb of her pussy as it nutted.

"Yeah baby, let that shit out," he told her.

The driver tried not to look, but Tina's ass was so fat. He had seen Souped fuck a girl in the whip before, but he knew that this nigga was feeling Tina. He laughed to himself, proud of Souped. *He back there making love.*

Tina was in la-la land. She had just experienced the best nut of her life and he still had not even pumped her pussy yet.

"Aye! Driver, find somewhere ducked off to pull over," Souped said. Tina almost forgot about the driver, but when she remembered that he was there she still didn't give a fuck.

The driver pulled over in a ducked off parking lot of some apartment buildings. He pulled to the darkest corner of the lot and turned the engine and head lights off.

He wanted to help them set the mood so he grabbed his CD's and popped in Tina's favorite song out right now.

"Turn the fuck up," Tina whispered.

Souped took his shirt off and opened the car door.

"Get your ass out of this car," he said, stepping out, ass naked, with some brand new Timbs on.

<u>Chapter 12</u>

Dred sent out a group text message to the 15 boss niggas he had running different sections of the state:

TOMORROW 8AM FIRM

Dred thought, *It's time to clear the fucking air. If you ain't fucking with me, then it's fuck you flat the fuck out.* He prided himself on making loyalty the top purpose of the group. He held retreats yearly, all-expense paid just to bring niggas together. *I run this shit like a real corporation,* he thought.

He had to set the meeting for tomorrow so that everyone could have time to fly or drive to the secret location. Firm was code word for be there or you are going to get found and brought there.

"D," Tessa said, stirring in her sleep, "I feel so safe with you in the room. Please come lay with me."

"I want to, but I need to straighten things out." he said. "I need to head out for a second. You remember Ol' School Joe? He coming to protect you until I get back.

"After this is over we going on vacation," he told her. "Anywhere you want, just me and you."

"YES!!" Tessa screamed like a child. "Can Tina and Souped come too?"

"See, that's why I fuck with you. Hell yea!!!" Dred said.

She was his light, he thought. He knew that Tessa was a bad ass bitch. He could not wait for her to get back to one hundred percent and take her place on the throne. They were lucky she was out of commission, because she got a dangerous ass side to her too. The difference between her and Mila is that Tessa is a ride or die.

No fake phony shit popping with her!

****

Across town the five bosses shook Mila's hand and started to head out.

"Hey Mila," Rocko asked. "Can I stay behind and holla at you for a second?"

"About what?" Mila snapped. "The meeting is over." she said, trying to show her boss status.

"I got some info about Dred I think you need to know," he said.

"Alright, my ears open," Mila said, thirsty to know where Dred was and what he was doing.

"Can we talk in private though?" Rocko whispered to her. They were off to the front of the room. It was still an of couple people there saying goodbye to each other.

"Alright," she said. "Wait here. Let me see these niggas to the door."

Outside of Dred and Mila's house looked like a car show room floor.

"Damn, it smells like money out this piece!" she said, closing the door behind the last boss.

Halfway down the block all of the bosses' phones went off at the same time.

TOMORROW 8AM FIRM

"OH FUCK!" one yelled!

****

In the house Mila walked into the room where Rocko was waiting for her.

"Where did this nigga go?" Mila said.

Rocko came from behind the door and grabbed Mila up.

"I miss this pussy," he said.

Mila could feel herself getting moist.

"I missed you too." She said, kissing him and thinking to herself, *Fuck this nigga.*

****

Souped grabbed Tina's hand and pulled her out of the car. "Bend that ass over right here." he directed. He opened the 5th door of the truck so he could bend her over.

He slid his fat dick in and began to stroke her really slowly.

Tina was so caught in the moment.

"Harder," she said to him.

With her permission, he began to pound her back out. *Oh shit*, he thought, *I can't hold that shit no more.*

He put his dick all the way in her and let his nut off. Thinking to himself, *Got damn, this pussy good.*

When Tina felt Souped's warm cum fill up her pussy she began to cum again herself. The force of his nut had put so much pressure on her g spot that she could not help but squeal. Souped slid his half limp dick out and stretched his legs out.

"That was soooo good!" Tina said.

"Was? We ain't done yet!!!" Souped said, pulling her closer.

****

"Come on, let's go to my crib," Rocko said, smacking Mila on the ass. "You need to get the fuck out of this house, A.S.A.P.!"

"I am not scared of shit, point blank," Mila said. "We got this house set up like Fort Knox!" Mila laughed.

Fuck he mean? she thought. *Reinforced steel door, bullet proof windows.*

"I'm good," she said.

"For old time's sake?" he asked, with his puppy dog eyes.

Mila looked him up and down. That dick did used to be good back in high school. She thought, *Maybe I should fuck him and turn him into a puppet.* That shit was so funny to her she laughed out loud.

This sick, fucking twisted ass bitch, Ion want your ass. he thought. Dred already knew he used to fuck with Mila back in the day. That shit been over for years now. That was some kid shit, and he never looked at Mila like she was sexy. He knew from way back when that she had a couple issues. *Beauty is a motherfucker he said, I'll take a loyal seven over a dime any day!*

"Man, get your purse and come on, ride with me. You need a nigga like me on your team," Rocko said.

"True!" Mila said, grabbing her purse as instructed.

They walked up the steps to Rocko's town house door. Mila was light weight excited. She was pregnant, but on the outside she still was fly and fine as hell. As soon as Mila stepped inside a nigga waiting in the shadows swooped down on her, putting a bag over her face.

Rocko quickly grabbed her purse. *If her old Wild, Wild West ass had got that gun out we would be dead.* He laughed, knowing he scored major cool points with Dred. After all, Dred was the realist, fairest, nigga he ever met in his life. Ain't no pussy worth losing that connect.

Rocko caught a glimpse of himself in the full length mirror on his wall. *Damn, I am ready for that next level.* His green eyes sparkled as the light from his cell phone turned on. He was having the best week of his life.

Word on the Street today was Carlos was missing, and that was a good thing. It left room at the top.

"Dred," Rocko said into the receiver. "We got her."

"Good work. Get her in the car and don't stop driving until you get to Doc's crib," Dred responded. It was 2:30 am and he wondered if Doc was still working, but instead of asking a dumb question, he shut up. That nigga can make anything happen.

His boy already had Mila wrapped in duct tape. She was kicking and screaming. He was trying to get the tape over her mouth but she kept trying to bite his ass.

"Let's get her the fuck out of here before somebody call the boys," Rocko said.

****

When Mila woke up she was strapped down to a hospital bed in Doc's private penthouse offices.

"Dr. Bruce, somebody just kidnapped me," she said.

"Oh, like you kidnapped Tessa," he shot back, with his pretty, blue, eyes.

"Night, night," he said, injecting her IV with something to keep her ass knocked out.

Doc drew her blood. He wanted to be respectful, because if the DNA test came back and it was Dred's baby, she would still have status. He really didn't give a fuck about all the drama. All he knew was that he just made 350k dollars in total that night for the services he provided Dred.

He dialed Dred, "It's done. The earliest I can get the results back is tomorrow morning. I've got a team together to work on it. I already received the payment. I'll keep her knocked out until you get here."

"Damn," Dred said, still sitting next to Tessa, "I just accomplished everything from here." He could get some sleep now.

Tomorrow would either make him or break him. He had to play his cards right.

Before he laid down he called Souped. He still did not get an answer, so he left a voice message saying they had Mila.

Tessa heard Dred lay down. "I heard everything baby." she said. "I am feeling much better now. That rest energized me. I need to go with you tomorrow. I need to make sure you are safe."

****

Souped and Tina got dressed after fucking for almost two hours. He smacked her on her ass, "You know this my pussy right?"

"Not just yet," she said, "You got a little wining and dining to do," she laughed. "I got your nose open off this good shit."

Women know when that pussy on point, she thought.

"Shit, I'm down with that babe, just say where," he laughed.

They got back in the car and the driver pulled off. The driver could not believe what he just saw. "I got the best fucking job in the world," he said. "I am going to retire from this job."

Souped paid him nicely. He was trust worthy and very dependable. Souped knew that he was his boy for real. They spent a lot of time together going to and fro.

"Got damn!!!" Tina snapped. "I am so fucking happy they got Mila ass!"

"I feel like going over to the hospital and fucking with her," Tina said. "Didn't yo brother say that Doc had her knocked out?"

"Aye, you so fucking crazy. You mine. I'm claiming this shit now." he said, grabbing her face and looking into her pretty ass eyes. "Say that shit ain't so. Say it ain't. My next song gonna be about you." he laughed.

She stared out the window, unable to contain the smile on her face. "Maybe I'm yours. We will see," she said sweetly.

"But for real doe, let's go up to that hospital!" Tina said, her dickmatization had worn off and she was thinking about fucking with Mila. "I don't wanna hurt her. I just wanna fuck with her a little."

"Fuck with her, like how? You got that damn clown mask with you?" Souped asked.

Tina reached into her book bag and pulled it out.

"Ion know. I'm getting light weight tired," Souped said.

"Oh, you fucking party pooper, but somebody need to guard her ass." Tina said, determined to get her way.

"Alright," he said. "Check it. They got some comfortable ass beds there too," he said, looking sneaky.

"Rob, take us to Docs!" she said.

Chapter 13

In the morning Dred woke up at around 5 am. Ol' School Joe had shown up in the middle of the night, and Dred decided to have him stay over at Souped's crib. He was not yet sure if he was going to let Tessa come with him to the meeting.

He wanted to stop by Doc's. He knew Doc would not be there yet, but a nurse should be able to find out the status. He paid a large amount of money for the test, as well as for Mila being kept asleep.

When he got to the top floor he could already see the commotion going on. Tina was in the hallway fooling.

"Why is this bitch woke?!" she yelled at the nurse.

Dred walked up and diffused the situation. Tina and Souped stood with their backs against the wall outside of Mila's room, pissed as hell.

"If she not yours, I'm shooting her ass," Tina said, as Dred went into the room.

He laughed. "Cool with me, but we gonna have to be more creative than that." he said.

He peeped his head into Mila's room and saw her looking fucked up, restrained to the bed. He wondered if that was his baby. If so, how much stress was it under?

Just then, a call came through the nurses' station.

Chastity, a nurse that worked in Doc's penthouse for 10 years, she knew Dred well and did not like seeing him having a hard time.

"Dr. Bruce is on the line and has your results," she said, handing him the phone.

"Hello," Dred said, his heart beating out of his chest.

"Dred, You ARE the father!" Doc said.

****

Tessa rolled over in bed wanting to cuddle up next to Dred. She reached her hand out only to have it land on an empty bed.

"Did he leave without me?" She asked herself, feeling irritated.

Doc said all I needed was fluids and 24 hours' rest, she thought. *I'm good now. They tortured my ass but my mind strong as hell.* She thought back to the small trap room she spent days in. *I refused to let they wack ass break me, especially when all four of those niggas dead as we speak.*

"Maybe we should donate Los' house to charity or some shit, he doesn't need it," she said, getting weak. *I'm sure Dred can DBO that shit,* she thought.

"I need to be at the meeting," she said, calling Tina.

"Sis," Tina answered, feeling bad. How would she feel knowing that the baby was Dred's?

DAMN, Tina thought.

****

The secret meeting space had been set up by a member of Dred's team. He had bottled waters, finger food, and fruit for everyone.

Monty, a little up and coming young dude on the team, looked at the set up like, *damn, what is this? Don't even look like a boss nigga meet up. This shit look like a company lunch meeting or some shit.*

He was happy to be assigned the task, because he knew whatever was about to happen in this room was going to the illest shit ever.

At the hospital Dred dropped to his knees with the phone in his hand.

He was shaken, devastated, but happy he could not call it. He respected life though. He was a real stand up nigga, and everyone in the room knew it.

"What we gonna do?" Souped asked.

"I need a second to think man," He said, walking away. He went straight to the rooftop deck and was very relieved that there was no one else up there. When he grabbed a chair he thought, *this being my baby makes life a hell of a lot more complicated.* He leaned back and watched the sun rise as he thought of a way out of this situation.

****

Doc sat at the desk in his home office refreshing the screen. He had bags under his eyes but he was so far having the best day of his life. He could not wait to close up that illegal ass office and get the fuck out of dodge. He was going to purchase a condo in Hilton Head, North Carolina and chill his ass out.

He had been stacking his money for a while. The majority of the money he made came from Dred, and he was partially sad that he would never talk to him again. He was a very intelligent brother. He had to give it to him. This was the first chink he ever saw in his armor.

He started to feel a little nervous but he figured shit was cool. He weighted the risks of what he was doing. Last night when Mila offered him 10 million dollars to fake the test results he jumped on that shit immediately. He figured that he could always say the lab made a mistake if it ever came back on him.

That fucking baby was not Dred's. "This shit better than Grey's Anatomy!" he said aloud. He asked Mila if she even knew who the kid's father was. He could still hear her say, "I don't fucking know, I never knew and I don't fucking care. I make the rules! You want the 10 million or not? I see you around here every day looking drained and wore out. You starting to age quick as hell. So what's up?"

They completed the transaction and he briefly untied her so that she could call her personal banker and arrange for the wire to go first thing in the morning. He didn't know how much money Dred and Mila really had but he knew it was a lot.

For some reason every time he thought of the name "Dred" he felt a sort of nervousness build in his stomach. *Damn, this is what all people that cross him must feel.*

"It'll be fine," he said, reassuring himself as he refreshed his computer screen on more time. All of his troubles washed away as his online account reflected a deposit of $10,000,000.00.

"Was it worth it?" he asked himself one final time. "Hell yeah," he said.

He stood up and started to pace. He prided himself on being an intelligent man, but something told him this was a bad move. He kept turning the wheels in his head. He kept picking up the smartphone to call an UBER to the airport, and stopping right after dialing a couple of numbers.

His conscious told him one last time that if he fucked Dred over he would be on the run for the rest of his life if he found out. After seeing what he did to that Fooley fellow he knew that would not be him.

His eyes shined and a huge smile returned to his face as he figured out the perfect solution to his issue. If he called Dred and told him that the lab fucked up, he had them retest a couple times, blah, blah, blah, and that it was really not his kid, they were gonna fucking kill Mila!!

He could keep the money!

He snatched up the phone and dialed Dred's cell.

"What's up, Doc?" he answered.

"Umm, we have a problem......" Doc began.

****

"A problem? What you mean a problem?" Dred asked, sitting up in his chair.

"Well, the lab just contacted me and said the results were flawed." Doc said, sweating bullets. "It turns out that you are actually-"

BZZZ! BZZZ, Dred's phone vibrated, just as Doc was talking, from a text message.

"Say that again. I didn't hear you." Dred said, standing up now.

"As it turned out, the baby Mila is carrying is not yours." Doc repeated.

"WHAT, ARE YOU SURE?!" Dred said, feeling a wave of relief wash over his whole body. *It's not mine,* he thought. *I am free of this bitch.*

"I had them run it twice just to be sure, and congratulations. I know this was a fucked up situation man," Doc said, feeling relieved.

"I will email you a confirmation letter now." He said at his desk, attaching the test results to an email to Dred.

"YESSSSSS!!!" Dred screamed, in his heart he felt sorry for the baby, but that was no longer his concern.

Dred said goodbye to Doc and went to check the text he just received, wondering if it was from Tessa.

$10,000,000.00 has been successfully transferred from your account ending in 1242, TEXT STOP TO OPT OUT OF NOTIFICATIONS.

Who the fuck accessed that account? he thought. "What the fuck is going on?" he said.

He was still so hype about not being Mila's baby daddy. He wanted to see that email for himself.

"Man… Hell yeah!" he said, looking at the attachment. "WOW."

Just before he was about to close the email, something caught his eye. The time stamp on the letter read *4:29 am.*

"Oh really…" he said, heading back to Tina and Souped. He walked slowly as he called the Banker.

"Who authorized 10 mil out of my account, and where did it go?" he asked.

The banker could hear in the tone of Dred's voice that something was off. "Mila called and said that you were buying a house from a Mr. Bruce O'Hare." the banker responded.

"Recall the wire and restrict Mila's access to all of my accounts immediately!" Dred yelled into the phone. He was so pissed, he just hung up.

"Nigga, I helped you eat and you trynta fuck me over?" he said.

"Aye Bro, stay here and guard Mila. Tina, come with me." Dred said, not asking but telling.

Souped was cool with that. *I'm tired as hell*, he thought.

"Where we going?" Tina asked.

"To Doc's house really quick. I will fill you in on the way there." Dred said with a mean mug.

Chapter 14

Tina hopped in the whip next to Dred.

"Soooo, how you feeling?" Tina said.

"Happy as fuck and mad as fuck at the same damn time," Dred replied.

He ran through the whole series of events to her before he pulled out of the parking lot.

Tina sat there in shock with her mouth open like, "WHHAAATTTTTTT!"

Instantly she grabbed the door handle, trying to open the door, but the door was locked.

"Aye, where you going?" he said, laughing.

"I'm going upstairs to kill Mila ass right now. Why wait? This bitch got it coming!" Tina snapped.

She also felt the pressure lifting. She wasn't going to have to call Tessa back and tell her that fucked up shit. Earlier when she had called she decided it was best if he told her.

"T, we got special plans for Mila. Right now though, Doc gotta get it. That was the most disloyal shit ever. I put this nigga on, T. He was not shit before he met me. He was a Doctor, I'll give him that, but his ass wasn't ballin' out. This nigga used to be in an old ass basic ass office. That shit was like the trap office." Dred said, feeling salty, for real.

He trusted dude, and now that he knew he was shady he had to be dealt with as soon as possible. *He knows too much*, Dred thought.

"So, let's tag team this shit, then head over to the meeting," Dred told her.

"Why Souped ain't coming to the meeting?" she asked.

"Souped not in the drug game. Your new boyfriend is a rapper only, that's it. Ion want him in this shit." Dred said.

"So damn, can we have fun with this shit then?" she said, pulling the mask out of her book bag grinning.

"Man, fuck that clown shit," he said, laughing. "Let's do another theme. Aye, you ever saw that movie called 'The Purge'?"

"Where the fuck we gonna get purge type masks at 6am?" Tina asked.

"Aiight, Aiiight, hold up I got it," Dred laughed sharing the plan.

"Ahhhh! My nigga, my nerve, let's go!" Tina sung.

Doc lived in the outskirts of town. He actually had two houses, this one being the smaller of the two. It was still a nice property surrounded by two acres of land. There was a decent sized manmade lake in the back yard. Dred had been in Doc's boat before. It was ok, but it did not compare to Dred's.

Tina and Dred parked down the street and approached the house. Dred gave Tina a bag of small rocks they collected, but he kept one for himself.

"Alright, you go left and I'll go right." Dred said to Tina.

On cue, they began to hail rocks into all of the windows. Every window they saw they threw rocks in. Dred figured that Doc should still be in his office or the bedroom, one of the two.

Doc was knocked out in his bed. It had been a long day. *It all worked out great*, he concluded.

****

The sound of glass shattering jolted Doc out of his bed.

"What the fuck was that?!" he said.

Doc stood up as he heard his windows breaking around his house simultaneously.

"Did he find out?" he said in a panic, grabbing the phone to call the police.

"Put that shit down!" Tina yelled, coming into the room with her nine pointed at Doc.

"No – no – no, there's some kind of misunderstanding here," Doc stammered.

"Nah, I got somewhere to be," Dred said, appearing in the doorway. "I know what you did, so fuck you. Start walking nigga!"

They walked Doc outside barefoot by gun point all the way to the lake.

Dred took some rope out of the boat and tied Doc's feet as he pleaded for his life.

"Don't worry, we just going for a quick ride," Tina said.

"I was gonna give it all back. I came clean," Doc lied.

Once Dred finished tying his ankles together, she took the other end of the rope and tied it to the back of the small boat.

"You love this lake right?" Dred said, fucking with him.

Dred stepped into the boat and held the gun on Doc, and Tina eased out dragging Doc, squirming and screaming, into the water.

Dred got behind the wheel and floored it. The water pounded Doc as they sped through the water doing donuts. Doc couldn't scream but the look on his face told it all.

"Woo hoo!" Tina said. She had not been on a boat in years. "This ole disloyal ass nigga, end his shit D."

With that, Dred swung the boat around full force and maneuvered it so that Doc's body slammed right into the Boat Dock.

"Fatality!" Tina said in her mortal combat voice.

Chapter 15

Dred and Tina jogged back up toward the house.

"Damn, I need to call a cleanup team. We dropping bodies everywhere! Los' body prolly decomposing like a muthafucka, ugh. I know that house smell fucked up like nigga. Phew ewwww!" She said, holding her nose.

They hoped in the car and headed to pick up Tessa. He debated if he was gonna let her go. He decided that if she was gonna be his, she had to get used to this shit. "Naaah, not forever, though," he said, correcting himself.

"Run to my house on the way," Tina said, always looking out for her sister. "I know damn well her fly ass wonder what the fuck she gonna wear."

"I need to get Tessa something to wear, she my size." Tina said while lying back in the seat.

Once they made it to Souped's house Ol School Joe was in the living room chilling. Dred looked at him and thought no one can look at him and tell how dangerous he is.

Tina came in the house after Dred.

"Aww, is this y'all dad?" she said seriously.

"Nah, I just had him here protecting Tessa while we were out." he responded.

"What!!! You had his old ass protecting her!" Tina said, dead ass serious.

Ol School Joe was 5'5", around 150 pounds, and brown skinned with big, thick glasses on.

Tina thought, *I am usually not judgmental but I just don't see this shit.*

Ol School Joe saw the look on her face. "This lil firecracker got heart, let's see if she jumps." he said, reaching in his back pocket and pulling out a hand knife. He threw it into the wall inches away from Tina's face.

Got damn he did that shit in the blink of an eye! Oh snap, grandpa need to come to this meeting, Tina thought.

Ol School nodded with approval. *She was surprised when I threw the knife, but she didn't flinch.* He prided himself on being very observant. So far he felt that Dred was on track with bringing Tessa and Tina into his circle.

"I'm just glad he done with that Mila bitch," he said as he headed towards the door.

"Sis," Tina yelled. She came into the bedroom with the perfect "I'm-finna-go-fuck-shit-up-with-my-man-outfit."

"AHHHH!" Tessa squeaked. "You know me like a fucking book, I love it!!!"

"Guess what, he letting you come!!" Tina said, teasing her. "I can't wait to see the action that's about to happen in that room." She was glad she would have a front seat to Dred checking niggas. "Don't let it get messy," she said. "They ain't seen Tessa ass in action yet."

Tessa walked out of the bathroom freshly showered. She had a crisp Egyptian cotton bath towel wrapped around her body. She looked down at her outfit like, *yes, I really like this.*

Sis hooked me up. I love her man. She sat on the bed close to tears. "She found m. She found me!" She kept saying to herself. She was so happy to be alive, but not too long ago she thought she was dead.

"This bitch gonna tie me up and fucking talk all that shit" she said under her breath. "I can't wait to see that bitch again. All that shit I just went through over her petty ass. She thought back to how they snatched her off the street."

Nothing could compare to what happened to her at Los' house. She still had not been able to tell Dred or Tina what all happened to her. She did not know if she ever would. She thought about it, reliving the ordeal, "But fuck that shit, these RED BOTTOMS though," she said happily.

Dred stood at the door looking at Tessa. Her body was so fucking banging. She could barely close the towel around that round firm ass.

He bit his lip thinking about sliding up in her. *Damn, I wanna eat that pussy though so bad.* He could feel his dick getting harder. He was overdue for some of that wild ass sex they had together. He grabbed his dick and tried to hide his erection.

"Damn, calm down nigga," he said to his dick.

Tessa turned, startled, and laughed when she saw Dred. *Look at my man, got damn, is that all mine? Man, this shit too good to be true… I could not ask for a better man.* The only problem that she had was the fact that his business activities were questionable. Tessa was willing to help him get out the game in any way she could when he was ready, of course.

"You almost ready, boo?" he said, hugging her.

"Yes almost." *We gotta hurry*, she thought.

Dred was willing to make those niggas wait just so he could make love to her. He wanted their first time as a true couple to be special. He wanted to plan something nice for her. *She deserves it*, he thought.

"Alright, we will be waiting down stairs sexy." he said.

****

At the hospital Souped sat on a chair outside Mila's room. He was so tired he could barely keep his eyes open. He kept nodding off.

Chastity, the nurse, had been lurking around Mila's room all night. She was drawn to the drama. She thought she had figured out everything that was going on here.

"Unt uhhhnn," she said. *Something going down in here.*

Her nosy ass got a cup and a pitcher of ice to take to Mila, knowing damn well she was not supposed to go in there. She was just going to talk to her for a little while. *I mean, she is pregnant why are they holding her here like that?* she thought.

Chastity had seen a lot working for Dr. Bruce, but she just could not get with drugging a pregnant girl.

She crept past Souped stretched out on the chair, who was looking very uncomfortable. "He is out like a light," she said. "Hpmm, he should be. All that fucking they was doing in that empty room last night."

"Hey hun, I am just going to check your vitals. You feeling ok?" *This is a crying shame,* Chastity said.

"Yes, can you loosen the straps? My arms hurt really bad," she said, sounding like a whole other person. She looked Chastity in her eyes and mustered up some tears as she whispered, "Help me!"

Chastity stood frozen for a second. She looked around the room, trying to make a decision. *I have to do what's right,* she thought.

"Ok, I will loosen the restraints, but it's up to you to get out of here. I will try to distract the other staff and *he,*" she whispered, pointing towards the door, "is sleep."

"Ok, thank you so much," Mila cried, looking like a wounded BIRD.

****

Down stairs at Souped's crib Tina took a look around.

"Okay. Okay, I can definitely live here," she said, smiling. "This is the fucking life!!!!!"

She sat on the couch and wondered where they were. *Damn, we gotta get going. I know everybody already there.*

Out of nowhere it seemed her phone started to blow up. What the fuck is going on?

Her Facebook notifications went ham. The phone started to fill with notifications, her eyes got wide as hell as she realized that she had just went fucking viral.

"Oh shit," she said. "What picture they post?" She was excited. She pulled up one of the main sites to see a fire ass picture of her and Souped in the back of the truck snuggling.

"AHHHHH! All you hating ass hoes, run, tell that!!!" she said, felling hyped up as hell.

Let me call Souped.

****

Souped flinched out of his chair as the phone rang. He grabbed his phone and glanced up to see Mila running full speed toward the elevator. He caught her as the doors were opening and pushed her in the elevator.

"Bitch, you coming with me." Souped said. He was ready to go home, and he did not see the point of him being there anymore.

Souped opened his front door and shoved Mila through it. Tina was standing there waiting for her with her arms crossed. She knew he was on the way.

"Yeaaaaaah bitch," she said, pacing. "Tessa get down here, this bitch here!"

Mila stood her ground in a room full of people who hated her guts. She could care less.

"Tessa!" Tina yelled. "She down here."

"Who down where?" Tessa said, walking down the steps.

"Wow," she said, with a big Kool-Aid smile. "You wack ass bitch!" She screamed at Mila. Tessa got in her face.

Mila stood there with her head up and her chest out like she was still the baddest bitch. "These hoes won't see me buckle," she said.

"Oh, you hard you bubble head ass bitch?" Tessa said, skipping back a few steps. With all of her momentum she kicked Mila right in her face.

Mila hit the floor hard as hell. She felt like her head had been split in two. She had no choice but to scream and hold her head.

"I though they said crazy people don't feel pain," Tessa said, laughing.

Dred stepped in and told Souped to continue to watch Mila. They were already an hour late for the meeting.

"Alright baby," Tessa said, kissing Dred. She went over and bent down next to Mila. "Hey bitch. Hey bitch. Look up. Yeah bitch, look me right in the eye. When we get back, I am going to spend 24 hours killing your ass."

"Damn!" Souped said, "I wanna go with y'all. Ion wanna baby sit this bitch."

"Yea!" Tina said. "I want him to come too," she said, grabbing Souped's arm and laying her head on his shoulders.

"No, he stays here. I already told you." Dred said with authority.

"Alright, you right my bad, D." Tina said, heading for the door.

After everyone left he sat on the couch as Mila still laid in the same spot on the floor.

"UGH!" Souped breathed. "This bitch is nuts. Man, where my pistol?"

Mila sat up on the floor and began rocking back and forth mumbling.

I am tired of looking at her ass, he thought. *I gotta tie her ass up or something.* He grabbed her arm and tried to make her stand up, but she would not move.

Finally, he had to forcefully drag her by the arm to the bathroom.

He had a half bath in the hallway with no windows. He figured that he could prop a chair under the door and keep her in there.

Once he had her secured in the bathroom he walked back in the Den and stretched out on the couch. He needed the rest. He had a concert that night.

Chapter 16

When they got to the meeting place they were not surprised to see everyone still there.

When Dred walked into the room he looked at all 15 niggas. There was a reason he chose these men in the first place. He tried to figure out where he went wrong. He prided himself on being able to read people.

As he sat down at the head of the table, simultaneously, all of the men raised their hands in the air.

"White handkerchiefs?" Dred said, "Oh, y'all want peace, y'all waving the white flag?" he laughed.

"What about the four of you that met up with Mila last night?" "Y'all wanna end me?" Dred said. "You can't fuck me over without fucking yourself over."

As Dred spoke, Tessa, Tina and Monty walked further into the room. They positioned themselves near the four disloyal niggas who, ironically sat next to each other.

"So now, what is the best piece of advice I could ever give you?" Dred paused. "DIE SLOW."

With that, each of the 4 got a bullet to the back of the head.

Blood hit the tables and splattered all over the other bosses there, but no one said a word.

"Do any of you have a problem that needs to be worked out?" Dred said.

Having seen Dred at these meetings before, they knew that sometimes saying nothing was the best idea. Each man, one by one, raised their arms and waived their white handkerchiefs in the air.

They ain't want none, Dred thought.

****

When they got back to the house they found Souped laying on the couch passed out. Instantly, they woke his ass up.

"Where she at bro," Dred said.

"Oh, shit," he said, half asleep. "I locked her in the bathroom." Souped said, adjusting himself and dozing back off.

When they opened the bathroom Mila was laying on the floor with empty pill bottles next to her.

Tessa reached down and took her pulse. She didn't feel one, and Mila was foaming at the mouth.

Tessa was pissed beyond belief. "Fuck it then," she said. "At least she gone for good."

"Man, let's get the fuck out of here." Dred said. He was ready to go home and get some rest.

Tina went and shook Souped, "Nigga she OD'D in your bathroom, Mila ass dead."

"Fuck that bitch," he said as he got up. "Let's go get some breakfast, babe."

In the bathroom, Dred got a white sheet from the closet and covered Mila's body. She was crazy, but he just shook his head at all the potential that she wasted.

The two couples walked out arm and arm.

"Aye, y'all coming to my concert tonight?" Souped asked.

"Hell yeah. We will be there." Dred said as he got into his whip. *Damn.* He was wondering why the Cleanup crew dude hadn't called him back yet. These fucking bodies were piling up, and he needed a new connect for that shit he thought as he was pulling off.

****

As the effect of the beta blockers that Mila stole from the hospital wore off, she got up from under the sheets.

"Got damn, I'm a smart bitch. They really thought I was dead." she said.

She knew it was a strong possibility Dred would leave her there. This nigga doesn't ever touch dead bodies.

Let me get the fuck out of here while I can, she thought, looking around.

Chapter 17

Dred cruised the streets with Tessa by his side. He had so many plans in store for her.

I can't take her home for real, he thought. At least not to the house he shared with Mila. He would have to sell that crib, and he knew that Tessa didn't want to live there. *Shit, I don't even want to live there,* he thought.

He turned the music up and just cleared his mind. He decided that they were going to book a few nights and a five-star hotel in the city. He hoped she was cool with that. He wanted them to spend a few days looking for a new house.

"Sooo, babe I was thinking that we could go to The Perianne, that new hotel down town for a few nights. You cool with that? It's whatever you want, though, for real." Dred said sincerely.

"Oohh, room service!" She said, clapping her hands together, and feeling excited. She heard that The Perianne Hotel had the best food and spa services in town. "Yes, let's go! Are we really going to Souped's concert tonight?"

"Hell yeah!" Dred said. He had to support his brother, and he was performing his new single for the first time. People were coming from all over to see him, and this was a big deal.

Tessa looked around shyly. "Imma need something to wear," she said. She still had no clothes with her, and the modest house she owned was on the outskirts of town.

"Babe, know something right now, real talk, as long as we together you don't ever have to ask for something you need. Just tell me. I have a stylist in mind that Souped fucks with, and I could have her come bring you a week's worth of nothing but the best shit! Is there anything else you worried about?" he said reassuringly.

Tessa's mind was reeling as she thought back to the ironic way they first met. *Is this gonna be my fucking husband?* She thought. The sheer thought alone gave her chills.

"A stylist!" she squealed. "I am good. That and food was all that was on my mind."

Dred pulled up to the valet of the hotel relieved to be getting a little rest and some alone time with Tessa. This hotel had just opened its doors, and the line to check in was full of good-looking people in town for Souped's concert.

As they waited Dred pulled out his phone and downloaded *Sugar Loops* from the app store. He loved that game.

People in line began staring at Dred suddenly. Someone screamed, "That's Souped's brother, AHHHHH!!!" as pandemonium broke out.

"Oh fuck," Dred said. He looked at Tessa hoping this did not make her uncomfortable. She was smiling ear to ear, *Damn,* he thought, *she a breath of fresh air.*

****

Rocko was at his mom's house eating some home cooked breakfast. "Mom's food is bussin," he said, fucking that shit up.

As she walked past he reached in his pocket and pulled out a stack of 100 dollar bills.

"Here Ma," he said, handing her the money. "Buy yourself something nice."

He loved his Moms. She was currently the only woman in his life at the time. He had bitches and he wanted to settle down, but he knew he was not ready for love. He didn't want to use the word "hoe" to describe himself, but if the shoe fits he had to wear those muthafucka's like they were custom Jordan's.

He was thinking about what he was going to wear to Souped's concert that night. Dred called and personally invited him. *That's my nigga*, he thought, *I ride for him*.

BUZZZ! BUZZZ!

Rocko's phone went off with a text message:

Come Fuck Me.

Rocko got up and put his plate in the sink, ready to go put it down on this little freak.

"Boy, if you don't wash that damn dish, I'm gonna go upside yo head!" his mom snapped.

****

The hotel manager thanked Dred for his stay. They received a special check out once the hotel found out who Dred was. Souped had a room at the hotel as well, so that he didn't have to go far to get to and from his show. Dred requested the same floor but on the opposite side. He wanted to have a little alone time with his woman.

As soon as Dred got in the room he went straight to the desk. He needed to make a few calls.

Tessa could not believe her eyes when she saw this room. She was expecting nice, but not this nice. There was a full living room with high end furniture. In the bedroom there was a king sized bed with fluffy white pillows and a high end down comforter.

"Oh wow," she said. "I could stay here forever."

Dred looked at her from the desk. He was happy to see she liked it. *This ain't shit though,* he thought, *compared to the house I am going to buy her.*

Dred keyed in the number to the cleanup crew. He wanted to check on the status of things. He had so far requested the sterilization of five crime scenes: The penthouse, Los' house, the crib next to the chicken spot, Doc's house and Souped's house.

"Yeah, FAM what's the status?" Dred said into the receiver.

"Well, we cleaned up four spots so far. Our locksmith was not familiar with the type of lock on Souped's door. The windows are fucking bullet proof or something. They are actually still on the property. Can you bring down a key?" Tony said, the owner of the crew.

"Nah, I don't need to do that, hold up." he said. He had the pass code to open the lock from his phone. *Technology these days is a muthafucka,* Dred thought.

"It's open! The body in the half bath right there on the first level." Dred said as they disconnected the call. There would be no trace that a murder had ever taken place.

RINNGG! RINNGG!

"What's up?" Dred answered.

"Um, Dred… My guys said that there is no body in the bathroom." Tony said hesitantly.

Chapter 18

Tina and Souped spent all day chilling. They were having so much fun together. They were behaving as if they had been together for a lifetime.

"Alright babe, I need to go to the sound check," he said, flopping down on the couch in their suite. "The turn up is going be real tonight." Souped said. Dred and Tessa were on the same floor. "Man, this shit is what's up."

"I wanna go to sound check too. That sound live as fuck," Tina said laughing. "Wait, what the fuck is sound check again?"

"Shit, I just go to the area and drop a few songs just to make sure the audio and layout is bomb, you wanna come too?" he asked. It was something about this girl… He just could not get enough of her company. He loved the way she could look so sexy like that, with just a fitted tee and some jeans. "Man," he said, "I got a rider for real."

****

At the sound check Tina watched Souped do his thang. *Damn, he is talented as fuck,* she thought.

"That mouth was spitting bars now, but earlier it was licking pussy," she said. She walked over near Souped on the stage.

He took the Mic away from his mouth and gave her that pretty ass smile. *Damn, that smile go in. Ahhh, this shit is bananas,* Tina could not believe things had turned out so well.

"AYE!" Tina yelled over the music. "Let me try that!"

"Let you try what?" he said, grinning. *She wanna spit?* He thought, walking towards her.

"Oh you got bars, baby?" he said, handing her the Mic. *She cool as a fucking fan.*

"Uh uh uh!" Tina started, giggling.

"Body real big, dick real little, PANTS DROP DOWN BALLS LOOK LIKE SKITTLES!" she began.

"HHHAHHHHAH Hell na," Souped said, getting super weak off of her. *That shit was funny but she also sounded good.* He wondered if she could sing to her tone and shit was near perfect.

"He looking for a nut, all he wanna do is fuck! When it goes down he take it in da butt!" she continued.

"Gimme that shit" he said, feeling weak, snatching the Microphone away from her. "Yo silly ass!"

"Nah, I was just fucking around with that," she laughed. Their eyes met and she felt that same spark she felt every time. *They say the eyes are the windows to the soul. If so, this gotta be my soul mate,* she thought.

****

"Man, search the whole fucking house!" Dred yelled into the phone.

"D, we don't do that, we just clean up," Tony replied.

"You heard what the fuck I said, now do I have to say it twice?" Dred said, his voice booming with authority.

"Alright man, I'll take care of it." Tony said, shaken up. He cleaned up enough of Dred's crime scenes to know that he was a cold blooded killer. *Piranha's in a tub* he thought. His boys were so surprised when they reported back to him. They said the tub was full of mush and blood. He got the chills just thinking about it. *Still, we gonna have to talk about this later. I'm a fucking boss too,* he thought.

****

Mila's petite frame fit perfectly in the cabinets under the sink. She heard someone pounding on the door. When the pounding stopped she felt her best move was to stay put. Her stomach was aching, but she had a high tolerance for pain.

About 20 minutes passed before she decided to crack the door open and peep out. She could not see anyone from her vantage point, but she definitely heard footsteps.

"Tony, there is nobody here." a male voice said. "There is just a white sheet on the ground. I see some body fluids, but not a lot."

"Why you cussing at me, I just got here?" he asked, continuing his conversation.

Damn, Mila though, *that's just the Cleanup crew.* She felt she could probably take these niggas pregnant and all. She knew Souped's house like the back of her hand, because she had been there several times.

Mila closed her eyes and took a deep breath before she stepped out of her hiding space.

Mila ducked down by the kitchen island as she heard one of the niggas go upstairs. She tuned everything out except for the sounds the men were making. Focused, she could tell there were only two people, one man near the bathroom and one upstairs.

She grabbed a knife out of the drawer and an apple out of the fruit bowl on the counter. The bathroom was in the hallway next to the kitchen so there was no way she could see him. "I have to bring him to me," she said.

As quiet as a mouse, she crept over near the entrance to the hallway. "Fuck you bitch," she said to under her breath, rolling the apple around the corner. The man, startled, came toward the kitchen thinking it was his coworker, but as soon he got near Mila she jumped out and stabbed him directly in his throat. There were no screams, only the sound of his body hitting the floor.

"Hey!" someone said.

Mila turned around to see the second man there. He looked pale, and she was sure he was shocked to see a pregnant wild haired women covered in blood. The thick red blood seeped out of the man's neck and pooled around her feet. It was the thing horror movies were made of.

With lighting speed, just like Ol School Joe taught her back when they were cool, she hurled the knife at the second man and hit him right in the middle of his forehead.

"AAHHAHHHHAHAHAHAHHA!" she laughed wildly, as his body crumpled.

Tony tried to call his men back to check on the search he told them to do, but he got no answer. He felt it in his bones that something was up.

"Get me my car," he yelled at his assistant.

Chapter 19

Tina waited and watched in awe as Souped completed his sound check. He was so captivating that she could not take her eyes off of him. She loved his broad shoulders and toned body. He was so polished. She thought, *you could always smell him from a mile away.*

Souped winked at Tina as he finished his set. *Damn, she over there looking so juicy. With her thick ass.* He wondered if they had time for a session before the concert later that night. He wanted it whenever he could get it. Every time they fucked, each time, was better than the last.

Souped completed his sound check and walked over to Tina.

"So, are you enjoying yourself? I want you to have a fire ass night." he said.

"I am!" she said, smiling from ear to ear.

"Damn baby, them jeans looking right!" he said, coming close to her, whispering in her ear. She was moist and ready to feel that big dick inside her again.

"I know they looking right, that dick print looking right too!" She replied, smiling.

"Oh really?" he said, pressing his dick against her leg. It was hard and thick.

"Aw fuck this! AYE, listen up! I need everybody to exit now. Go back stage." he commanded.

There were cleaning crews and security guards around as well, but not within ear shot.

Souped grabbed the Mic and repeated that everyone needed to leave now. Souped had power in this industry. When he spoke, people listened.

After they could see that everyone left Souped dropped his pants to the floor.

"Bring that ass here." he said.

"On the stage?" she asked, feeling the chills going through her body.

"Yep, get your ass here!" he demanded.

Tina walked over to Souped taking her T-shirt off. *He don't have to tell me twice,* she thought.

He tried to bend her over first but she stopped him. She wanted to suck that dick. She got down on her knees in front of him. Tina had never sucked it before, she wanted to save that. *Niggas tend to go crazy after some good head,* she thought. Hers was better than good. Shit, hers was better than better.

She slowly licked the tip of his dick, teasing him.

Her lips feel soft as hell, her mouth all warm and wet. He looked around and got a rush that he was about to fuck on stage. He never did that before.

She snapped him back into reality when she started sucking. He had to put his hand on his face. Her whole motion was so different than what he experienced from anyone before.

As Tina sucked Souped's dick she took her tongue and flicked it all over his dick. It tasted so good and smelled so fresh. She began to deep throat his dick. She went all the way to the base. He held the back of her head as she stayed there.

"Damn, what the fuck," he moaned. *How the fuck she breathing?* he thought. He got his answer when he felt her inhale through her nose. She began to slam the dick in her mouth. Her mouth almost felt like a pussy, he thought.

"Get your ass up!" He said, helping her up. He walked over with his pants at his ankles and pressed a button on the equipment. One of his songs began to play from the enormous speakers. He turned it down a little.

"Here, bend over this lil speaker right here," he said. He wanted the hum of the medium-sized subwoofers to vibrate his song on her pussy as he fucked her.

He pounded her as she screamed for him to give it to her harder. His thick dick was covered in Tina's cum. He kept looking around, thinking he would never forget this shit.

Chapter 20

Dred hung up on Tony. He was furious. He almost regretted telling him to have his guys search the house, because if she was still alive they were in trouble. At one point in time he loved her so much, but he realized that she was a master manipulator. *Hell, she had to be, she damn sure fooled me.* Somewhere inside of him he regretted not putting a bullet in her head. He knew some of her family and at the very least he wanted her to have an open casket funeral.

He could not help but to conclude that she was still alive, because dead bodies do not just get up and walk away. *It's getting ready to be a war,* he thought. She is going to try and turn anyone she can against me.

"Bitch," he said. When he caught her this time there would be no mercy spared. "I am gonna stand until she bleeds out completely," he said.

Tessa was so happy he planned to not ruin everyone's night telling them this. *He would have to beef up security for sure though,* she thought.

He got up from the desk wanting to be closer to Tessa. He could hear the shower running as he neared the bedroom area of the suite. She had left the door open, and he stood there and watched her through the foggy glass. He could see the shape of her brown body. Her ass wiggled a little as she washed her hair. He wanted to get naked and hop in the shower behind her.

He had to get focus. *Nah, it's not the right time,* he thought, *she deserves more.*

****

Mila ducked down in the seats at the top of the arena. With the naked eye all she could see were two figures on the stage. She knew Souped and Tina was fucking. *How creative,* she thought. Her heart jumped a little when she though back to her and Dred's first time. She almost loved him, but she quickly had to admit to herself that she just was not built for romance.

Mila had no regrets about her plans this night. She would make them all pay for ruining her fucking plans. They would regret the day they met her. She decided to pick them off one by one. She wanted them to have to morn and bury one body after another. She would save Dred for last so that he could endure the death of everyone he loved.

She put her hood on and grabbed her bags, then headed toward a nearby utility closet. There she would wait patiently in the dark until it was time.

****

Dred waited patiently as Tessa showered and styled her long natural hair. He was not as worried about Mila. He had lived in a home with her and her craziness. *She was always on the loose,* he thought. His mind went back to the child. He wondered who it belonged to. Who had she been sleeping with? He felt almost sure it was probably someone he knew but then again he knew a lot of nuthackers.

KNOCK! KNOCK!

Tessa ran over to open the door.

"Hold up!" Dred said, jumping up and stopping her. *That could be anybody,* he thought. *Hell nah, I can't protect her 24 7, Mila ass got to go ASAP.* The feeling he had when she was about to open the door was frightening. He would have to make some calls and put a real contract on her head.

"Who is it?" Tessa said sweetly.

"It's Summer, I am the stylist," she said.

Tessa opened the door to two racks full of clothes and shoes. *OMG, this concert is going to be killer!!!*

Chapter 21

"Aw fucking shit," Mila said, stretching her legs in the closet, while breathing hard and giggling to herself. "I can't wait until Dred see this shit. This shit is gonna be national news epic."

****

Everyone walked in the back to the area VIP of the concert. The arena was quickly filled with people. They could hear them chanting Souped's name, waiting on him to come to the stage. Dred and Tina were feeling great about the night, and they both looked and smelled like new money.

In his dressing room, Souped looked in the mirror feeling oh-so fresh! He had on the new black out Yeezys, and an expensive ass Givenchy T-shirt on.

He was iced out with over 250 thousand dollars' worth of jewelry on.

I gotta go out here and rock this shit, he thought. His dressing room was empty, except for Tina who was sitting on the sofa. Usually it was filled with his niggas and a bunch of half-naked females. They were all in the building, just not in the room. He wanted to ease Tina into his lifestyle.

"Damn, it's thick out there," Tina said, talking about the hallway. She was wondering why nobody was in there with them as she expected more excitement.

"Aye, I will be right back. I wanna go and see if Dred and Tessa made it, and I can't wait to see what outfit she got on." she said, smoothing out her leather Tom Ford tube dress. Her hair was in a neat bun that made her cheek bones look to die for. She had a fresh face beat. A nude lip and smoky eye had her looking like she was off the cover of a magazine.

"Got muthafucking damn, nigga!" She said to the stylist, Summer, earlier that day. She and Souped had to get there earlier than everyone else. *I been in muthafucka all day*, she thought.

"I will be right back," she said, walking out the door.

The bitches lingering in the hallway looked at her like, "who the fuck is she?" *Little did they know they had better shut the fuck up talking to me,* she thought.

One girl said, "I used to fuck him to a while back," popping her gum.

"Well, damn? You been out here waiting for some dick that long?" Tina said.

Souped could hear her talking, "Don't talk to them hoes baby," he said to her. "Fuck them, she a fucking stalker. Why is she out here?" he asked security.

****

Tessa and Dred actually planned to stand on the side of the stage during the first few songs of Souped's show. They talked and laughed as they headed up to their designated area.

"Oh my," Tessa said. "This is the livest shit that's ever happened to me."

We really just on the side of the stage for the biggest concert of the summer, she thought. *Somebody fucking pinch me, right now!*

****

As the music dimmed and Souped's song started to play, the crowd went wild. When he appeared on the stage, it was madness.

"Alright, put y'all MUTHA FUCKING hands in the AIIIIRRR!" He shouted, holding the Mic with one hand! His diamond's glistening, voice all sexy and smooth.

"Y'all fuck with ya boy. If y'all fuck with ya boy, make some fucking noise right now!" He said, smiling as all the women screamed.

At the very top section of the arena Mila cracked opened the door to the utility closet. Using the scope on her shit she scanned the stage looking for Dred. *Yeah nigga, fuck yeah,* she thought, *and he here with the bitch. I should shoot her ass right now*, she said laughing. *I win and you lose nuthackers!*

She pointed the tip of her long range rifle out of the door and winked her eye as she looked out of the scope. She lined Souped up for a clean ass shot. Her piece had a silencer on it. She thought no one would hear where this shit came from.

Pop!

Just as Souped started his first bar, a bullet tore through his right arm. *Oh shit!* Souped thought, "Cut the lights!" he said into the Mic.

The crowd went nuts, everyone scattered trying to get away but not knowing what the fuck was going on.

"Somebody just shot him!" a woman screamed.

"He hit!" a man yelled.

"He dead!!" another man said.

The crowd screamed as they headed for the nearest exit. Even though the stage was dark, there was still light coming from elsewhere. Some people even pulled out their phones to catch the action.

In the closet Mila braced herself to take another shot. At this point, she did not give a fuck who she hit on the stage. She pointed at the outline of a person on the stage. "Damn I should have got some fucking night vision," she said.

Pop!

The kick back of the gun pounded her shoulder so hard, she leaked piss on herself. *Got damn*, she thought, *what the fuck? Wait a minute, this ain't no dam piss.*

Chapter 22

Mila not yet feeling any contractions sat on the closet floor in shock. *I should be mad right now, but I am really feeling relieved,* she thought. *I don't have to deal with this pregnancy shit no more. I got to get the fuck out of here.*

Mila knew security would be doing sweeps of the arena. She figured it was still a lot of people running around and she could easily blend in. She hoped no one there would recognize her. She had a reputation to maintain.

Her pants and shoes where soaked with fluids. She was happy that she was dressed in all black. She hoped no one would notice it.

Like a pro, she broke down her rifle and packed it in the large back pack she brought with her.

"AAAHHHHAAAHH!" she screamed, in pain now that the first contraction hit her. It was the worst pain she had ever experienced in her life. She looked at her watch because she knew that she needed to keep track of the timing of the contractions.

As she opened the door to the utility closet she could see a lot of people still wandering about. Like a ninja she slid sneakily out of the closet and headed for the nearest exit. As she walked another contraction hit her and it stopped her in her tracks. She felt more fluid running down her leg as she winced in pain.

"Ma'am, are you OK?" A nearby concert goer asked.

"Mind your own got damn business!" Mila snapped.

The young women looked at her in confusion. *She looks like she is in labor,* she thought. She could see a faint outline of water in the shape of Mila's shoe print on the floor. *Did her water break?* She thought.

"She may be in denial, but she needs help," she said under her breath. The woman headed for the nearest security officer.

This nosy ass bitch, Mila thought, hurrying away from the closet. She felt a wave of relief when she finally made it out of the arena. She was walking towards her car in the parking lot as another contraction hit. "Damn," she said as she looked down at her watch. The contractions are now five minutes apart. This baby is coming.

She had no concern for the baby. She kept thinking about how much pain this would be for her. As soon as she got into her car she pulled out her phone and called Chastity, the nurse who helped her at the penthouse.

No answer.

She didn't know if the staff knew that Doc was dead yet. She was mad as hell to find out when Souped caught her trying to sneak out of the hospital.

"Hell yeah," she said, "I got his ass." *This wanna be Jay Z ass nigga, that's what the fuck he gets,* she thought.

"Ahhh…" Her insides were throbbing as another contraction hit. She put her car in reverse and pulled out of her space. She did not yet know where she was headed. She did not want to go to a real fucking hospital. "Fuck that," she said.

She cruised through the streets, calling the penthouse hospital number hoping someone would pick up. She decided that she was in route, and if someone was there she would make them help her, even if she had to do so by gun point.

At the elevator another contraction hit her, and she cursed everyone and everything.

"Come on out you little muthafucka," she said to her stomach. She stood at the elevator for five minutes and no one sent it down to pick her up. She knew the elevator was secured and it required the press of a button to be lowered to pick someone up. She resolved that there was no one up there.

I am about to have this baby I have to do something. The pressure in-between her legs was unbearable. She could barely walk straight. It was like her insides were falling out. She knew right then and there that she would never get pregnant again no matter what purpose it served.

Ducking into a nearby stairwell, Mila collapsed on the floor. She wanted to get this over with, and she figured that soon this night would just be another fucked up memory in her life that she would repress.

"Ughhh!" she screamed as she began to push the baby out. She took off her pants, held her legs up like she saw on TV, and pushed. After a few minutes she could feel something had slid out of her onto the ground. Without looking down she continued to push as she could still feel the pressure. Soon after, something else plopped out of her sore vagina.

She was shaking and sweating, still in pain, when at last she looked at the aftermath of her pushing. She could see a small baby girl lying on the cold, hard, concrete. Next to it, laid a something that resembled a brain. *What the fuck is that?* She thought.

She knew that she had to cut an umbilical cord. She reached into her back pack and got her knife, then cut the cord that was attached to the baby. She almost hurled three times as she cut through the thick cord.

"Waaaa!" The baby began to softly cry. It was about the size of man's hand.

"Bastard!" she screamed at it. She took a deep breath and stood up. Once on her feet a lot of fluid and blood began to rush down her leg. She fought through the pain as she struggled to get her pants back on. Once she did she took off her hoodie and wrapped the premature baby in it.

"Fuck, fuck, fuck!" she screamed as she pulled out of the parking lot. She drove to the closest hood of the city and went into the nearest alley.

Mila pulled her car down the dark, wet and deserted alley and stopped at the nearest trash can. She cut off her car headlights and grabbed the baby that was wrapped and screaming in her passenger seat. Quickly, she got out of her car and headed straight for an old, dirty trash can.

Numb to the world, she placed the baby in it and covered it up with the fowl smelling trash.

Chapter 23

As Souped began his performance he was the happiest he had been in a while. He thought about all the fans that were there to support him and his lady standing on the side of the stage.

"I been in the game a long time, hustle strong you know I earned mine, Hungry, grab a plate and get in line...... AHHHHHHHHHHH!" Souped screamed as he felt the bullet tear through his right shoulder.

"Cut the lights!" Souped screamed into the Mic. His heart was beating fast as he rushed to exit the stage holding his wounded arm. *Somebody just tried to assassinate me,* he thought. *What the fuck is going on?*

He could hear the screams of the people at the concert. Dred, Rocko and Tina rushed to the stage to grab him. Rocko used his body to block as Tina and Dred helped him off stage. He didn't know where the next shot was coming from but having Rocko block him eased his mind.

"Tina, get off the stage!" Souped screamed at her.

A second shot hit Rocko in his back. His adrenalin was running so high he felt it but did not yet feel the pain. The security team finally made it over to help them. Two huge men picked Souped up and carried him the rest of the way.

"I'm hit!" Rocko yelled out as they finally made it to the protection of back stage. He took off his bloody shirt to reveal a wound through his upper left shoulder. The bullet went through his shoulder and hit one of the nearby speakers.

Dred felt sick to his stomach. No one but him knew that Mila was still alive. He knew for a fact that she was behind this. The hatred built up for her in his heart. Whereas before he had still felt sorry for her, now he only wanted revenge. He would find her, he resolved. *She will regret the day she ever met me.*

The EMTs loaded Souped and Rocko into two separate ambulances parked in back of the arena waiting area. Tina hoped into the ambulance with Souped and held his hand as he lost consciousness.

She knew that whoever did this would be in her hands one day soon.

I am going to kill a muthafucka ASAP, Tina thought. *They fucked with the wrong family.*

****

Maybelle saw a car pull into her alley. She was out on the fire escape smoking a joint with headphones on. She saw a woman get out of her nice car with something in her hand.

"Well, what the fuck is going on?" She heard Mila cussing to herself. *Did I just hear a baby crying?* She dismissed it. She had saw a lot of weird things go on in this alley. As she watched her stuff something into the trash can she could not shake a feeling that was coming over her. Something said go look into the trash can.

As the car pulled off she sat her joint in the ash tray and got up. Maybelle was 38 years old, and stood 5' and 7" tall. She was 280 pounds with a deep chocolate complexion. She had a short natural afro that she kept well moisturized and neatly done. She climbed through the window slowly, as she was starting to get stuck. She started her second diet this year, and so far she lost eight pounds.

Maybelle walked through her neat and tidy apartment. She was very proud of her home. "Just 'because you live in the hood don't mean you can't have a nice home," she would always say.

As she neared the trash can in the alley she could definitely hear crying. She opened the lid of the can to find a small, premature baby covered in filth.

"Oh this trifling bitch. Oh LORD I pray for this child in your name. LORD protect this child, let her live LORD," she said as she felt chills come through her body.

The child was crying and that was a good sign, she thought. Its lungs were strong. She picked up the bundle carefully and headed back upstairs.

"Belle got you lil baby, I got you."

****

Dred hopped in his whip and sped out the parking lot headed towards the hospital. His heart was racing and he could not help but to feel responsible for the whole situation.

I brought this bitch into our circle, he thought. He knew that she had to be behind this. He was happy that the baby was not his. He did not have to live with fact that he was the one that killed the child's mother. He knew that she was relentless and one day it would come to that.

I gotta kill her before she fucking kill me, he thought. He shook his head to clear his thoughts and turn up the music. He could not let this bitch get him off of his "A" game. He needed a calm mind more, now than ever.

Mila touched the person that she knew he most loved, his brother, and for that she would have to face the consequences.

****

Maybelle hurried into her apartment with the small child. By the time she got to the top floor she was out of breath and felt light headed.

Oh LORD, she thought, *what do I do now?* She was torn on whether she should call the police as she looked down at the small child.

"LORD, if it was meant for me to find and keep this child let it be so, in your name," she said, raising one of her hands to the sky.

She caught her breath and got up to head toward the sink. She layered the sink with towels as to give the baby something soft to lie on. She tested the room temperature water before she laid the baby in the sink, carefully holding its head.

She smiled down at her as she watched her facial expressions. *LORD, she so small,* she thought, *this has to be a miracle that she seems so fine.* She washed the filth off as she stared into her eyes.

"What are we going to call you?" she asked. "I know, how about 'Heaven,' for the LORD surely sent you from above."

KNOCK KNOCK.

Belle's heart beat increased dramatically as she wondered who could be knocking on the door this time of night. Had any of her nosy neighbors saw her with the child? She resolved that she would not answer and let them knock. She continued to clean Heaven as she hummed one of her favorite gospel songs in her ear.

KNOCK! KNOCK!

The door rattled on its hinges as the person hit the door with all their might.

What in the world? she thought...

****

At the hospital Tina held Souped's hand as they rolled the stretcher towards the operating room.

"Ma'am, you will have to wait in the hallway. You can't come in here, please wait in the waiting room. We will be out in a couple of minutes," one of the nurses said.

Tina was five seconds away from catching an attitude. She held it in as she walked away. As she walked back toward the waiting room pissed off she bumped into Dred. She had tears streaming down her face. She figured he would live, but she was still hurt nonetheless.

"D, he's in surgery. He will be in there for a while. We need to go find out who the fuck did this, and do we know if the venue has security cameras? Let's get on this shit." she said in his ear.

"We gonna handle it, Tina" he said, hugging her, *she must be really feeling bro,* he thought. She did not seem like the type of woman who would cry.

"Let's go find them then!" she said, this time more forcefully and louder.

"I know who did it," Dred said, grabbing her arm and pulling her into the hallway. "It was Mila."

<u>Chapter 24</u>

"Mila? What is that bitch a ghost or something?" Tina snapped. She hated that she was taking her anger out on Dred. She decided to calm down a little bit. After all, it was his brother, and he is probably more hurt than she is. *What he means Mila, though? This bitch is dead,* she thought.

"What you mean Mila, nigga?" Tina said, this time with a calmer voice.

"She not dead." He explained to her how the cleanup crew never found her body.

"Are you fucking kidding me? We dropped the ball that heavy? Hell nah." Tina said. "So, where the fuck you think she at?"

"If I knew where she was, do you think I would be standing here?" he asked. "I cut off her access to my money, but who knows if she has some stashed elsewhere. She could be anywhere right now. What I do know is she want me dead, so she gonna show herself very soon."

"Alright, so what's the plan, man, where should we start? Where her momma live at?" Tina said, thinking of a grimy ass plan. "If we get her momma, you think that will bring her ass out?"

"Nah" he said, "That bitch hate her momma with a passion."

"Fuck, let me think on this shit for a second," Tina said, rubbing her temples. "I ain't just about to wait around for her ass to pop up. Nah, fuck that."

"Alright, I got a fucking plan!" She said.

****

Maybelle stood outside of her door with the baby wrapped up in a towel. Whoever was out there was knocking still. She decided to lay Heaven comfortably on the couch. As she walked back to the door she felt fear building in her heart. She could not recall anyone ever pounding on her door like that before.

"Oh LORD, I know you hear me. Protect me and this baby." she said under her breath, walking to the door. A floor board creaked and she froze in place. *Oh no!* She thought. *I hope they didn't hear that.*

When she finally got the courage to look out of the peephole she could not see anything but an orange blur. She knew then that someone must have had their finger over the peep hole. She got down on her knees and tried to look under the gap in the door to see if she could see anything. She saw black shoes. They looked small like a woman's shoe size...

Is that the mother? She thought. Paralyzed with fear, she began to recite the Lord's Prayer under her breath.

****

At the arena, Tessa was surrounded by security. Dred forced her to stay put and that shit pissed her off. *I am not a stay put type of female,* she thought. *I wanna know what the hell is going on too.*

She asked the security guards at least five times to take her to the hospital, and they refused. *They think they are about to hold me up in here, they are fucking wrong!*

"I am going to use the restroom! Move out of my way!" She snapped at the three big burly guys Dred left her with.

"Uh, Tessa we need to stand outside of the door. We don't know if the threat is still in the building." One of the men said.

"The threat?" Tessa laughed. "I'm the muthafucking threat!" She said, quickly snatching his gun out of his holster, and pointing it towards them as she hastily backed away. Once she got to the door she kicked her heels off and ran like it was no tomorrow. She knew for a fact that they big asses could not keep up with her.

As she neared the exit, she heard a woman giggling. "This lady is barefoot," she heard them say.

"I done seen it all tonight," one of the girls said. "I still can't believe that other skinny bitch was coming out of that closet going into labor. Her pants were wet and errr thang girl, that shit was cray!"

Tessa said "ugh" to herself as she kept walking. She did not have a car there. Dred took the car. *Damn,* she felt stuck. She decided that the hotel was not too far of a walk away. She was disgusted to walk on the dam nasty ass ground with no shoes on. "Fuck," she said!

****

Mila was glad that she had doubled back around the block. She saw that heffa get that baby out of the trash can. When she went into that ghetto ass apartment building she did not think she would be able to find her, until she saw her fat ass shadow closing the upstairs window.

As she knocked on the door she knew that she would have to shoot them both.

Chapter 25

Tony, the owner of the Cleanup Crew, arrived at Souped's house followed by two all-black trucks. He could see his van outside the house parked. He began to rub his chin, the wheels in his mind turning. He remembered his boys that he sent on this job had been working with him for years as he got out of his car. Juno, one of the men inside, was like a son to him. He did not have a son of his own and he hoped to groom him to convert from cleaning to businessman. He kept him on the field to teach him the value of hard work and the nature of their business from the ground up.

Tony made millions of dollars a month with his cleanup crew. They were known for being a professional bunch that could handle any crime scene and make sure there was no evidence left. Over the years Tony had become well connected. His client base included celebrities, politicians and CEO's.

Six other men hoped out of the other cars and ran ahead of Tony to scope the scene out. He was dressed in a traditional 3-piece black suit. He was clean and he prided himself on his Rat Pack fashion sense. He was in his early 40's, but not many could tell. He was mixed with White and Puerto Rican, although most could not tell what nationality he was that well.

Tony pulled out his own pistol as he walked cautiously to the door. He did not know who could still be in the house. He was hoping that there was just a reception issue with the phones and everything was just fine. That actually happened to him before. He was very protective of his employees, and he expected respect and decency from his clients.

Even though Dred was in the upper class of his clientele, Tony did not know if the small amount of fear he had would hold him back from retaliating. He respected Dred, but in some way the fear he had of him made him feel less of a man over the years. If Juno was harmed on this job, he and Dred would need to have a face to face. What troubled him was he did not know if he wanted to go to war over Juno, or his pride.

****

Mila could hear her ass breathing on the other side of the door.

You should have minded your own fucking business, she thought. Mila almost thought she heard her praying.

"Enough of this shit," she said. She knelt down in pain. Her stomach and pelvis were extremely sore. She wanted there to be no trace of her baby. *I should have not put it in the trash can,* she thought. She knew the moment she pulled away that it was a bad decision. She thought of the aftermath of a premature baby being found in a trash can by the local trash man on the news.

She sweated as pools of blood ran down her leg and collected in her shoe. She could not wait to get home and wash this night away.

"AAHH," Mila moaned quietly as she shifted the wrong way while unzipping her book bag to retrieve her rifle.

****

Belle had her faced pressed to the door as she saw Mila opening a book bag. When she saw the handle of a gun she knew she only had seconds to react.

"LORD protect me," she said, believing in her prayer. She grabbed her car keys and stuffed them into her pocket then ran over to the couch to pick the baby up. She cradled baby Heaven in her left arm as a tear escaped her eye.

Belle ran towards the door and with her right hand grabbed the wooden bat she kept by the door she called, "Sally." She never had to use Sally before, but she threatened a few people with it before.

Quickly, she flung open the door as Mila knelt putting her rifle together.

Whack!

She knocked Mila out cold with a one handed swing of the bat. She did not even bother to close her front door as she took off down the steps towards her car, praising the LORD the entire way.

****

Tessa walked into the lobby of the hotel bare foot. She hurried to the elevator hoping no one would see her.

Once she got in the room she stripped off her clothes and took a quick shower. She was pissed at the situation, and Dred. If they were going to be together, he would not control her movements. She would be included in everything.

After she got dressed in comfortable clothes and her Nike running shoes she called an Uber to take her to the hospital. She felt like shit without a car to even hop into.

"Hell nah, I gotta have my own too," she muttered under her breath as she waited on her ride.

Brring! Brring!

"Sis," Tina screamed into the receiver. "Take off the damn dress and come down stairs, we need you! It's time to ride. That bitch Mila ain't dead."

"Hell YEA!" Tessa screamed, hanging up the phone. My sister is my bitch, and she had to know that I wanted parts.

****

"Ion know. I don't want her involved in this," Dred said to Tina.

"D, Tessa is who you chose. You can't take who she is away from her. She does not wanna stay at home and wait for you. She wanna be a part of the action. Let her be her, if you try to change her, you're gonna lose her."

"You right," he said, knowing that Tina was being honest with him. "Tonight will show me if she can take care of herself in these streets, for real for real."

"Oh, she can." Tina said in a matter-of-fact way as she opened the door to hop out and let Tessa sit in the front.

Mila woke up on the hallway floor a few minutes after Maybelle got away. Her head was pounding, and she was starting to think that she needed serious medical attention. She got on her feet, grabbed her gun and stumbled into Belle's apartment, closing the door behind her.

Unsure if there was anyone else in the apartment, she locked the door behind her and began to search each room. It was not much to go through, as it was only a one-bedroom apartment.

"Fuck!" She screamed at herself. "This bitch got away." She looked down to see she had left a trail of blood on Belle's carpet. Quickly, with all the strength she could muster, she grabbed a few towels and proceeded to wipe the blood off of the hallway floor.

"This bitch ain't coming back here no time soon. Fuck it, I ain't got shit to lose," she muttered under her breath as she began to look though Belle's closet for something she could possibly wear. She chose a huge T-shirt and some battered draw string jogging pants. She was irritated with the big ass clothes, but at least they were clean.

In Belle's shower she washed herself clean as best she could. The pain and weakness was getting too much to bear, and at this point all Mila wanted to do was sleep. She figured that she would have to get a hotel room for the night. As the hot water from the shower massaged the soreness away she figured she would have to try to find Belle tomorrow. At some point she would have to come back home.

Her tiny frame was lost in Belles clothes, but it felt good to be clean. Luckily Belle had a new pack of cotton underwear that she had to tie on the side to make herself fit. She stole pads, socks and house-shoes as well. She was decked head to toe in Belle's gear.

"This is so fucked up," she said, preparing to go. She grabbed Belle's purse on the way out so she could have all of her personal information.

Once she reached the new fancy hotel downtown, she could not wait to get a room.

"Um, Ma'am are you looking for someone?" the clerk asked. He was not used to seeing bums book rooms. *Is she homeless?* he thought. *She looks like a crack head.*

"Yes, I am at the fucking right hotel! Get me a room, I could buy this hotel." Mila said, pulling out her wallet. She did not want to use Dred's account, that way he would not be able to find her. Good thing she had been squirreling away money for years. She had a huge ass bank account in her name that Dred knew nothing about. *Yea nigga,* she thought, *I was not doing that much shopping.*

"I am sorry ma'am, my mistake. Welcome to The Perianne." the clerk continued to check her in. *Well,* he thought, *you never know who is a millionaire. She must be one of those extreme cheapskates.*

****

"Punta!" Tony shouted in Spanish as he stepped through the front door of Souped's house. It did not take a long walk for him to see that both of his men had been executed in cold blood. He rubbed his chin and pondered what would his next move would be.

He needed time to form a solid plan or else fucking around with Dred would have him dead as well. He needed an assassin, and a damn good one fast. One with no prior dealings with Dred, and he thought he knew just the person.

****

Monty sat on his baby momma's front porch smoking a joint and talking to some of the neighborhood niggas. He had been on a high since he helped Dred merk those disloyal niggas in that meeting. *I'm in the door*, he thought. He wanted in Dred's team so bad. *The nigga was a good nigga,* he thought. He knew that as long as he stayed loyal he would not come under any harm. Some of these top niggas didn't give a fuck. Nowadays they would shoot your ass if you looked at them funny.

He and his baby momma had been fucking like rabbits since that shit happened earlier in the day. He was turned up because he knew that it was only a matter of time before Dred cracked the door open for him.

Beep! Beep!

A black Benz pulled up on the other side of the street. Monty stood up wondering what the fuck was going on. The window rolled down a tad, so much so that he could see the driver's eyes. *Oh fuck that's D. I thought this nigga up.*

He jogged over to the car. "What's up, Family?"

"I need your help, nigga you down?" Dred said in his usual cool manner.

"No questions asked my nigga, let's go," Monty said, hopping into Dred's back seat.

****

At the hotel, Mila walked towards her room as two women carrying an ice bucket walked past her.

"Oh," one of the women whispered. "That's that fucking lady, what the fuck? She doesn't even look pregnant no more," she said to her home-girl.

Mila heard every word. *Will this fucking night never end?* She thought. *Now I gotta kill both these bitches. They know too much,* she said. She stalled outside of her door so she could peep what room they were in.

Once they went inside their room Mila pulled a pocket knife that she had out of her book bag and walked calmly towards their door.

KNOCK! KNOCK!

"Room service," Mila said in her nicest voice.

"We didn't order any room-service," one of the girls said, walking toward the door.

Hesitantly, she opened the door to see Mila standing there looking deranged with the knife out. Before she could close the door Mila already had the knife at her neck daring her to make another fucking move...

Chapter 26

Souped laid in the hospital bed, unconscious. The surgery had been successful and the medical team decided to let him sleep through the night. He was located in the private wing of the hospital, which was usually reserved for celebrities and high net worth individuals.

Rose crept down the hallway past the gossiping nurses looking for Souped's room. Once she got near the nurse's station, she sneakily glanced at the nurse's board looking for Souped's room number.

"Aha, room 585," she said excitedly under her breath. *I am going to make sure I be here for my nigga. He knows dam well he cares about me.* She popped her gum as she rushed to his room. She didn't know who that bitch was earlier coming out of his dressing room, but *she had better fall back.*

She played back in her mind the one night she slept with Souped. It was the best dick she ever had in her life and she could not wait to get another piece of it.

"Aww, poor baby," she said, entering the room. "I know what will cheer him up," she said.

She lifted his hospital dress and started to rub on his soft dick.

"Nothing like a little head to wake a nigga up," she said, laughing...

****

"Back your ass up," Mila said quietly, shutting the door behind her. "Don't touch that fucking phone. This what nosy bitches get," she said, slicing the girl who answered the door's throat.

The girl who had seen her at the area and told her friends tried to run passed Mila into the bathroom.

Mila powered by craziness stabbed the girl repeatedly as soon as she came within arm's reach. She stabbed her for all the frustration she felt that night.

"Now, I can finally fucking sleep." Mila said, stealing some of the girl's luggage.

She peeked out of the room before dashing down the hallway to hers. She was covered in blood and could not afford for anyone to see her.

She went straight to the phone to call the Cleanup crew.

"Tony. It's Mila, I just fucked someone up at The Perianne Hotel," she whispered into the phone.

"I need you to come ASAP to get this shit, please Tony," she said sweetly, happy that he was not able to see how she looked right now.

"Mila, I am sorry but Dred is no longer a client of mine. You will have to find someone else to do it," Tony replied.

"Fuck Dred, F-U-C-K that nigga! I want his ass dead! I don't fuck with him. I have my own money and I need someone to clean this shit." Mila said. "You don't believe me, check the news. That was me who shot his brother."

Hmm, this is interesting, Tony thought, *seems I am not the only one with revenge on the brain.* This could work to his advantage, plus Mila was a pretty ass bitch, and he liked his women crazy.

"Alright, give me the details and I will help you, but it's gonna cost you." Tony said.

Mila rattled off the details to Tony.

"Alright, so we will clean up the scene and wipe any video footage from the hotel cameras," Tony spoke softly into the phone. "I will call you when it's done. We also have other business to talk about." he said, hanging up the phone.

By the time Tony disconnected, Mila was feeling faint. Before she knew it, she collapsed on the bed.

****

Rocko woke up in his hospital bed.

"Damn," he said. "I fucking hate hospitals!" He grabbed the intercom to page his nurse.

"Yes, what can we help you with?" the speaker on the wall relayed to him.

"I need my nurse." he responded.

"She will be right in," the voice said.

A tall, bubbly blonde, young nurse popped in the room a few minutes later. Smiling, she asked, "How can I help you, do you need something for sleep? How's your pain?"

"I need to find out where Souped is," Rocko asked her, knowing that he was such a celebrity she would know exactly where he was.

"Well, I think you need to get some sleep," she said, fluffing his pillows.

"Man, I'm a grown ass man. Stop with all this shit. That's my nigga and I need to go check on him. I am sore, but otherwise I feel fine." He said, smiling at her. He knew that women had a weak spot for his eyes.

Without asking another word, he stood up.

"Take this out of my arm." He wanted the fucking IV out, and he wanted to get the fuck out of there. He could go to his mom's house, and she could clean wounds and take care of him, he thought. It would not be the first time.

"You're not going to take no for an answer?" she asked, grabbing his arm. "Sit down. I will help you, but on one condition."

"What's that?" he asked.

"Give me your number," she asked, blushing.

"Hell yeah! Now get this shit out of me," he said, laughing as he smacked her on her butt.

Outside of Souped's room there were not many people around. He could hear nurses talking and laughing, but they must have been in the nurse's station stealing snacks and talking shit.

"This is it," she said, opening the door.

"What the fuck!" Rocko said under his breath. He and the nurse stood there shocked to see girl riding this nigga while he was out cold.

"Bitch!" Rocko said, reaching out to pull her off.

****

Click deep in Dred's whip they passed the joint around as they headed to Dred's house to search through Mila's shit to find out where she was.

"Sooo…" Tina asked. "Nigga, who is you?"

"Shit, I'm just a fucking hood ass nigga that is down for the cause. I would not be in this car if you could not trust me." Monty replied. *Damn,* he thought. *This is one pretty ass female. Look at them thighs and that pretty ass smile. I would eat her pussy like an apple pie*, he said, picturing Tina sitting her pussy on his face.

"Boy!" Tina snapped at him. *Is this nigga staring at my titties?* She thought.

"What up," he said playing it off. "I was just over here thinking about whoever fucked with my nigga got it coming to they ass."

Dred chuckled upfront in the driver's seat, *wrong girl to crush on,* he thought. He would have to have a talk with Monty later and make sure he knew that she was Souped's girl. *Shit, he should know, as many blogs was talking about that shit.*

Dred took out his cell and dialed Tony.

"Tony, I meant to call you right back my dude, but shit got hectic," Dred spoke as he blue toothed the call to his radio speakers so he could be hands free.

"Um…" Tony hesitated. Anyone could hear the fear in his voice even though he had said only one word.

"We have a problem, and I can no longer do business with you. Both of my guys, including Juno, was murdered," Tony said, thinking to himself that he meant to call a sit down meeting to discuss this shit. He resolved to himself that he was too rich to get his hands dirty. The reality, though, was that he was scared as fuck. He knew that a face to face with Dred meant there was a small possibility that he could never walk out that room again and he was not willing to risk that.

He had decided to set Dred up to meet him. When Dred got to the meeting there would be something else waiting on his ass.

"Tony, I am sorry for your loss man, but I had absolutely nothing to do with that. I--"

"Dred," Tony said, cutting him off. "I am in the area and we need to speak about this man to man. Can you meet me tomorrow?"

"Yes, that's fine, we need to clear this shit up." Dred said, starting to get irritated at this nigga.

"Alright, I will send you the location tomorrow." Tony said, hanging up the phone.

"You gonna let that nigga talk to you like that," Tina said, talking shit.

"Fuck you," Dred said playfully.

Tina laughed and tried to seem cheerful, but she could only think of Souped. This shit was taking too long, and she wanted to go check on him. She made up

her mind that they would have to stop there next. She
didn't think Dred would deny that request.

In the mansion that Dred and Mila shared the
group went straight to the bedroom.

"Alright," Dred said. "We are looking for bank
statements, receipts, anything that could give us a clue
to where she is."

Monty went straight to Mila's laptop that she had
sitting on the night stand. "Now I can show how useful I
am," he said. In his younger days he was a straight up
gamer computer nerd. If she had something in this
computer to be found, he would get straight to that shit.

He opened her computer.

"No password," he said. She had no password to
get into her computer. That mistake on her part saved
him time.

"This is going to be too easy." he said, confidently
smiling.

As the group destroyed the room looking for
documents, Monty invaded Mila's Laptop.

"Got something," Monty said, grabbing
everyone's attention. "D. do you bank with Chase?" he
said, logging onto Mila's account.

"Hell no!" Dred said. "What the fuck is that?" he
said, looking at an online Chase bank account profile
with a 2-million-dollar balance. "I knew it," Dred said.

"This account was last used at the The Perianne
Hotel, Today." Monty said, looking at the shocked faces
in front of him.

Chapter 27

Rocko winced in pain as Rose lay on the floor, shocked.

"Hey, I'm Rose. I been fucking with Souped, ask him!" she yelled, holding her arm.

Rocko looked over at Souped. His arm was in a cast, and he was knocked out in the bed with his hospital gown up.

"Man, bitch, this nigga sleep!" he said, walking towards her. "I ain't never fucking seen yo ass around this nigga."

"You fucking with the wrong bitch! He gonna be pissed at you," she said back to him, looking him dead in his eye.

He sized her up for a second. He guessed that he didn't know everyone this nigga was fucking with. *She is a ten*, he thought, looking down at Rose. Her skirt was raised up, and he could see her fat juicy shaved pussy. *I don't fucking know.*

He walked over to Souped and tried to shake him.

"Aye, can you wake this nigga up?" he said to the nurse. He thought to himself, *I don't even know her fucking name.* He glanced down at her name tag, it read, "Asha."

"Asha, help me wake this nigga up." he said. "Ion know what the fuck is going on here, but I think this nigga was getting raped or some shit," He thought, *damn*.

"I think we need to leave him sleep. Let's just get her out of here. I don't want to lose my job," Asha said.

"I'm not going no fucking where until my man wake up!" she said, standing on her feet. She walked toward Asha, "you won't touch me bitch."

Asha didn't hesitate. She cocked back and knocked Rose dead in her nose. Her shit instantly started to leak as she moaned in pain.

"Shut up, bitch!" Asha said, grabbing Rose's neck.

Damn I got me one, Rocko said as he looked at Asha, grinning.

****

Dred's fucking wig was blown back. "This bitch been at the same hotel we at now…" he said.

"That's our hotel," Tessa said to Monty. *We got this bitch*, she thought. Her head began to dance with thoughts on how she would pay Mila's ass back for what she put her through.

She zoned out for a second and thought back to that small room in Carlos' basement where they held her. She thought about the darkness and how she kept her head from being consumed by it. The first night she spent there, Carlos came down and pulled her out of there. She remembered crying, telling him to let her go.

"Naaah," Carlos said to her. "You my personal pussy stash."

"Tessa," Dred called, waiving his hands in front of her face. He could see the pain on her face, and wondered what thoughts had her facial expressions looking pissed. He was waiting on her to tell him what happened to her. He didn't want to ask. He wanted her to trust him enough to know that her mind and her body were safe with him. He walked over to her and held her in his arms.

She buried her face deep in his chest and took a deep breath. She knew more than anything, that when she got her hands on Mila it would be a slow and painful death for her. She was almost happy she was still alive. She felt like suicide didn't do her justice. *This bitch deserved an epic death, one for the history books,* Tessa thought.

Dred grabbed her hand and held it close to his chest as they headed for the front door.

"Let's get this bitch!" Tessa said through her tears.

****

Maybelle had been driving for an hour. She didn't know where to go. She didn't want to go to one of her family member's house.

Belle was still unsure of what she should do with the baby. A part of her felt like she found the baby for a reason. She was so shaken that the only thing that she had to go on was her instincts, and they were telling her to go back home.

She kept looking at her phone and keying in *911,* then deleting it.

LORD, show me the way, she pleaded, *I trust you LORD.* With that thought Maybelle turned her car around and headed back towards her house. It was the only place she felt safe. No one would take her home away from her. She was hoping that since that lady had just had a baby and got knocked in the head, she would still be out cold, or even better, dead.

She didn't know what she was getting ready to walk into, but her heart said to go home. She could not go to a hotel and she had left her purse. As she pulled up outside her apartment building she said a silent prayer of protection as she grabbed baby Heaven out of the passenger's seat.

****

Mila's ringing phone woke her up.

"Tony," she answered, sounding sleepy.

"My guys are there. I am in the area and I need to cover a lot of ground in a short amount of time," he said.

Mila touched her hair and face. *Oh shit,* she thought. *I look a hot ass mess.* Her eyes glanced in the direction of the luggage she had just stolen from the now, dead girls down the hall.

"Uhhh," she said, walking over to open the luggage. There was some cute shit in there. A makeup pouch was tucked in the side compartment.

"Hello," Tony replied, wondering what the holdup was.

"Yea, come on," she said to him, thinking she could try to be presentable. It was eleven thirty pm, and she guessed that she had been asleep for a couple of hours. She was still sore as hell.

"I have a headache. Do you think that you can bring me some pain meds? Anybody on your crew got some?" Mila said, in her sexiest voice.

Mila heard talking and shuffling on the phone as Tony asked the niggas in the car with him.

"Yeah, we got some perks. I will be there in about 30 minutes..." he responded.

****

Dred and his team valeted the car outside of The Perianne hotel. They hopped out and headed toward Dred's and Tessa's room to plan how they would find out which room she was in. This was a big ass hotel, but for the right price any information could be purchased.

****

Mila quickly hung up the phone and headed towards the shower. She felt disgusting, and she felt that she would have to take ten showers before she would feel clean again. As she washed her body she looked down at her empty stomach. It was still a little pudgy, but she could see her shape again.

"Aww shit, a bitch is back." she said. "Annnd this pussy still tight." She was referring to the fact that she had just pushed out a small baby.

She was almost on a high because she was so relieved that she was not pregnant anymore. She almost forgot about the problem that she had on her hands with Maybelle.

It hit her like a ton of bricks. "Shit," she said. She fucked up. "Why the fuck did I put the baby in a fucking trash can?" That was a bad move that she was really regretting. She wondered if the fat lady called the police yet.

"Fuck it," she said. "I live in the moment and not the past. Right now everything is cool, and everything is still under my control. I need to find that bitch, asap though."

She brushed that shit off of her shoulder and resolved to let the chips fall where they may. *Shit, the old bitch probably wanted to keep the baby. Ion know if I can let her ass live,* she thought. If she had called the police when she first found the baby, they should have been there before she left. Mila added the time as best she could. Laughing, *I took a shower in that bitch and everything.*

Turning off the water she realized that she was starting to feel a lot better. She still felt like she was the shit, she still felt like she was unstoppable and she still felt that she had a good enough hand to go all in.

Mila took her time rummaging through the women's clothes. She was happy when she found some panties her size. She tossed the clothes that she stole from Belle in the trash can.

"Nah, she can't keep that baby. If a child of mine gonna walk this earth, it won't be with a bummy bitch," she said under her breath, wondering why she was even thinking about that baby still.

Once she got dressed and put on makeup to cover the dark circles around her eyes, she looked in the mirror. Mila knew she was bad as fuck. She had brushed her long hair so that every strand was in place. When it came to her appearance she knew that she had fucking OCD. She felt the shittiest she ever felt in her adult life. *I can't wait to this fucking day is over,* she thought.

Mila had on a nice pair of damaged True Religion Jeans and a fitted black polo tee. She was surprised to find a pair of brand new Polo Buddies in the suit case as well. They were a size too big but she knew she would have to make it work.

TAP! TAP!

Mila walked over to the door knowing that Tony was on the other side of it.

"Hey Tony," she said, letting him in. She opened the door and strutted away so he could get a good look of her ass as she walked away.

"Milaaaa, nice to see you," Tony said after he told his men to wait in the hallway.

"I thought you were pregnant," he commented.

"I was but I had a miscarriage," Mila snapped back at him.

"Aww... I am sorry to hear that," Tony said, trying to sound sincere, but really, he was happy as hell because he had been digging her for a while.

"So let's discuss why I am here..." he continued.

****

As Asha choked Rose out, Souped slowly began to regain consciousness.

"What the hell," he said, groggy, wiping his eyes hoping that he was seeing things. "This better be a fucking dream."

"Naah bruh, this ain't no dream and do you know ol' girl, cause my, nigga, we just walked in here to see her riding you my nigga, like *really* riding you," Rocko said, while he made motions with this unhurt arm.

Souped looked down at his hospital gown which was raised, and then looked at ol girl.

"Haaa haa," Rose laughed as Asha let her neck go. "Told you that he knew me. What's up baby? I came up here to give you some of that feel good."

"Man, did I fucking nut? I don't remember shit." he said, ignoring Rose. "That's all the fuck I wanna know." His worst fear after seeing what Dred had been through recently was having a baby by a crazy bitch. This was like a nightmare come true. *Damn Tina*, he thought. Would she believe that he had basically been raped? *We gotta get this bitch out of here. This bitch gotta die, she gotta pay the price for this shit, ain't no fucking way.*

"Man, nigga, this stalker ass bitch. I fucked her one time and she been following me around since then," he said as he got up. *I got to get the fuck out of here*, he thought, opening the hospital closet door.

Rose kept talking, but Souped was so pissed and disoriented, he just ignored her. She was definitely gonna be dealt with, but the biggest problem he had was who the fuck shot him. Somebody was out for his neck, and for all he knew he had no enemies.

"Man, we gotta 86 this bitch," Souped said to Rocko.

Rose was standing there looking crazy ass fuck, talking about, "I don't know what an 86 is, but I know what a 69 is."

Pow!

Rocko used his good arm to knock Rose ass clean the fuck out.

"I don't hit women," he said to Asha. "But this bitch here is as good as dead. We need to get out of here."

"Yeah," Souped said in deep thought. "We need to get to that hotel now. I don't know why they ain't here but they gotta be there." Souped didn't have his cell phone or anything. Dred changed his numbers often, and he didn't have the chance to get familiar with Tina's number. He felt ass out.

"Yo, you got a phone bro?" Souped asked.

"Hell nah," Rocko said, finally realizing it.

"I got one." Asha said, offering hers up.

"Nah, I don't got they fucking phone numbers. They at the hotel though. Some shit is going down. I can feel that shit in my bones."

"I can help you get out of here," Asha said to them. "There are a lot of paparazzi near the front entrance. I can take y'all to the employee parking lot where my car is," Asha said. She knew that she was a risk taker, and she wanted to live a little any way. *Shit, I can get a job anywhere. I am a fucking nurse, and they not gonna fire me over this shit.*

Asha went to go get a wheel chair for the crazy bitch.

When she got back, they dropped her limp body into the chair.

"Follow me," Asha said.

She took them through all of the short cuts straight to her car. *Good thing its third shift,* she thought. The only other people they had come across so far were environmental services janitors, and they could fucking careless about what was going on.

They all loaded up into her car as she got the fuck out off of the hospital's premises.

"What are we going to do with her?" Asha asked.

"We gonna kill her ass," Rocko said. "You got a problem with that?"

"Do what you gotta do," Asha said, smiling. "Damn, he is a real fucking thug," she mumbled.

Once they rolled through the hood on their way down town, Rocko asked her to pullover near the first small time dope boy they came across.

Rocko hopped out and made a quick exchange with the young dude and got back in the car quickly.

"Aye, here. Stop in this alley," Rocko said. He had purchased 75 dollars' worth of crack and a needle from the young dude. He picked Rose out of the car and laid her next to an old trash can. Using what he could find he melted the rocks down and injected all 75 dollars into Roses arm.

"I think that should be enough to kill a muthafucka," he said, walking away.

Maybelle stood with Heaven in her arms looking out of her window. She had been standing there because she also had a view of the cars driving past on the main street. She could not believe what she had just seen.

"I hate this alley!" she said. She wondered if she should go downs stairs and help another person left in that alley for dead.

****

Once Dred and everyone got to the hotel room, Dred went straight to the phone and called the front desk.

"Can someone bring some fresh towels up to our room?" he said politely. *Whoever the fuck was going to bring those towels up stood to make a lot of money if they had the access to the right information.*

****

Mila walked over to the mini bar in the hotel room.

"You wanna quick drink? "she asked, winking at him. *Hell yeah,* she thought. *I need another boss in my life. Fuck Dred ass, this nigga rich too.* She winked at Tony and smiled.

"Do you have time for that?" she asked sweetly.

"Sure, why not?" he said. His voice was deep and smooth with just a hint of his mother's Puerto Rican accent. *Look at that fucking body.* He felt like, *fuck Dred, and what better way to say fuck you than to steal your bitch.*

She poured Tony a stiff drink and placed it in his hands as she sat close to him on the sofa. She placed her hand on his leg and asked him, "To what do I owe this pleasure?"

"Well, this is going to be a tough conversation. Wait. First, let me ask you again… What's up with you and Dred?" Tony said, wanting to look Mila in her eyes as she told him they were over. He knew he could spot a fucking liar from a mile away.

"We have been done for a while, but we stayed together because I was pregnant. He could not handle a bitch like me. He wanted a stay at home, goody two shoes ass hoe. This nigga cheated on me, and he with the bitch right now. Fuck both of them. I am just happy that we didn't bring a baby into the situation. I lost love for him a long ass time ago, and to tell you the truth, that nigga better off dead. He thinks he's the fucking king of this city. He ain't the only boss around these parts," she said sweetly, stroking Tony's bruised ego.

Tony looked her in her eyes as she spoke and there was nothing there. She was telling the honest truth. She did not care what happened to Dred. He could not be happier. He decided then and there that he would let her in on his plot to wipe this nigga off the earth. All of the close contact he had with her had his dick feeling like he was about to stand up. He heard of

Mila's handy work before, and he knew of the side bitches that she had killed over Dred. Hell, his men had been the one to clean up afterwards. *She was ruthless but she obviously was a fucking Queen and if Dred didn't see that then, his fucking loss*, he thought.

"So, what's up?" he said to her. He wanted to cut straight to the chase. He had so much status that he didn't have to beat around the bush.

"Let us get to know you better, I peeped you out for years now." Tony said, putting his arm around her.

"Whatever you want to be up," Mila said, blushing and putting on her classic innocent act.

"Alright then, this is Dred's last day alive. I am cutting his shit short tomorrow. This is what I have set up," he began as he laid back in his seat, and took the drink to his head. *No turning back now,* he thought.

****

Maybelle paced the kitchen floor. She laid the baby down on the couch. She had to clear her mind.

She didn't know if she should call the police and report that she had the baby. Now she had to worry about if she should call the police and report the woman that was clearly dying in the alley. She peered out the window to see the woman shaking and convulsing.

She began to sweat beads as she picked up the phone and keyed in 911.

"911, what's your emergency?" The operator asked.

"Yes, I need an officer and paramedic immediately to 233 South Lane Street." Maybelle spat out. *Oh no,* she thought. *This is going to be a long ass night.*

****

Souped, Asha and Rocko pulled into the parking lot of the hotel and cut the engine off.

"Aye, I can't walk in there like this with this hospital gown on," Souped said, feeling lost.

"I need you to go up to my brother's room and knock on the door and tell him I am down here," he said to Asha.

"Cool, I am down, what's the room number? "She asked.

Souped gave her the information and laid back in the car seat. He was in so much pain. He almost wished that he had stayed his ass in the hospital. He thought about Rose in that alley. He didn't know if that had been a smart move. *Should we have just left her there like that?* The pain had his mind all over the place. He needed his brother bad at this point. He knew Dred would be able to set shit straight.

Asha walked into the hotel and could not believe how nice the lobby was. She was feeling Rocko and star struck by Souped at the same time. Her heart was racing and the thrill had her smiling from ear to ear. Fuck Netflix and chill, this was some other type of shit.

She pressed the button for the elevator. When the doors opened a cute couple walked off arm and arm.

Damn, she cute, she thought. *I like them shoes, I ain't never seen Polo Buddies like that before.*

****

Mila and Tony decided to go to the bar for a drink and continue their conversation with a bite to eat. On the ride down she felt salty that she could not fuck just yet. It was getting hot and heated in the hotel room, and she had to use this as an excuse so he wasn't wondering why she was not going all the way. *This pussy doesn't flake on dick,* she thought.

As she got off the elevator she noticed the pretty blonde starring at her. *Damn, what the fuck she looking at?* She was hormonal as fuck. She had popped the Perks that Tony had given her, and she could not feel an ounce of pain.

They went straight to the bar and ordered a couple of drinks.

"So, do you think the plan will work?" Tony asked.

"Hell, but we don't need to get just him. We need to make sure they off, the bitches that I was telling you about too." Mila said, winking at him. She knew by then that Souped was still alive. That shit was all over the news. She was had a back story behind a world-wide trending topic, and they ain't even know it.

"Alright, whatever you want. I am a provider, unlike his ass. I will make sure you are taken care of in every way," Tony said, dead ass serious.

****

KNOCK! KNOCK!

Asha stood at the door not knowing what to expect. She wore scrubs with smiley faces on them, and it was the middle of the night. She shook her head at the thought, laughing. As she stood waiting for someone to answer, a hotel employee walked up right behind her holding a pillow. *Damn, good timing*, she thought.

"Who is it?" Tina asked.

The employee behind Asha called room service.

Tina opened the door and let them both in.

"Actually, I am not room service," Asha said, a little out of place. *That bitch look like she doesn't play*, she thought. "I have a message for Dred from his brother."

"I'm Dred. What the fuck is going on?" he said with authority.

She walked over to him and said quietly, "Your brother wanted to leave the hospital and he is down stairs in my car. He didn't come up because he had on the hospital gown. He needs clothes."

"Fuck," Dred said. He would need to go to the bar and get a drink soon. This shit was getting so deep. "Aye, can y'all handle this?" he said, pointing to the room service person, and then handed Tessa a white envelope full of money.

"We got this, baby." Tessa said, and then kissed him on the cheek.

Dred grabbed a couple pieces of his clothes and headed out the door with Asha.

"Now, tell me what the hell is going on?" He asked, getting on the elevator.

Asha began to replay the night just as it happened. As they got off the elevator Dred glanced towards the bar ...

Chapter 28

Dred looked over at the bar and thought how bad he needed a drink.

****

As Tony laughed at Mila's jokes, thinking everything was going great, he caught a glimpse of a familiar face out the corner of his eye. Dred?

"Excuse me for a second baby, I need to use the restroom." Tony said, patting her on the back.

This Bitch, he thought as he walked into the men's restroom in the corner of the bar area. He turned on the water in the sink and splashed his face. He was fucked, he thought. "This bitch is trying to set me up," he said, peeking out the door.

Mila sat at the bar and joked with the bartender. She almost looked like she was flirting with him. While she had her head in the other direction he slipped out of the men's room and headed towards the elevator.

As he crept around the corner into the main lobby of the bar, he could see Dred walking out of the front door. He damn near ran his ass over to the elevator and pressed the button repeatedly until the doors opened. Once he got into the elevator and the doors closed he felt relieved.

"That bitch almost got me," he said, heart beating fast, and hands shaking. He knew then that he was terrified of Dred and that had his mind fucked. His dad always told him, "A scared nigga is a dead nigga." He knew now that Dred had to already know the meeting was a setup and he would be coming after him. He had to come up with a new plan, and quick, he thought.

****

Mila sat at the bar for almost 10 minutes before she began to wonder where Tony was. Is he shitting or something in there? She was beginning to feel sleepy and wanted to bring the night to a close. Her body needed rest. She didn't wanna go into that shock shit she heard about before.

She got up and walked over to the bathroom and knocked on the door.

"Yooo hoo, you in there dropping bricks or what?" she asked, laughing. She didn't get a response, so as bold as she is she opened the door. It was a nigga in there pissing and she just walked right in to see that Tony was not in there.

"What the fuck?" she said.

"Can I help you with something?" the weird ass man said, turning around with his dick still in his hands.

If this was any other night, I would cut his dick off talking that shit. she thought.

"Fuck you," she snapped at him as she spat on the ground near his feet.

Mila was pissed. She felt confused and vulnerable. "Oh, you on some bullshit, Tony." she said.

****

Maybelle waited with the baby in her arms as the police ascended up her stairs. All she could do was pray.

"Ma'am, did you call 911?" the tall Caucasian officer said in a friendly tone.

"Yes, well… This has been a long night. There is a girl downstairs in the alley who is overdosing off of drugs." As Maybelle spoke each word she kept going back in forth in her mind about whether or not she was going to tell them about the baby.

"I saw it out of my window." she said, looking down.

"Ok, did you see anything else?" he asked.

Are you really about to do this? she thought. "No, I didn't see anything else," she said softly.

"Ok ma'am, thanks for being a Good Samaritan. Go back to bed. We will take care of it." he said.

Maybelle said goodbye to the officer and closed the door. She went over and picked up baby Heaven. She was so small. She had been suckling and she would need to eat soon. She didn't know what she could do, what she could feed her. She figured that there had to be some kind of formula that babies that small could drink. She turned on her computer. She had a lot of Googling to do. She also had to figure out how she was going to make this child appear to be hers.

"LORD, I know this baby is with me for a reason. Use me LORD. Bless me with the wisdom to fix this mess." Maybelle said, crying softly.

****

Tina looked the hotel employee over and she took the pillow.

"Sit down, we have some talking to do..." she said.

Chapter 29

Maybelle could see the lights of the ambulance bouncing off the wall of the alley and filling her living room with color.

She glanced at Heaven lying on the couch asleep. The thing that concerned her the most was that the child was so small. In her head she wondered how much she weighed. A light bulb went off in her head. She had been trying to lose weight for so long that she owned two scales. The best quality one was the digital one that she ordered off of Amazon.

She ran in her bedroom and grabbed the scale, then a towel out of the hallway closet. She decided to try and get the most accurate weight of the baby. By the pictures she saw online just then of preemies, she looked to be between 30 and 32 weeks old.

She covered the scale with the towel and adjusted it so that it read 0. Carefully, she laid Heaven on the scale.

3.11

"Ok, so that is not that bad," she said, trying not to wake the baby. She laid her back on the couch and ran back to her computer.

An hour later she had a list of all of the items that she would need to take care of the baby.

"I am doing the right thing," she said. She could feel it in her spirit. The next website she went to was

Craigslist. She knew that she had to get out of this apartment as soon as possible. "The lady took a shower in here and everything," she said, walking over to the bathroom.

"LORD, she done stole my clothes," she said, looking in her bedroom. "Oh no! No! No! She done took my purse to!!"

****

Tony got off the elevator and rushed over to his men who were still stationed outside of Mila's room.

"We need to get the fuck up out of here. It's fucking set up. That rat bitch," Tony said, pissed off.

"Fuck her fucking crime scene. Let them catch her dumb ass. Who kills a muthafucka in a hotel anyway?" he continued.

"Well, I think they are almost done anyway," One of the men said.

"Let's fucking go now!" Tony said, heading towards the stair well.

***

Asha took Dred to her car. Inside, he could see his brother laid out in the back seat. He was furious. This shit was getting out of control. Two fucking bullet wound having ass niggas in the back seat. This was the moment he regretted killing Doc.

He hopped in the back seat and helped Souped get dressed.

"Bro, he just killed a stalking ass bitch." Souped said. "This hoe came up to the fucking hospital and fucked me while I was sleep bro, you can't make this type a shit up!"

"Y'all killed her in the fucking hospital. This nigga is a celebrity. He can't move like we move," Dred said, mean mugging Rocko.

"Nah we killed her in an alley, my nigga, I am not dumb," Rocko said, irritated by the pain his body was in.

"Aye miss lady," Dred said nicely. "Pull up to the back door of the hotel. We need to bring him in that way. If we bring him in through the front, it's all bad. His fans all over this damn hotel."

****

Mila decided tonight she would get no sleep. There was no way that she could go back to her room with Tony on this weird bullshit. She had to tie up these fucking lose ends and she needed her fucking privacy.

She could not even get her piece out of the room right now. She would have to pay for another night and leave it there until the coast was clear. She could not risk an employee finding it if she just abandoned the room. There was a boat load of bodies attached to that rifle. She would have to risk it and stop by Dred's ducked off crib by the Chicken Spot to get more ammo.

Mila was happy as fuck she had the perks in her pocket. She would need that shit for sure. Her first stop was going back to that dumb, nosy ass bitch apartment.

She was team no kids and would remain that way. *They both gotta fucking go tonight,* she thought as she headed for the hotel exit.

Chapter 30

Mila hopped in her car and leaned back against the seat. Her eyes were so heavy she could barely keep them open. Her body hurt and she needed to change her pad immediately. All of her shit was upstairs in the room. She felt homeless and completely ass out. She thought, *that fucking bitch... I should have put the bullet in her head my fucking self.*

She leaned back and remembered the time when she first found out Dred was fucking with ole girl.

2 Months ago

Mila lay floating on her back in her and Dred's pool, looking up at the cloudy sky. Small drops of rain started to gently hit the pool. She didn't want to get out yet. It was the perfect temperature outside and the rain felt cool against her skin. The wind softly blew over her body and she laid there thinking to herself.

What's up with him, he used to be so affectionate. He used to worship the ground I walk on. Something is fucking going on. She tried to tell herself it was just her hormones that had her thinking this way. Mila could not believe that she was tripping, that something was definitely off. This was the second time this shit happened, this distance between them. She could not have him falling out of love with her. Dred was her meal ticket.

She rubbed her belly wondering if it was a good idea whether she should have gotten pregnant.

Dred looked out of the patio window at Mila in the pool. He started to pay more attention to her ways ever since she had gotten pregnant. Dred started to notice that she was detached. Something was not right. He had expected her to settle down and be more of a home body. It was as if the cloud of her beauty had come from over his eyes. There would be no greater love for him than a child. In thinking of the child's best interest he started to see that Mila as a mother was a no go. He could not help but fall out of love with her. She kept up a front for a long time, but the first three months of pregnancy she had been sick and the real Mila came through too many times to ignore.

Dred realized that he did love her, but just more as a friend. He started to date outside of the relationship, which he felt guilty about, but he could not help himself. After all, they were not married, and as far as he was concerned they were done. He just could not break it to her yet.

He stepped away before she could see him standing there and headed out the house. *Tessa,* he thought, smiling. *She the first woman I had to damn near chase down in a long time.* He hopped in his car on his way to take her lunch to her job.

Mila got out of the pool and wrapped a towel around her. She heard Dred's car start up and was pissed he didn't even bother to say bye when he was leaving anymore.

"I don't give a fuck," she said, lying to herself.

"What the hell you looking at?" She snapped at the maid who was cleaning the kitchen and minding her own business. "Go somewhere. I want to be alone."

I bet you do, the maid thought. "No problem with me," she said. She headed to an empty bedroom to watch "Days of Our Lives."

Mila headed toward the kitchen to grab an apple. On her way there she noticed Dred left his phone on the counter. She picked it up and went straight to his text message. Mila sat there for 5 minutes, face red, reading all of Dred and Tessa's text messages. She heard the front door open and quickly sat the phone down and stepped away from it.

Taking a bite of the apple, the room remained silent as Dred came in and grabbed his phone then left right back out. As soon as she heard his car pull over she threw the apple so hard against the wall that it left an indentation before it dropped to the floor.

"AAAHHHHHHHHHAAAAAA!" she screamed while tugging at her hair.

She quickly grabbed a pen and pad and wrote down Tessa's phone number, job and address that she memorized from the messages in Dred's phone.

"You Bitch!" Mila said, and then picking up the phone to call Carlos, "Yo, I got another job for you. Not just yet. I am going to get all the details, then hit you up in a few weeks." She chatted with him for a second. She knew he was down. She just wanted to confide in Carlos. She liked hanging out with him.

"I don't know why you still with that nigga. Didn't you just merk that other bitch!" Carlos said, hating on Dred.

"Ion know either. We need to talk in person. I am going to come over there a little later, is that cool?" Mila asked.

"Yeah, just call before you come. You know Dred be popping up over here," Carlos snake ass laughed.

She ended the call with Carlos. She felt a little better, but she was still salty. She was not the jealous type of mad. She was being possessive. She didn't love him. She just didn't want anyone else to have him or his wealth. She was on some Beyoncé ring the alarm type shit.

She grabbed her keys and headed out the door. She knew exactly where Dred was heading and she was on his ass!

Chapter 31

A car pulling in next to Mila snapped her out of her daydream. She started her car and pulled out of her parking spot with murder on her mind.

Mila's first stop was Dred's apartment spot in the hood. She opened the lock with the spare key she had. She immediately rushed into the apartment. Her heart was beating fast, and she was on high alert. A few people had access to this spot and she was hoping no one was there.

When she walked into the apartment she could hear snoring in the bedroom. "Fuck. That could be anyone." Dred didn't snore so she knew it was not him. "Shit!" she said. She had wanted to relax here for a second.

Mila crept over to the kitchen cabinets and retrieved the cereal box that held small hand guns and a few rounds of ammunition. She grabbed what she could and crept back out of the apartment, leaving the door wide open. *Fuck em,* she thought.

She cruised back to the hood where that lady lived. She didn't know if she was going to be there, but if she was, she was a stupid bitch. As Mila turned down her street, an ambulance and a few police cars zoomed past her.

"What the fuck?" she said.

She didn't know if the lady came back and called the police, but she needed to know now. She needed to know if that was the baby on its way to the hospital! This is the fucking hood though. That ambulance could have been for anybody.

She didn't give a fuck. She was on her way to ole girl's house, and there was nothing that could stop her.

Mila parked her car on the opposite side of the street, where it could not be viewed from the alley. She knew this bitch liked to look the shit out of her fucking raggedy ass window.

She checked her gun and made sure it was loaded. *Dred didn't fucking play,* she thought. *This shit had a silencer and everything.* He always thought two steps ahead.

Mila got out of her car and closed the door quietly behind her. Her stomach started to cramp as she jogged up the stairs in the stinking hallway. She could feel a drop of blood run down her leg as the pad shifted. "This some real live bullshit," she said under her breath.

Mila stood outside of Maybelle's door. She was not going to knock this time. That shit had not worked before. The fact that the door was now closed she knew that someone had to be in there.

"Got your ass bitch," she said. " Lights the fuck out."

She pointed the pistol at the door knob and fired one round. Thankfully, the majority of the sound came from the door knob falling off. *This cheap ass shit,* Mila thought.

"Ohhhhh!" Maybelle yelled.

Mila heard a woman on the other side of the door yell out in surprise. She pushed the door and it flew open easily.

"Put the baby down!" Mila yelled at Maybelle who froze in the process of picking up the baby.

"You don't have to do this. I can take care of Heaven myself and I would never say a word to anyone," Maybelle begged.

Heaven, Mila thought. *This bitch named the baby and everything.*

"I know that you don't want nothing to do with her but she is beautiful. Just look at her, she looks just like you," Maybelle pleaded, tears streaming down her face.

Mila stood there holding her weapon like a professional. He fingers tightened around the trigger.

"Why didn't you mind your own got damn business," Mila said, feeling pissed. "I said put that fucking baby down."

Maybelle slowly placed the baby on the couch and stood back up with her hands up.

Belle thought, *if it is my time LORD thank you for my life and I pray that you protect Heaven and forgive this woman for she knows not what she does.*

Mila turned this situation over in her mind for a second. *Could this work? Could I let this lady raise this child?* She obviously had not called the police yet.

"I have a list," Maybelle said calmly. "I have a list of everything that I need for the baby. I will take care of it. I don't even need help. I will never tell her about you. She will grow up only knowing me as her mother," she said, trying to convince Mila to let them be. Belle was fearful for the child who had not yet gotten a fair shake to live her life. But for herself, she was not afraid of death. She knew that she had lived a righteous life and she had a mansion in Heaven with her name on it.

"Hmmmm," Mila thought aloud, with her gun still aimed for Maybelle's head.

Chapter 32

Mila's temples started to throb as she stood there about to make a big decision.

She felt like she was at a crossroad in her life, and this was a big deal. She could feel the weight of it on her shoulders.

A lonely tear slipped from Mila's eyes as she squeezed her trigger and shot Maybelle in her face.

Mila ran over to the couch and pointed the gun at the child. She could not help but notice how beautiful she was. She had a thick head of hair and big pretty eyes. Mila's hands shook as she tried to shoot the child.

"Just do it," she kept saying to herself. "Just pull the fucking trigger. Fuck this little bitch." More tears started to fall from of her eyes as she lowered her gun.

"Fuck!" she screamed at the top of her lungs as she scooped the child off the couch.

****

Maybelle had a split second to process the fact that she was about to die. When the bullet hit her in the head the first thing she saw was a white light.

Her spirit floated out of her body and hovered over the room. She looked down and she could see her body lying there on the floor. In the next second she felt herself being pulled upward. As her soul propelled forward through a tunnel of brilliant light, there were colors that she didn't have a word for, and she had never seen in her life.

Maybelle felt care free and as light as a feather. There was a peace that surrounded her that she never felt before in her life.

At the end of the tunnel there was a hand there waiting for her. A man, he grabbed her hand and said, "You must go back, it's not your time yet."

Before Maybelle knew it she awoke with EMTs around her and her nosy ass neighbor standing over her.

"Her eyes just opened. They open y'all," the elderly neighbor said.

Maybelle could feel the pain searing on the side of her face.

"The baby, where's the baby?" she sputtered out.

"Oh, she done lost her mind. There ain't no baby here," the lady said.

Maybelle lost consciousness.

Chapter 33

Mila jogged down the steps breathing hard. She got in the car and speed off with the baby lying on the floor of the passenger seat.

The first corner that she hit the baby screamed as she rolled on the floor.

"AAAAHHHHHH!" Mila said, screaming louder than the baby. Her head was pounding, and all she wanted at this point was sleep.

She pulled in a cheap motel on the side of the road and left the baby in the car while she went to go pay. She got a room on the far side of the parking lot. All of the hotel room doors were outside so she could take the baby straight in the room.

Once she got in the room she lay on the bed and put the child next to her. The throbbing in her head had gotten worse, and her pants were soaked at this point with blood. With the child lying so close to her she could hear its shallow breathing. She didn't want to touch it or look at it.

Her breasts felt hard as a rock as they had filled to capacity with milk and began to leak.

"Fuck," she said.

She picked up the baby and attempted to put her boob into her mouth. She didn't care about feeding her she just wanted the pressure to go away in her breasts.

After a few minutes the baby finally latched on to Mila's nipple.

"Ahhh," she said, feeling angry. It hurt like hell, but she could already feel the milk flowing out of her.

After she fed her baby she laid her back on the bed and stood up to take a shower. When she did, more blood and clots fell out of her. She began to feel faint.

Am I dying? Mila wondered. She was too selfish to die.

Mila reached her capacity, and the blood was starting to frighten her. She was afraid to go to sleep. What if something was wrong and she never woke up? Mila began to fear for her own life and that drew the line for her.

She picked up the phone and called 911,

"Yes, I was pregnant and I just went into preterm labor. I need a paramedic," she whispered into the phone and felt relieved.

****

Tina and Tessa walked right up to the hotel employee's face.

"What is your name?" they asked.

"Ronnie," the employee said softly.

"Ronnie, our sister is in this hotel and her phone went dead" Tina pouted. "We need to know what room she is in," she said, describing Mila.

"Um, I think that there was a woman who looked like that earlier, but I don't know if it was your sister.

She had on some other type of gear," Ronnie said, starting to feel comfortable and hoping she could get a nice tip.

"Ok, that is probably her sometimes. She just doesn't care, you know," Tina said reaching into her pocket for a one-hundred-dollar bill. *Hell*, she thought. *This might not cost up that fucking much.*

"I believe she is in room 521. There has been a bunch of dudes standing outside the door for a minute now." Ronnie said, taking the hundred dollars out of her hand.

"Alright thanks, bye now," Tessa said while rushing Ronnie out of the door.

Once the door closed, the sisters looked at each other. They were both thinking the same thing.

Should we wait for Dred?

"Hell naw," Tessa said, grabbing her gun and sticking it on her waist. Let's leave a note and go get this bitch.

"I'm with you sis," Tessa said, preparing to leave.

Once they arrived on Mila's floor they could see a group of guys heading toward the back stairwell door.

"Who the fuck she got with her!" they said as they hit the wall like cops. They were going to kill everyone with her if they had to...

Chapter 34

"Shhh, bitch you walking all loud and shit," Tessa said, geeked and laughing.

"Girl, I am creeping. I am the best at this shit." Tina said, laughing. They had action and she was ready for that shit.

"We in this muthafucka like top flight security of the world," Tessa said, laughing. She was really having a good time. She was so happy that she had Mila in her sights finally. She was going to do some damage to this hoe bag.

Tina and Tessa neared the stair well. Tessa peaked in the small square glass window. There was no one immediately within her view.

"The coast is clear water head," Tessa said, smiling.

"Hawaii 5-0, 86 over and out," Tina said, talking shit. She was enjoying this shit. It was like old times.

They slipped through the door quietly and began to descend the steps quickly. Tessa stopped suddenly.

Tina bumped into her, giggling, "Move yo ass," she whispered.

"Shhhh," Tessa said with a serious face. She heard the men talking then she checked her gun one more time. *Safety off. Ain't no one safe in this bitch.*

Once Tessa and Tina reached the second to last stair case, they could hear men clearly talking.

"Where my fucking car?" a scary ass voice said.

"Yo, get Tony's car here ASAP," a deep voice said.

"Tony," both Tessa and Tina whispered to each other at the same time.

"What the fuck he doing here?" Tina said, feeling some type of way.

****

The manager of the cheap hotel that Mila was forced to pull into on her way back from Maybelle's house stood outside the door of Mila's room.

"Ma'am your ambulance is here!" he yelled, knocking on the door.

"Just open it. It could be life or death," One of the EMTs said.

Once they got inside, they saw Mila passed out on the bed with a small newborn lying next to her asleep.

"She's lost a lot of blood, get the stretcher." The still room came alive with men clamoring to see if Mila still had a pulse.

****

"The car is here," the deep voice said.

"It's now or never bitch," Tessa said, peering around the corner at the men standing at the bottom of the stair case.

"Shit," Tina said. There were about five to six niggas down there. "Do we just come out bussing or what?" They had not heard Mila's voice yet, but from where they were standing they didn't have a complete view.

She also wondered why Tony was here after he talked that bullshit on the phone to Dred earlier. *Talking about he doesn't fuck with D no more. I should merk his ass off general principle.*

"Now," Tessa said, creeping down the steps.

"Alright fellas," Tessa said, with her gun pointed in Tony's direction. Tessa figured that Tony had to be the most important of the bunch. The gun on him gave her leverage. "Drop your fucking weapons before I show you what PMS really looks like," she said, smiling with Tina behind her.

One of the big ass white dudes tried to be a hero and pulled his gun. Before he could get it out his side, Tina put a hole right through his fucking hand.

This lil pussy, Tina thought as he began to scream his ass off.

"Shut yo ass up, or the next one is for your head." she said with authority.

****

As Dred, Souped Asha and Rocko got off the elevator they thought they heard a scream.

"Somebody getting pounded out," Rocko said, happy to be headed toward this nice ass hotel room.

"Nah, that sounded like it came from the stairwell," Asha said, raising her eyebrows.

"That's none of our business. Let's stay on course." Dred said, heading towards the room. He was hoping they got the information they needed from the employee. He was hoping when he opened the door they didn't have her ass tied up, trying to take the information by force. He laughed at their crazy ass.

When the door opened, it was as quiet as a mouse.

They fucking hard headed, he thought, before he bolted off towards the stairwell. *I guess that shit was my business. Good thing it was a man screaming.* That thought only had him fucked up more, *what the fuck is going on...*

****

"All you niggas, on your knees now!" Tessa said forcefully. That pretty face could not take away from the authority that she had.

Instantly, these niggas dropped to their knees.

"Unt, not you Tony, you stay where the fuck you at!" she yelled.

An employee of the hotel suddenly opened the door at the bottom of the stair well where all of the action was.

"Whhhatt?" he said, dressed in his house keeping gear.

POW!

Tina shot him point blank in-between his eyes. His body laid there half in, and half out of the door.

"Tina, yo trigger happy ass, what the fuck you kill dude for?" Tessa said.

"I had to. He saw too much, and this is business. What else could we do? Pull out our Men in Black memory erasers bitch? He had to go." Tina said.

"You right sis, now hopefully no one else has to take they last breath today." Tessa responded.

****

As Dred opened the door to the stairwell he heard the gun shot...?

Chapter 35

Monty came out of the bathroom in the hotel room.

"Where Tina at nigga?" Souped asked.

"Shit, I thought they had gone to the bar," he said rubbing his stomach. *Fucking Mexican food,* he thought.

"Why, what's up my nigga, everything cool?" Monty asked.

"Shiiit, based on the way that Dred just ran out of here, Ion really think shit cool, my nigga." Rocko said. "Me and Souped need to lay our ass down for a second. Go make sure everything cool. He just ran down the stairwell."

"Nigga, hurry up," Souped said, shading Monty. *That's mine, if I had of been here she would still be in my sight,* he thought.

Souped looked down at his bandage which had begun to bleed through. *I should have stayed my ass in the hospital.*

"Did anybody get my phone?" he asked, grabbing Monty's shoulder on the way out.

"I don't know my G." Monty said, trying to be understanding. He was not about to be a fucking peon for no damn body.

"Give me your phone to you come back. I need to make a few calls," Souped said, impatiently.

"I got respect for you because you're D's brother, but watch how you come at me. I'm not one of those type a niggas. I don't take orders from you. You can use my shit but if I am part of the family, I need my respect." Monty said. He felt that if he didn't start saying something about that shit then, it could eventually get out of control. He had to be a man and play his cards right, so right then and there he set his boundaries.

"I can respect that," Souped said just to calm him down and to use his phone. He was so curious about what the world was saying about his concert and how he was shot. *Shit, all the cameras in that bitch there could be a picture or video of who did this shit easily.*

"I need to find out who the fuck did this shit," Souped said, thinking out loud.

Souped and Rocko still did not know that Mila was alive, Monty thought.

"I got a little info for y'all before I head out. Mila, that bitch is still alive," he said, closing the door, which left Souped and Rocko shocked and Asha wondering, *who the fuck was Mila?*

****

"So, are you Cleanup crew Tony?" Tessa asked. She had never seen this nigga a day in her life.

"Yeah, shit don't take no fucking Albert Einstein. These the niggas that was outside her room. Where the fuck is Mila?" Tina asked, beginning to sweat in the hot ass stair well.

****

Dred was so close that he could hear everything. He could tell that Tessa and Tina were okay after he heard them talking. It sounded like they had shit under control.

He decided to hang back and check them out in action without him.

"I hope they don't kill Tony," he said under his breath. He already needed to replace Doc. He felt like he could repair the situation with Tony once he told him Mila was behind this shit.

****

"I don't know where she is," Tony said. "We were called here to do a job. She killed two hoes here. I am not lying. Their bodies are still in my van."

"Nigga cut the bullshit," Tessa said. "You don't work these jobs yourself, why would you? And you own this shit."

"Fuck Mila," Tony said, looking right into Tina's eyes.

"Yeah, you should feel that way. She the one who killed your crew at Souped's house," Tessa said. "You were supposed to be cleaning up her body. We left her ass for dead there. She killed your peeps. I running shit right now, why lie?"

Tony thought about it for a second. *The way they were killed... With the one stab wound to the head or neck... That shit had Mila's name all over it!* He felt like a dumb ass. It was her all along. *This rat bitch,* he thought, balling up his fists.

"So, are you with us or against us?" Tessa asked.

"He with us," Dred said, rounding the corner. He didn't want to lose Tony as a connect. *Shit, maybe I been too hard on this nigga. I got to cut him a fucking break.*

Tina and Tessa dropped their guns to their sides as Tony and his crew breathed a sigh of relief.

"You ol Casper the black ghost ass nigga," Tina said, feeling relieved to see him.

Dred laughed at their goofy asses and walked towards Tony with his hand out.

"No disrespect, let's get together and talk about any and everything at a later date. I value your service, Tony," Dred said, shaking his hand. "Much respect."

Tony felt better about shaking Dred's hand after he heard the word "respect." That's all he had been looking for this entire time.

"Mila's at the bar," Tony said.

It only took a split second for it to register before everyone bolted up the steps.

Tony looked back at his crew. "Clean this shit up!"

Chapter 36

Dred, leading the pack, entered the bar area of the hotel. His eyes quickly scanned the bar for Mila.

"Fuck," he said, turning around to them. "Her ass gone. Man, we all need some fucking sleep." Dred said. They had all been up since the concert, and it had been a long couple of days.

By then Monty had also found the crew and was hanging in the background so that he could figure out what the fuck was really happening. So far he knew most of the story, but he still had questions that he did not want to ask directly.

"We gonna need some more rooms. Tony, what's your plan? You crashing here tonight?" Dred asked as they walked slowly back toward the elevator. *Pissed and tired that this slippery bitch had been in the same fucking building as them.* He thought.

"Yeah, I need to get my own room," he said, rubbing his eyes. "I will meet up with all of you over breakfast."

Dred gave Tony a dap and they parted ways on what seemed to be good terms.

Inside Dred's room Tina walked over to Souped sleeping soundly on the couch. Mila had her so angry that she didn't even know if she would be able to sleep tonight. "Look at my baby," she said softly.

"Wake up. Let's go to our room," Tina said, rubbing his back.

"Bae," Souped said, still in pain, but super fucking happy to see Tina's face. "Come on," he said, standing up, ready to be alone with her.

****

Mila woke up in her hospital bed. She nuzzled her head in the pillow. Her body felt so much better.

Even though so much shit was going on she still did not give two fucks. Her wheels were turning, and she wanted to form a fucking plan unlike any other. Mila was crazy, but she was also somewhat smart. This night had made her realize that she just didn't want a team, she needed a team. Mila, unlike Dred, had a sick and twisted idea of what a team consisted of. She could not do this shit by herself. Shit, why should she? *I can sit my pretty ass back and chill while someone else gets revenge for me.*

She sat up a little in her bed and turned on one of the reading lights over her hospital bed. She grabbed the pen and paper from what looked like a child birth packet and began to write.

Over the years she met many men in the business. Mila was front and center for any beef that Dred experienced during his time with her.

By the time Mila finished writing she had several names on her paper, with notes and lines pointing to how all of the people were connected to each other. Mila stared at the paper. Who wanted Dred's head on a platter the most? Who was the dumbest? That way she could be in control of how and when it happened. Dred won the first round, but she was planning a TKO.

She hoped Tony might be another boss that she could get on her team. Mila didn't want to put in the work to start her own organization. She wanted to do a hostile takeover on one that was already made.

"Fuck that, I don't grind, I shine," she said, thinking she sounded witty.

An idea popped in her head that she thought was brilliant. None of the niggas on her paper so far fit the right profile for her. She could see shit going wrong.

There was someone who had as much power as Dred. The problem was there was no beef.

"Where's the beef?" she said, chuckling to herself. Mila decided that she would create the beef.

"NoNo," she said, rubbing the pencil eraser against her lip.

NoNo was a big drug lord who served to more upper-class clientele exclusively. There were no traditional dope boys on his team. He ran his shit like a delivery service or concierge.

Mila would go after his fifteen-year-old daughter.

"That prissy bitch," Mila said, thinking back to the first time she met her. *This bitch asked me if I was born in the 1900's,* Mila thought. *I am petty as fuck. I almost sucker punched her little ass. Fuck her,* she reasoned. She was built like a grown woman, and Mila heard she was already being a fast ass.

"Yeah, she deserves it," Mila said, finalizing her plan.

She hopped on her feet and walked out her room headed towards the nursery. Mila knew for a fact that anyone who just had a baby could turn it over to the hospital, no questions asked.

"Y'all take care of its ass, I got shit to do," Mila said, sounding just like her mother.

Chapter 37

Mila walked toward the nursery in her hospital gown. It was three am in the morning. She was happy about the policy that usually the maternity ward is the busiest place of the hospital. At this hour it was quiet, with the exception of another baby crying.

Mila walked up to the nursery room window. She didn't see the baby in there.

"Uggghh," she said, ready to get this shit over with.

"Are you looking for your baby hun?" A round, short brown-skinned nurse asked her with a sweet smile.

"Yes ma'am," Mila said, putting on her innocent act.

"Your baby was premature. She is in the NICU on the other side of the ward," she said with a kind voice.

"Thanks. I can find my way," she said, heading in the direction that the nurse was pointing in.

Mila pulled out her phone. She received a few mixed calls and messages. One from Troy, the only person she would consider a friend.

Ever since Mila saw that damn baby in the hotel while she was feeding it she knew who its father was. "My night fucked up, so I am going to fuck his up as well," she said, preparing to send him a text.

Tina's Story

THE BABY WAS YOURS I JUST HAD IT PREMATURE. I CAN'T DO THIS. IT'S AT THE GRADY MEMORIAL HOSPITAL. FUCK YOU VERY MUCH!

Mila smiled. He had some good dick, but he was not on her level. She knew if this baby looked like Dred she would not hesitate to keep it. It wasn't though, and she knew that for a fact.

****

Tina and Souped lay on the bed looking up at the ceiling. All the bullshit they had just gone through had somehow brought them closer together. It had advanced their new romance, and tonight she could honestly say that she felt at home with him.

"The fucking blogs are going crazy, the news and everything." Souped said, feeling salty. He didn't know if getting shot would boost his rap career or dead it. A lot of times a rapper being shot was a good thing, but at his concert though, he wondered to himself.

"I bet everything, Mila was the one who shot me, that tacky ass bitch. I been trying to tell Dred ass for years. I'm happy as fuck they done. She would have ended up killing his ass." Souped said, realizing to himself that he had been very close to death that night.

"Yeah bae, what goes around comes around, and she gonna definitely get her Karma." Tina said. Her mind was still working even though she was so tired. She could not get her body to fall asleep. "Damn, this is what people with insomnia must feel like," she said, thinking that at least she was lying next to him. Tina didn't wanna be funny, because she knew he was in pain, but she could not help but think a good as orgasm would knock her ass right out.

TING! TING!

Tina grabbed the phone on the bed.

'It's a damn text" she said, "I thought that was Facebook or some shit."

She handed the phone to Souped who opened the message and read it out loud.

"THE BABY WAS YOURS I JUST HAD IT PREMATURE. I CAN'T DO THIS. IT'S AT THE GRADY MEMORIAL HOSPITAL. FUCK YOU VERY MUCH!"

"Oh shit! Hell nah," Souped said, laughing.

"Baby, a fucking baby. You didn't tell me you had no fucking body pregnant!" she said, jumping off the bed.

"Not me goofy ass, this ain't my phone. I still don't know where my phone at," Souped said. "This Monty phone."

Tina breathed a sigh of relief, grabbing the phone out of his hand.

"Whhatt? That shit is deep, but we should take him his phone," she said scrolling loosely through the text messaged to someone saved under the name, "Good Pussy 1."

"You stay here. I think I should go take him this shit. This nigga is a daddy. This some emergency type shit. I think he a good dude. He need to get up to the hospital. I mean, what would you do?" Tina asked.

"Shit, I would be up at that fucking hospital ASAP cussing that bitch out." Souped said, standing up about follow behind Tina.

Chapter 38

Souped and Tina headed out of their hotel room down the hall to Dred's room. They knocked on the door hoping that Monty would be the one to answer since he was supposed to be the one sleeping on the couch. Tina knocked on the door softly as she looked back at Souped and stuck her tongue out.

"Aye, this shit is so crazy," Tina said, whispering to Souped.

"I know; I'm starting to get sleepy now. I don't know who gone take this nigga to the hospital." said Souped, holding his shoulder.

The door swung open and Tessa stood there with one of Dred's t-shirts on.

"Hey sis, what's wrong?" Tina said in a sleepy voice

"This nigga had Monty phone, and it's an important text message that he just got. We need to wake this nigga up." said Tina, pointing at Souped, sorry that she had to go wake her sister up. Tina knew she had to be tired.

Tessa stepped out of the doorway and headed back to the bedroom area, while Tina and Souped walked over to Monty lying on the couch.

"Psst... We weren't trying to be in yo business or nothing, but Souped still had yo phone. But you just got this text in yo phone and I really think you need to read it right now." Tina whispered.

Monty sat up rubbing his eyes. *This shit had to be important,* he thought. Monty grabbed the phone and read the text message.

His mind was blown. He felt his head pounding, PREGNANT! He thought. I barely know this bitch. *Nah, I ain't coming up to no fucking hospital. I'm gonna need to see some DNA results.*

I only fucked that stuck up bitch a couple of times. Every time I hung out with her it felt like she was lying about shit, I don't even know shit about her.

Tina and Souped turned to leave the room, figuring that he needed time on his own, plus that burst of excitement was starting to make her think she might be able to go to sleep now.

After Tina and Souped left, Monty had lain back on the couch, turned off his phone and went to sleep. He wasn't on that shit.

****

Once Mila arrived at the NICU she headed straight to the front desk.

"My name is Mila Jones and I just had a baby today. I don't know what room the baby is in." Mila said, softly bringing some fake tears to her eyes. "But I am in no condition to take care of a child, so I want to turn the baby in to the hospital and be on my way."

The nurses looked at each other in shock. They knew of the hospital's safe haven rule, but they had never seen anyone use it before. They knew exactly who her baby was because the gossip of how she was found in the hotel had spread quickly throughout the staff on that floor. They were just talking about that shit on their last break.

"Well ma'am-" one of the nurses started to say.

"No fucking questions asked!" Mila snapped at them as she turned and walked away.

Mila quickly headed for the hospital exit where there was a taxi stand outside, which was usually filled with cabs earlier in the day. At this time of night, it was lucky for Mila that there was still one out there.

Mila hopped in the back of the old yellow cab and gave the driver her destination. She pulled out the phone to call Troy as the driver took off. Mila was happy that she had Troy as a muthafucking best friend. Sometimes she was distant from him, but for real, he was like the only family she had.

"Hello," Troy said.

"Wassup, can I come crash at yo place for the night? It's a bunch of bullshit going on," Mila said.

She knew that he wouldn't have a problem with her coming over there.

"Bitch, it's three muthafuking thirty in the AM, what the fuck is yo ratchet ass up to?" Troy said, curious as to why Mila was calling him so late. "Oh, what's the Tea?"

"Bitch, I hope you got yo edge control. You gone need to get them baby hairs on fleek because this Tea about to push yo wig back to yo neck." Mila said, laughing.

"Well bitch... Get to pouring. I got my muthafuking cup ready. You ain't been answering yo phone. Imma punch yo ass dead in yo ear when you get here." Troy said, lightweight happy to talk to Mila.

Child... This bitch probably killed somebody. Ain't no fucking telling what she done did, he thought.

"Alright, your hooker. I'll be there in ten minutes." Mila said, hanging up the phone.

****

Maybelle went through extensive surgery on her head to have the bullet removed. It was lodged in her right cheek. She pulled through the surgery just fine, but currently she was asleep dreaming of baby Heaven.

****

In another area of the same hospital, Rose lay on the table in the morgue. She was dead on arrival upon entering the hospital. Rose had not survived what Rocko had done to her in the alley.

****

The nurses in the NICU gathered around the nurses' station as one of them dialed child protective services. They could not believe that she just left that baby.

"That's a got damn shame," one of the nurses said.

"Well, at least she didn't put her in the trash can. If she could not take care of the baby this was the best thing she could have done," another nurse said. Little did she know, baby Heaven had been in the trash can at one point in her short life, but she was still right. Mila leaving her at the hospital was the best thing that ever happened to her.

Chapter 39

When Mila pulled up outside of Troy's apartment building she started to feel more relaxed. It was a four family apartment building on the edge of the hood in what was considered the good part of town. She knew that she could tell Troy everything and his ass knew better than to tell ANYONE. Mila didn't have many friends, because by now, people discovered she was a dangerous friend to have.

She took the little bit of money she had tucked in her bra out and paid the driver the 90-dollar fare. Mila had not ridden in a taxi in a minute.

"I can't fucking stand this nasty shit," Mila said. "I am used to the finer things in life, not this bootleg shit."

She got out the car shaking her fucking head at what she had been reduced to that night.

Troy's building looked like any other 4-family house around the way. There was nothing special about the building or the landscaping.

"This nigga better gets on his hustle and step his game up," she said under her breath.

At least it will be clean and cute inside, she thought. Troy had a colorful style that Mila liked. He had a comfy tiffany blue sectional sofa with a ton of decorative pillows that matched the theme of the room perfectly. There was a white IKEA TV stand that looked very classy for what it cost, and spanned the main wall of the room. He had a big ass black and white picture of himself in full women's wear. Mila had to give it to him, that picture was dope. He almost looked better than her. The focus walls where the painting was hanging had splatters of colorful paint splashed artfully over the wall.

His decor was definitely out there, but somehow it worked and he had turned his small apartment into a work of art.

Mila stood on the doorsteps and knocked hard on Troy's door. The door flew open and Troy stood there with a fluffy, white hotel style robe on.

"Damn bitch, why you ain't call? You know we keep this hallway door locked." he said.

"Well hoe, you should have been waiting on me at the Door," Mila said, cocking her head to the side, laughing.

"Move the fuck out of my way with that stolen hotel robe on," Mila said, pushing past him into the hallway headed straight for his apartment door.

****

In the morning Maybelle woke up in pain. It felt like her whole face was covered in bandages, and she could barely move her jaw.

Before Belle did anything she said a prayer and thanked the LORD for saving her life. She knew what she saw last night was not a dream. She had touched HIS hand.

Maybelle knew without a doubt that her purposed centered on baby Heaven. She prayed that GOD would give her direction and she was sure that he would. She grabbed the remote and switched on the TV. She was wondering if they caught the lady who shot her. She had no clue where the baby was, and she didn't know who to ask.

She was not concerned about her wound. Her faith was so strong that she knew she would make a full recovery. *Why believe anything else?* She thought. *Where will believing anything else than the perfect outcome of this situation get me?*

Maybelle watched the TV for about 30 minutes, not really paying attention, but mostly thinking and waiting on the morning news to come on. She guessed that she had been in the hospital for about 6 hours or so.

Once the news finally came on, Maybelle suffered through two commercial breaks before she heard about the shooting that happened to her on the news. They showed the outside of her building. The news must have recorded last night because there were still police cars outside. The part about the news cast that stuck with her the most was when the Anchor said, "We have no details on the suspect of this horrible crime. They are still at large."

Maybelle looked out of her hospital window and debated on whether to call the nurse to ask about the baby. She had remembered asking the EMTs as she lay on the floor of her apartment, but she still remembered the look on their faces which read, *what is she talking about?*

"In breaking news, the second baby this year to be turned in shortly after its birth for the hospital's Safe Harbor program happened last night at around 3am. The baby will be turned over to child protective services in hopes of finding it a new home..." a reporter continued on the TV.

Maybelle's eyes popped out of her head, "Oh thank you Father." She hoped with everything in her that the baby they spoke of was Heaven. If it was, she was right in the same hospital as her. She had to find a way to get her back, she thought. She picked up the hospital phone on her night stand....

Chapter 40

Monty woke up in the morning with a headache so severe it felt like a hangover. Ole girl had never even told me she was pregnant, and now she had a baby. What the fuck is going on? I am not gonna let that shit get to me whatsoever.

"I only fucked her a couple times, and then she just skied up. It was like she used me for the dick and got missing, that was not even nine months ago." Monty told the group over breakfast at the hotel.

When Tina woke up she was surprised to find that Monty had not found a way up to the hospital to check on his baby. As she listened to him explain the whole situation to everyone, she was still calling bullshit.

"Nigga. Point. Blank. Go see about your baby. Even if it ain't yours there is a chance that it is. You would let your fucking baby go into the system? No nigga, in my circle gonna be no dead beat ass fucking daddy." Tina said, covering her mouth because she was still chewing. She could not believe that this nigga sitting here was trying to use the fact that it was a one-night stand as a sorry ass excuse.

Tina looked over at Dred, she knew for a fact the D was about to let his ass have it. Dred didn't fuck around about kids. He would go hard for his people. His eyebrows were scrunched up and he had a sour look on his face. That shit was giving her the straight *fuck you* face.

"Monty, I don't care how it came to be. You need to get up and head out to see your seed. You are excused from the table bruh; I don't fuck with that type of shit. You go do the right thing first, and then come back an' holla at me. You don't need to help me handle mine if your own shit ain't even handled." Dred said, snapping on Monty's ass for not giving a fuck about his baby.

Everyone at the table looked at Monty like he was a sore thumb.

Dred could see the blank look on his face. This was a young black man, and he didn't know any better because he was not raised that way. *He probably doesn't even know what a father is,* Dred thought. Monty's whole line of conversation had him feeling like he was nobody he wanted in his circle. As he continued to size up Monty's reaction, he felt more compelled to draw him in, instead of pushing him away.

Dred got up from the table and grabbed his coat off of the chair.

"I will be back. I am gonna take him up to the hospital to see what's up," Dred said calmly. "Tony, I still got a lot I need to holla at you about. You wanna roll, or you got somewhere to be?"

"Nah, I'll roll," Tony said, what he just witnessed Dred do was shifting his opinion of him. *Maybe I can let this shit go,* he thought.

****

Maybelle listened as the Doctor told her how lucky she was to be alive and how her wound was just a flesh wound and there was no major damage. It felt reassuring to hear them say that out loud.

"You should be out of here in 2 days. We want to keep you for observation and make sure that your wound is healing properly. The police would like to speak to you. If at any time you want to stop the interview press your call button. I understand that you have been through a lot tonight."

"Ok," Maybelle said, not knowing what she was going to say to them.

****

Dred, Tony and Monty stepped off the elevator and entered the maternity ward.

Monty felt nervous as hell. In the car he called ole girl many times, but got no answer. He didn't even know her real name. How would he find the baby?

Almost like he heard Monty's thoughts, Dred said, "If she left the baby like she said she did then everyone will know who her ass is for sure, so that should be easy. If not, you can just describe her to them and maybe they will know. Any way it goes, we gonna find out what's up."

Monty appreciated Dred helping him, but he hoped with all his heart this was not his baby. He was in the streets. He could not take care of a baby with a bum ass mother. Fuck that. He could not be a single father. He didn't know if he wanted to put the burden on his

Mom or not. He was pissed beyond belief. He could not wait to catch up with Ole Girl. He was praying that she was here and he could talk to her stuck up ass...

Chapter 41

"Biiiittcchh," Troy said, sitting down on the couch.

Mila looked over at him thinking, *look at my friend.* He was definitely good enough to be her gay bff. He kept himself up with the latest gear.

Troy was about 5'7", with smooth tan skin. He didn't have his wig on, but his short curly hair was tapered for the Gawds. He had pretty wide, brown eyes with a beautiful white smile. On any given day you could catch him with some colored contacts or hair just because he loved to look outside of the box. He was bad, and he pulled the baddest niggas Atlanta had to offer.

His fashion sense was to die for. Mila told his ass several times that he should be a fashion designer.

Even though he identified more with being a female, he still liked the fact that he was male, and he decided not to change his name. Troy actually loved his name and thought it fit him just fine. Nobody could hate on him for who he was. He wore that shit well.

"Miiiillaa, what's up honey bunny? You look like you just got hit by a bus," Troy said, his eyes finally reaching her stomach.

"Hold the fuck up, why your stomach flat?" he said, with his voice full of concern. "Girl, get to fucking talking." *Poor baby,* he thought. *She got on a fucking hospital bracelet and everything!*

"I don't even know where to fucking start, to be honest with you," Mila said, exhaling.

"How about you start by telling me why you don't look pregnant anymore?" Troy said, feeling for her. Something had to be down bad, because he had never seen her crown tilted like this before.

"Well, I had the baby and it was premature. I just had it a couple hours ago," Mila said, looking him dead in his eye.

What the fuck? Troy thought. *Is it dead? Bitches don't have babies then be out the hospital a few hours later.* He knew with Mila, anything was possible. Troy put his hand over his mouth as Mila continued to talk. She told him everything that happened over the last couple days with blunt honesty.

"Now Bitch, I am pissed at you! I know damn well you didn't put no baby in no fucking trash can?" Troy was shocked at everything that she just told him. He was not surprised that she and Dred were at war. He remembered her trying to poison Dred that one time. He always knew he was good as dead fucking around with her.

Troy sat there speechless as Mila hit him with the cold hard fact. He was disappointed in her, but he also knew why she was the way she was. The apple doesn't ever fall to far from the tree. He knew Mila's mother, and that bitch had fucked her daughter up in the head. Regardless of what she had done, he decided that he was going to help her as much as he could. Deep inside of her, somewhere was a good person, and she had done a lot for him over the years.

"So, what the fuck Dred do? Is he at the hospital with the baby?" Troy asked.

"No," Mila said, "That ain't his baby. I tried for years to get pregnant by him, that nigga shooting blanks."

"What!! You didn't tell me that fucking shit!" Troy said, surprised that she kept that secret. He knew for a fact that he was her diary. He knew all her deep dark shit.

"Yeah, I tried everything to get pregnant by him." Mila continued. "That shit didn't work. I didn't tell you because I was trying hard to convenience myself that it was his and if I told you that would fuck shit up. I didn't want anyone to know."

Got damn, she is hard as fuck. This bitch ain't even fucking crying, Troy thought. *She saying this shit like we talking about the weather or some shit.*

"So, since I could not get pregnant by him I started to fuck niggas that looked like him. Dark skinned niggas with the same build and nose shape type of shit," Mila said, figuring that she would let all this shit out so she never had to think about it again.

"There was this one nigga, he works for Dred. He is a little corner nigga. With the hood he was from I thought it would be only a matter of time before someone shot his young dumb ass." Mila said, letting lose a nervous laugh. "His name was Monty. I had seen him a few times around the way. But, you know I don't fucking waste my time talking to broke niggas."

"So, what you about to say? You fucked him?" Troy said. "Did you get tested, because you know them downtown boys about that life."

"I'm good nigga. You met him before. You were with me the night I met him," Mila said, looking in his eyes "Halloween, the nigga we kept calling 'little thug' who was drinking at the bar with us. I fucked him right in that club bathroom."

"What? Bitch you are scandalous," Troy said, leaning back on the couch. This shit was better than Love and Hip Hop! "So, did he know you was Dred's girl? This nigga must be bold as hell because most niggas that know Dred won't even look at your ass."

"Hell no he didn't know." She shot back. "I had on the fucking mask. He never saw my face. Even if he did see me, I don't think he fucking knew me. I don't hang around those broke niggas. The second time we fucked I had on a fucking blonde wig and some other type shit I would not even normally wear. I know for a fact that he didn't recognize me. I handpicked his ass just to get some of that sperm. I knew that the fucking baby would still pass for Dred's even if it looked like dude. Shit I took a test 3 weeks later, and that was all she fucking wrote. I never talked to his young ass again and avoided downtown the best I could."

"Dammmmmnnn, so bitch, you just left the baby at the hospital, because I can raise her. You can't just let that baby go into the system like that Mila. That's some

bullshit, and I can't endorse your ass on that shit." he
said.

Chapter 42

"What you mean? That baby is in a Safe Haven hoe. I have the right to do that shit and it is completely legal. Bitches do that shit all of the time." Mila said, getting up heading into Troy's kitchen.

"Bitch, no the fuck they don't. Your ass is tripping Monkey Balls. I want the baby. I can't have one of my own. I would love to have a lil cute ass daughter to raise. I know she got to be pretty." Troy said, looking at Mila with the side eye.

"So, what the fuck you gonna do though? I know they looking for your ass. Do they know where I live? I am not trying to have them rolling through shooting up my shit!" Troy said, knowing that Mila didn't fuck with many people. *Shit, people was scared as hell of her, her tiny ass.*

"Nah, they don't know where you live. Nigga, they ain't never been over here." Mila said, cracking open a beer.

"Hell nah bitch put the top back on that beer and put that shit back, we are not done talking." Troy said, thinking of all of the questions that he still had.

Mila took the whole beer back to her head. She was surprised, she didn't really like the taste of beer but she was thirsty for some type of buzz, even if it was only imaginary.

As Mila sat on the couch Troy continued the conversation. "So, if Dred knows that ain't his baby, do he know who baby it is?"

"No, but I texted the dude Monty and told his goofy ass. He probably still asleep but he better go get his baby" Mila said, rolling her eyes.

"Nah bitch, you better go get your own damn baby. Or go get my baby. But you were not even fucking full term, honey what is the status of this child," Troy said, already really starting to consider if he could get custody.

"That baby good, I should not have even told your ass that part bitch!" Mila said, close to checking Troy's ass.

"I am not featuring that honey! So moving right the fuck along. So what are you going to do about this Tina and Tessa bitches? Mila, you better be careful, it's fucking real out here and I would hate to see something happen to you. You done shot Souped's bitch! That shit been on the news all day long. His fine ass!" Troy could not believe all of the damage she caused.

"I have a plan." Mila started. "I need to get them in a war with someone else so that they all can kill each other and I can sit pretty. I am getting ready to go to bed. I need some fucking sleep."

"Bitch, I guess you are sleepy. Murdering people makes you sleepy I heard." Troy said, talking shit.

"In the morning we got a lot of shit to do." Mila said.

"'We' bitch, did you really just fucking say we?" Troy said. "If I am going to help you I need for you not to leave that baby hanging like that bitch, and I want to go up there and see her."

"If you go it's gonna be by your damn self," Mila said, rubbing her eyes. *Alright,* she thought. *I am fucking done talking.*

Chapter 43

Dred, Monty and Tony walked up to the nurses' station.

"Oh shit, who baby daddy is that?" one of the patient care assistants said loud and indignantly. "That's a lucky bitch."

"Girl, say that shit," the co-worker said.

"Hi. How y'all doing? Who y'all here to see," the health unit coordinator said, leaning back in her chair.

"Well, we have sort of a problem," Dred said with this smooth, sexy voice, flashing that million-dollar smile.

"My friend here," he said, pointing at Monty. "This female that he used to mess with had a baby here. We up here to check on the welfare of the baby because she texted him saying that she didn't care about the baby, to be honest with you. We wanna check on the kid and make sure everything is ok."

Monty stood behind Dred like the young man he was with his hands in his pocket wondering how the fuck he ended up in this predicament.

"I know what baby you talking about." The patient care assistant said, popping her gum and switching her ass up to the desk. *Damn,* she thought. *You don't see them walking around looking like this too often.*

"Well, I don't know if we can release that information," the first lady said.

Dred reached down in his deep pockets and pulled out two hundred dollar bills.

"Shiiit, say no more, access granted nigga," the PCA said, talking one of the hundreds, and giving the other to the health unit coordinator.

"Let me take y'all there. So damn, she just gonna leave dat baby up here like that doe, that's down bad. What's her name again? Something start with an M. She just put on her shit and walked right out, straight fowl." The PCA said.

Monty didn't even respond. He didn't want to talk about this shit, let alone be here. He didn't understand what the fuck coming here was going to do. Dred was starting to get on his nerves with this daddy shit.

"Y'all, this is the NICU. The baby was born super early but I think she gonna be OK" she said.

"She," Monty said. *It's a girl,* he thought. He almost wished it was a boy. He felt like a boy could handle himself better in this world.

They walked over to the baby lying in the incubator. There was a pink card that listed the baby's information.

"Mila Jones?" Dred said with his face screwed up. "Nigga…."

****

Back in the hotel Tina and Tessa sat talking.

"So, I ain't been trying to pressure you but you know when you ready to talk I am all fucking ears.

Something is bothering you sis. I just can't put my finger on it, but I can fucking tell." Tina said, looking at Tessa as she applied her make up in the mirror.

"Sis, look… A lot of shit happened to me, and I am not trying to put that shit on your shoulders. If I tell you everything you ain't gonna never get that shit out of your head. They basically tortured my ass for days. Everything that you can think of happening," Tessa said, trying to hold her tears in.

"Tessa, you just can't carry that weight by yourself. Who the fuck am I going to be mad at though? Them niggas all dead already." Tina said, trying to lighten the air.

"Man. Alright. I will tell you everything," Tessa said, putting down her makeup brush.

"Ok," Tina said softly, sitting on the bed. She was going to try her best to keep a straight face. She didn't want to make telling the story that much harder, but she knew that she had to get that shit out. She was not going to go to no fucking therapy. Tina felt she would have to fill those shoes.

Man, fuck Mila, she thought. Once she got her hands on that bitch again, there was going to be no fucking Mrs. Nice Guy. She had been planning in her head the exact things she wanted to do to her.

"Alright, so when they first put me in the hole I was thinking I was going to die. I thought about you and how that would drive you crazy…"

Chapter 44

"Man, what y'all in here doing?" Souped said, walking over to Tina and kissing her on the cheek.

"Damn, it's cool sis. Now is not a good time anyway. I really don't feel up to it." Tessa said, getting up to head back in the bathroom.

"How your arm feel?" Tina asked him while standing up.

"This muthafucka hurt bad as hell. I got all type of shit to do today. I got to meet with my manager and publicist, they wanna know what the fuck happened." Souped said, feeling drained.

"Well shit, do you have to meet them in person? Just conference call they ass." Tina said, irritated with them. He just got fucking shot she thought.

"I got a few questions for you Bae," Tina asked, smiling at him.

"Mila, what you know about her so far? Who the fuck is she really? Like, I know D said that she doesn't fuck with her Mom, but she gotta be fucking cool with somebody. She got cousins, sisters, any fucking thing we can use to track her ass down?" Tina asked.

"Man, she been secretive as hell this whole time. I only met one of her friends so far. Some dude name Troy," Souped continued. "I think most of her family from New York."

"So y'all really don't think she would care at all if we just go roll up on her Moms, though for real?" Tina said. She was not able to believe that shit.

"I really can't say. I heard her mom batty as fuck. I really never paid Mila ass that much attention," Souped said, rubbing his eyes.

"Bosky, I got to step out for a second. I need to get on my private eye shit. I gotta find her. I mean, fuck she is looking for us, and there ain't no telling where the fuck she is. I can't let her blast on us like that again." Tina said with a mean ass face.

"Man, I know you hard headed and I am not going to try to stop you, but won't you wait on everyone else to get back?" Souped said. He knew that she was a bad bitch, but he didn't want her to make the wrong move.

"They gonna take all day, time is of the fucking essence. I gotta to do me Bae. You understand, right? I really got shit under control. I mean, I found my fucking sister, didn't I?" Tina said.

Tessa could easily hear their conversation in the bathroom and she poked her head out the door and said, "He right sis. You ain't fucking superwoman. You gonna need some help, somebody to cover you. I can ride with you."

"So, it's fucking settled. Me and her about to go find out what's up." Tina walked over to the desk in the live ass hotel room and got Mila's laptop that Monty stole. It was unlocked and she was hoping there was a contact list, Facebook, email or some shit that would give her some info on this Troy nigga or her Mom.

"I need to send someone else with you. I think we should call Old School Joe. That nigga know all type of shit. He will just give y'all that extra advantage." Souped said, grabbing his phone to text Old School Joe and tell him to meet them at the Hotel.

"So you tryna say we need a nigga with us to pull shit off. Oh, cause we women we can't do this shit?" Tina asked him, dead ass serious.

"No, don't take it like that. Since I can't be down I need someone to fill my shoes. That's all. I believe in you baby," Souped said as he walked over to her to wrap his uninjured arm around her.

"Yahtzee," Tina yelled as she invaded Mila's Google email account.

****

"Mila," Monty said, looking confused. "What the fuck?" he was overwhelmed. The sight of the baby and the name Mila sent his head reeling. In that moment he felt like a fucking dead man walking.

"What's good, Monty," Dred said, crossing his hands in front of his chest. He glared at Monty with the most hateful stare.

****

Ole School Joe pulled up to the hotel entrance in a decked out and restored 1969 Cadillac. He rolled down the window and motioned for the Tina and Tessa to hop in.

"Alright young ladies. Since I am in on this situation I want to make sure that we are clear on some things. I don't want us going into this all willy-nilly. Mila is more dangerous than she appears. I have taught her half of what she knows." Old School Joe continued, "Souped tells me you would like to talk to her mother. I know exactly where she is."

Chapter 45

Troy woke Mila ass up bright and early in the morning.

"You need to go up to this hospital with me." Troy said, nudging her in her ass with his foot. "Ion give no fucks right now."

"Troy, fuck you boo. I am staying my ass in this bed. Take your own stalking ass up there." Mila said.

"I can't just take my ass up there and see that preemie. The Mom got to be there bitch!" Troy said, cutting Mila with his eyes.

"Look nigga, you over here thinking you about to have a daughter and shit. Do you really want me as your baby mother? You live a wild ass life and you can't take care of no baby either. All them trips and tricking you do. Really, take a day and think about this shit, seriously." Mila said, acting like she was the rational one.

Troy starting to think about what she just said for a second. He knew that he was impulsive and shit. *Maybe she was right, do I really want a baby?* He had to be honest with himself and he was leaning towards yeah, he wanted her. He already knew the baby had to be super cute, looking at Mila.

Mila looked tired as hell to him. He guessed he could give her another day to rest he thought, flopping down in the bed next to her.

"Night night nigga," Mila said with her head stuffed in the pillow.

****

Old School Joe leaned back in his seat and cranked his music up.

"Girlll you know i-i-i- love you, no matter what you do, ohhh oh," Lenny Williams blasted through his speakers.

"Oh hell nah," Tina said defiantly. "We are not riding to this shit."

"I think this is cool," Tessa said, singing along.

"Y'all fooling, so are we there yet?" Tina asked from the back seat sounding like a kid.

"Few more minutes," Old School Joe said. He never said much but when he did that shit was right to the point.

"Now I usually don't ride out with people who don't understand how I roll. There is a method to my madness. We don't need to go around dropping unnecessary bodies, so ain't no reason to murder her mother. Let's keep this shit professional." he said, grabbing his pre-rolled joint out of the ash tray.

When they pulled up to Mila's moms house Tessa and Tina could not wait to open their doors. They were already tugging the handle before the car had even stopped.

"Yeaaaaah bitch," Tina said to Tessa.

"Aye, get in line youngin'. You got a lot to fucking learn," Old School Joe said, irritating the fuck out of Tina.

****

Maybelle got up the strength to sit up in her bed. She pressed the call button for the nurse.

"I know a child that was just born and she is in the NICU. It would make me feel a lot better if I could go check on her," Maybelle said sweetly.

"Ok, we will send your nurse in to talk to you about that hun," The loudspeaker on the wall replied.

****

"Maybe it's someone else named Mila Jones too," Tony said, trying to calm down the situation.

"Gotta be," Monty said. "I only fucked this girl a couple times and I don't know shit about her besides her phone number."

"What's her phone number?" Dred asked, getting right to the bottom of shit as usual.

Chapter 46

Mila's mother's house was a brick house with a nice front lawn. It had a wraparound porch with a few chairs sitting out front. They briskly walked up to the screen door. On the actual door there was an old piece of paper taped to the door that said, "If you knock and I don't answer you must not be important, so keep it moving."

Tina and Tessa looked at each other and got weak as fuck.

"I seen signs on doors before, but I ain't never seen one that said this bull shit." Tina said, laughing. "she off the chain already."

"Heeeelllll nah," Tessa said, thinking, *I hope she answer this door.*

"This paper ain't stopping shit," Tina said. "If she don't answer, we kicking this shit in."

"Yeah, we gonna keep it moving alright. Moving this muthafucking door." Tessa said, laughing.

Suddenly, the door opened and there stood a middle-aged woman. She was very pretty she had a caramel complexion and long wavy hair.

They both knew that it was Mila's mother, they favored each other. She was very petit. She had on a light blue button up pajama set with a silky blue robe to match.

Damn, Tina thought. *She is actually pretty. I expected her to be busted as fuck.*

Old School Joe slowly made his way up to the porch; he had a certain look in his eye that Tessa could not figure out.

"Joey, who the fuck are these bitches," Mila's mother said with a mean ass tone to her voice.

"Lola this shit needs to be settled. These women are after Mila. She fucked them over," Old School Joe said.

"Well, come on in girls, y'all want some coffee?" Lola asked. Any enemy of Mila was a friend of hers, she thought, *fuck her.*

"No, they don't want no fucking coffee." Old School Joe said to Lola. He knew that at Lola's house you don't eat or drink shit. If you did you might not ever make it out of the front door.

Everyone walked in and headed straight to the long black table in Lola's dining room.

****

Monty looked in his phone and pulled up the number, and, stuttering, he rattled it off to Dred.

"That's Mila, so you been fucking her the whole time. Are you a rat or something?" Dred said, stepping right up to Monty's face.

"No man, I fucked this girl a couple times. The first time was on Halloween and in a bathroom. Man, I had no idea the girl I was fucking was her. I was not even in your circle before. I heard of her and seen her drive by in a car before but I ain't never met her." Monty said, feeling like he was fearing for his life.

As Dred looked in his eyes he could see that he was telling the truth. He was just good with reading people. He had to keep his eyes open still because Mila had fooled him before. Either way, he had to cut Monty out the circle until he found out what the fuck was really happening around here.

"Alright, you stay here with your seed and finding out what's going on with it," Dred motioned to Tony to go.

The color drained from Monty's face as he watched Dred and Tony walk out the NICU.

"I'm a dead man if I don't find this bitch," Monty said under his breath.

Chapter 47

Lola sat at the head of the table laughing uncontrollably.

"Look, we ain't tryna be funny," Tina said, "but what the fuck is so funny?"

"Y'all two are what the fuck is funny. Y'all look mad as hell," Lola said, laughing. "She done pissed y'all off, come on tell me what she did. I've been bored as hell lately."

"Man bitch..." Tina started.

"Shh..." Tessa said. "Look, she tried to kill me and that's all you need to know."

"She tried to kill you and you still alive." Lola said, still laughing. "Joey, she must be losing her touch."

"Fuck a losing the touch, this bitch is touched, that one way!" Tina said.

Old School Joe sat back in his chair. He really didn't have much to say. All he could think of now is how he used to like Mila until he found out she was just like her mother. Now he could not stand her. He only tolerated Mila. He wished that she had never been born.

"What do y'all want from me though? What I got to do with this shit? She don't fuck with me, she stopped talking to me years ago." Lola said. "I don't know where she is and I don't fucking care!"

"Man, bitch yell at me one more time," Tina said, standing up.

"Fuck this spacey bitch," Tessa said, getting up. "Let's go. She doesn't know shit."

Tina and Tessa stormed out the house with Old School Joe.

"Aye dude what's up? Why you protecting this bitch?" Tessa said out on the porch. "I seen you grab your shit when my sister stood up."

"Oh hell naaa," Tina said, throwing her hands in the air.

"You involved in this shit some kind of way, man. How you know her mom my nigga?" Tina asked.

Lola stood at the screen door smirking at them.

"Go ahead and fucking tell them, or I will right now." Lola said, entertained by the whole situation.

"Me and Lola used to fuck around back in the day and Mila is my daughter. I didn't find out until a few years ago. Mila doesn't know," He said, sitting down on the porch steps. "I knew it would have to come to light one day. I been preparing for it," he said, taking a half blunt out of his pocket and lighting it.

"I found her and eased my way into her life working for Dred's business so I could be close to her." He started. "I didn't wanna just come out of nowhere tryna be her dad. After I got to know her I realized that she was a shell. I hate her guts. I could not bond with her. I could not get her. I could not make myself care about her. I'm very ashamed to say she is my daughter.

Dred turned out to be a cool guy, and I was sorry to see that he was with her. I knew that she didn't love him. It was not in her eyes."

"Man, what the fuck kind of twisted shit is this?" Tina said.

"Do Dred know?" Tessa asked.

"No, he don't know," Old School Joe said. "But I have been thinking about shit, and it's how she was raised. That bitch back there stole her innocence." Old School Joe said, thinking back to the first time he met Lola thirty years ago.

****

Maybelle's nurse came into the room.

"Did you need some assistance?" She asked.

"Yes I need to go to NICU to visit a child I know. I think I am okay. It would give me a lot of encouragement to go check on her and see if she is ok," Maybelle said, tearing up.

"Well, it's pretty quiet around here, let me get a wheelchair. I can probably take you up there for about 10 minutes max, ok?" the nurse said.

"Yes, oh yes! Can you please?" Maybelle said.

"Sure," the nurse said.

Chapter 48

1985

Joey sat back in the large black arm chair in his living room. It was his first night in his new apartment. He had stacked and flipped his money for months to save up enough. It was December and it was starting to get cold outside. He wanted his own shit.

He almost stayed at his grandma's crib a little longer to save up more money. She had begun to nag him about selling crack to the community and how he needed to get saved. He knew she was right, but he was not ready to make that change. Fast money was the only way to go as far as he was concerned. He could not see himself working a nine to five.

Joey saw himself more as a boss. He was fearless. People always looked at him as the quiet type, but really he always had a lot to say. But the shit that he had to say people never wanted to hear. They hate the truth.

He had just turned 19 a couple days ago and his grind was so strong that he didn't even celebrate. No one on the block even took notice. He had worked his corner from dusk 'til dawn that day. His feet hurt from standing up so long. His goal was to rise to the top, but of course that was most nigga's goal.

He pulled his socks off and grabbed his remote to turn on the TV. His apartment was a small one bedroom in the building right above the corner he hustled on. He loved his shit. He purchased a few pieces of furniture and he was very proud of the little shit he had. It had the basic shit you need to live comfortably.

Joey dozed off feeling proud of himself, only to be awoken by a loud bang against his door.

POW! POW! POW!

It sounded like someone was trying to knock his door knob off. He was scared as fuck, but he could not let that take over. Thinking quickly, he ran over to the coffee table and grabbed the knife that he carried everywhere with him. He didn't need a gun; he could throw this muthafucker like it was a bullet.

As he turned back toward the door the gun man walked in with the weapon drawn.

"Put that fucking shit down, befo' I light your ass up!" a woman yelled.

It was a bitch, he thought. *This bold ass chick rolling up in my shit like this.*

"Empty your fucking pockets, and give me that fucking watch too." Lola said, with her gun pointed straight towards Joey's head. *You fine,* she thought, *but money looks a hell of a lot better.*

"Why the fuck you doing this, baby girl," Joey said, flashing his sexy smile.

Before she could even blink, Joey threw his knife at the gun in her hand. It caught Lola completely off guard as he dove full speed at her. Both of their body's crashed to the ground as he fell on top of her.

"See, I gave you a chance to leave girl, damn!" He said, pulling the ski mask off of her face. *Damn, she beautiful,* he thought, his dick was getting hard against her stomach.

Chapter 49

1985

"Who are you, who with you?" Joey said, holding her down on the ground.

"Nobody. Word up, nigga get the fuck off of me," Lola said, squirming under his weight. She attempted to smack him in his head. She was not on this shit.

Joey grabbed both of her hands and held them down to the ground. He stared intently into her sexy brown eyes. "Damn, she don't got no fear in her," he said. He had not met many women that were this fucking bold. Other than his door being fucked up, he was not too pissed. She was so fucking fine. He was amazed at everything that was going on.

"Why you doing this baby girl? Who sent your pretty ass," He said, breathing heavily. She was giving him a work out trying to get out from under him.

"I sent my damn self, bro," she said, biting her lips and she tried to head butt him.

"Calm down, baby girl, calm yo ass down. I will let you up, but I am keeping that gun, and you need to pay me for my door you fucked up," Joey said.

"Alright, bet," she said. She felt his hard dick on her legs. She would have normally been pissed at some shit like that, but he was better looking than she expected. She had been watching the niggas on that block for a while. Lola had seen him before. He always kept his hood on and stayed in a lick face. As he talked to her his breath smelled like mint and his natural body odor smelled like the perfect cologne. Lola was starting feel a little tingling down below.

Joey carefully got off her and she stood up, straightening her clothes out.

"Fuck you," Lola said, getting up in his face.

"You wish," he said, grabbing his dick, before he stuffed her gun in his back pocket.

Damn, she thought, looking at his jogging pants, *why not? Might as well get something out of this shit.*

"No you fucking wish," she said, walking up to him and smacking him dead in his face.

"Your thieving ass!" Joey said, looking at her thickness. She had on a black T shirt and jogging pants. Her body was a perfect coke bottle shape. Her soft lips turned him on with each new word she formed.

Joey walked over and closed his battered door all the way. The door knob was gone, but he could still lock the dead bolt. He walked over to her, thinking that a broken door knob was worth the pussy that he was about to get.

"What are you doing, yo," Lola said, smiling.

"Look, I know your game. I've done the same thing before so I am not judging you baby girl," Joey said, walking to her and smiling. He had a fresh hair cut with a crispy white tee and grey jogging pants. He was lean and fit. You could see his toned arms and wide shoulders imprinted in the t-shirt.

"Judge this pussy," Lola said, stepping to his face.

"I plan to," he said, grabbing her face to kiss her. Lola put up a fight for all of one second before she was passionately kissing him back.

They stripped and kissed as they violently made their way to Joey's bed, knocking all of his new shit over.

In the morning Lola got up and got dressed only to never step foot in Joey's apartment again. She would not find out until months later that she was pregnant with an unwanted baby girl.

Chapter 50

Dred and Tony made their way to the hotel to meet back up with the rest of the group.

He wanted to care that Mila fucked someone from his crew, but he could not make himself. He was still too pissed that she shot Souped. He had the meanest mug on his face. He was tired of dealing with this bitch, tired of reliving her games.

He had not said a word to Tony the whole time they drove.

"Hey, Dred, my man. Let's stop by the store for a second." Tony asked.

"No," Dred said flat out, as he drove right passed the corner store.

Tony's blood was boiling. That one word and the way he said it had sent him back over the edge. He didn't like that shit. He didn't like for a nigga to boss up on him. Even though Dred was just a man of few words, insecure niggas just could not handle or understand him.

Tony pulled out his phone and texted his men to come and pick him up asap. He was done with this fucking Punta. He tried to conceal the pissed off look on his face as Dred continued to drive.

"Man, scoot your head back," Dred said to Tony as he was trying to turn at an intersection and could not see.

"Why do you keep talking to me like that?" Tony said, his voice barely above a whisper. He felt that if he didn't say something that he would feel shitty all day.

"Talking to you like what? You trippin'," Dred said. He had no feeling, no fear, no concern... No nothing for this nigga.

If it's fuck me then it's fuck you too, Tony thought. He could not wait to get out of this car.

Dred pulled the whip up to the hotel and hopped out.

"Park it," he said, tossing the keys to the valet heading straight towards the automatic hotel lobby doors. He got a couple steps and looked back to see where Tony was. *What the fuck is he on,* Dred thought. Tony was standing outside still with his hands in his pockets like he was waiting on something with the straight shit face.

"Nigga, what's up with you man? Why you still standing here," Dred said, walking up to him.

Before Tony could answer an all-black Benz van pulled up in front of Tony.

Tony looked back at Dred and put up his middle finger, "Fuck you BITCH!"

"Oh word," Dred said. He would usually keep his cool over some petty shit like this, but this nigga had him straight hot. Before Dred knew it he had dashed over to Tony, fists balled, ready to straight deck this nigga.

Dred snapped back into reality, but it was only after he heard the loud thud of his fist hitting Tony's face. *Something was definitely broken – nose, jaw, something,* Dred thought.

Tony's niggas jumped out the car and rushed over to break up the fight. One of the niggas who was still salty about being held at gun point by Tina and Tessa decided to flex on Dred.

"Nigga, you ain't shit. We gonna see your nigga." Dude said, looking like a broke Suge Knight.

"You see me right now, so what the hell is you saying bro?" Dred said.

The hotel Valet didn't even try to run and get help. They all had their cell phones out screaming World Star and shit. They were ready for some shit to pop off.

The combination of sexy and authority was too much for niggas to handle sometimes. On the outside looking in Dred had everything these niggas wanted and the fuck boys could not stand him because of it. Dred stood there daring a nigga with his eyes to jump.

Fake Suge Knight could not help himself as the two other niggas got Tony safely in the car. He decided to see if he could take Dred down. He knew that if he beat dude ass he was in for some major brownie points from Tony.

The first blow grazed the right side of Dred's face and he weaved that shit with ease. Dred had a mean ass left hook and when he put all his anger and frustration behind that blow he damn near took dude head off. The other two niggas jumped out the car and rushed to restrain Dred's arms.

But Dred was too smooth for these niggas. He swerved out of the way.

"Aye, come on," the drive of Tony's car said. "We need to get the fuck out of here."

"Yeah," one of the valets said with his iPhone out on record. "Y'all better gone on somewhere. You got knocked the fuck out nigga."

"Yeah, both they ass got knocked the fuck out," another nigga said laughing.

In the car Tony's pride was hurting something bad. Now he could see why Mila would turn on Dred's ass. He could taste the blood on his lips and he was almost sure his nose was broken. His pride was in shambles, and he almost wished that he hadn't said anything at all. He was embarrassed in front of his workers. At least he was not the only one in the car nursing a wound.

"Mila," Tony said under his breath. Maybe they could team up and take this nigga down after all. He had to find her before they did.

****

Mila and Troy had finally decided to get out of bed and head out.

"Nigga what's for breakfast?" Mila asked, heading into the bathroom to wash her face.

"Shit, you had me up all night I am not cooking shit. Let's go out and get something," he said, taking off his wave cap heading toward the closet.

"Owww, I know you got something for a bitch to wear. I don't want no bootleg shit neither. I got a few stops to make today and I need to look delicious," Mila said, licking her lips.

"Bitch, you stay up to some shit," Troy said, laughing. "I am down. I need something freaking fun to do," he said.

"OOOO bitch, did that baby give you a few extra inches around that booty, you looking thick," Troy said. "Ahhhh dab!" he said on cue. He and Mila hit the dab at the same time, looking cute.

See, Mila thought. *That's why this is my nigga no matter what I got going on. He always cheers me up.* She would need him around today. His energy would balance hers out and help her make all of the right moves.

"So, what's on the agenda today besides breakfast," Troy asked.

"Getting Dred fucked up," Mila said point blank.

"OMG that fine piece of man candy. What a fucking waste," he said, licking his lips. "You fowl. You don't love him at all, all those years y'all was together."

"Heeelllll no," Mila sang. "You about to find out just how much I hate his ass. Wait until you see what I got planned for his ass. This shit is going to be amazeballs." Milas said, cackling.

Chapter 51

Dred walked to the hotel elevator with his cool still intact. He didn't have time to give a fuck about Tony's weak ass. He had a lot of business to take care of. He was going to go upstairs get his people, and go the fuck home and figure shit out. He was the last muthafucka that needed to be worried about this shit. He was the fucking boss, and if niggas was forgetting that, he needed to let their asses know once again.

Dred rubbed his sore knuckles in the elevator. It had been a long time since he had to square up with a nigga. He laughed to himself.

"I still got that shit," he said, getting off on his floor. He didn't know what he was going to do about the young nigga, Monty. Before, dude seemed like he was promising, but now he didn't know about that shit. He still was trying to wrap his head around the fact that Mila had fucked him. Even though he didn't love her anymore, his pride was still hurt. The whole fucked up way she tried to play him with that baby situation was really fucked up.

When he loved her he tried for a while to get her pregnant after she damn near begged him for a kid. For some reason her ass could not get pregnant by him. Then all of a sudden she popped up pregnant. He didn't even think shit was fishy about it at the time.

"She really had a nigga fooled," he said. This dumb bitch went out and got a sperm donor though.

That was the wackiest shit he ever heard in his life. A nigga from his own crew, he thought shaking his head, *dirty bitch.*

Dred opened the hotel room door to see Souped on the phone and Rocko and Asha sitting at the table.

"Good thing you are a nurse," Dred said to Asha, thankful that she had taken the initiative to change both Rocko's and Souped's band-aide.

"I might have a job for you if you want it," Dred said to Asha sitting at the empty seat at the table. He was thinking about how he needed to get the Penthouse back up and running. *One doctor don't stop no fucking show, its mass muthafuckers out ready for this long money.*

"Where Tessa at?" Dred asked Rocko.

"Ask your brother," Rocko said, looking down at the ground.

Dred looked over at Souped wondering what he didn't know.

"Ahh, they went with Old School Joe to make a run really quick. I could not make them stay," Souped said.

Dred didn't say shit, else he figured they were out shopping or some shit. He headed over to the closet and picked out a fly ass fit to put on. Closing the bathroom behind him he started compiling a list of shit that he needed to do today, and all of the people who was on his shit list.

Dred stepped into the piping hot shower. He stood, leaning against the wall in the shower with his eyes closed as the water ran down over every part of his body. A smile spread across his face and he imagined grabbing Tessa and kissing her all over her body. It had been so long since he had sex that just the thought of her was making his dick start to get hard. He ignored and tried to think of something else as he lathered his strong, sexy, chocolate body up with soap. Dred got to his dick and began washing it off the more his slippery fingers touched it the harder it got. Before he knew it he was washing a long, fat hard dick in his hands. He looked down at his manhood knowing that he was very blessed to have such a big ass dick. He bit his bottom lip as he began to slowly stroke the head of it.

"Tessa," he said as he stuck his tongue out into the water imagining that he was licking her soft pussy. He tried his best to make his hand feel as much like her tight wet pussy as possible. He took his other hands and slowly massaged his wet, soapy balls, and the other hand began to pick up speed, massaging and stroking his dick harder and harder.

In his mind he could see her bending over shaking her round, soft ass all over his lap. He could see himself spreading her firm sexy cheeks open as he got down on his knees and let her shake her ass all in his face. He imagined licking her ass hole as she moaned in pleasure. He stood back up and slowly stuck the head of his dick in her pussy as he wet his finger and played with the outside of her asshole.

He grabbed his dick and flapped it under the water as he felt his nut building.

"Tessa, oh baby I love you," he said under his breath with his eyes closed tight. Still seeing her ass on his lap, he imagined himself grinding deeper inside her until he could see his dick covered in her juice.

He threw his head back as he began to pump furiously.

"That fat ass," he said over and over again to himself.

The last stoke of his soapy dick, released a hard nut. He had to put his back against the shower wall as he stretched his body out feeling good.

"Damn, I needed that," he said as he began to wash himself off.

Dred hopped out the shower and quickly got dressed. He threw on some True Religion Jeans and a Polo sweater, nothing to flashy.

After that release he was ready to see his baby. His mind kept going back to her voice and her body.

"Damn," he thought, nothing else really mattered besides him getting his business straight and settling down with Tessa.

****

The nurse rolled Maybelle off the elevator onto the NICU floor.

"What's the mother's name," the nursed asked Maybelle so that she could find the baby's room.

Maybelle had to think quickly, because she didn't know the mother's name.

"Um I don't know the mothers name," she said telling the truth. "I'll know the baby when I see her."

"How don't you know the mothers name?" the nurse asked, feeling awkward.

"Well, I only know her by her nickname," Maybelle said, hating that she had to lie. "I will know the baby when I see her though, can we just go look? She would have just been born tonight so that should help us narrow it down."

"Ok," the nurse said feeling kind. *This lady seems sweet,* she thought.

Maybelle and the nurse peeked in on two rooms before Maybelle saw Heaven in an incubator.

"That's her," she said, pointing to a room that a younger man was standing in.

"Hi," Monty said under his breath, not knowing who the lady in the wheel chair was. He was thinking that it had to be someone that Mila is kin to.

"Hi," Maybelle said with as big of a smile she could muster with the bandages on her face. "Can we have some time alone?" she asked the nurse.

"Sure," the nurse said, leaving the room to go speak to one of her friends that worked in the area.

"Who are you?" Maybelle asked, rolling herself over to Heaven.

"I might be the father," Monty said, ready to get the fuck out of here.

"Where's the mother?" Belle asked, looking around.

"She don't want her. She left her here and dipped out," he said, putting his hand above his head.

"Do you want her?" Maybelle asked slowly.

"I can't raise a baby right now," Monty said.

That was music to Maybelle's ears. She felt that if she approached this in the right way she may be able to get custody.

"Well, I am going to tell you a story about what happened to me tonight if you wanna sit down for a second," Maybelle said as Monty took a seat on a nearby chair. He was wondering why she was here and what she had to do with the baby.

Monty's mouth dropped as Maybelle told him the full, truthful, story about what happened and how she had been shot by the child's mother. He could not believe his ears. "A trash can," he said, looking over at the child who did sort of look like him.

"I would like to raise this baby for you. I will never keep her from you, and I won't ask for much," Maybelle said, ending her story with a proposition that she felt solved everyone's problem.

****

Tina and Tessa stood on Lola's porch as Old School Joe peered off into space.

"It's time to fucking go. I don't give no fucks about this shit," Tina said, walking down the walk way to the car.

"Yeah, I'm with her," Tessa said, following behind.

"Hold up," Old school Joe said, pointing his gun at their back. "We need to talk about this shit. I don't like her, but I can't let you just kill her."

"Oh, for fucking real Grandpa?" Tina said, turning around.

They all could hear Lola's cackling in the background. "Ahhh ha ha ha, you dumb hoes," she said, barely able to catch her breath.

"So, what are you saying?" Tessa said, crossing her arms over her chest.

"How can we dead this shit between y'all? I got some money stashed away and I can pay y'all to let this shit go," Old School Joe said. He thought, *if he only had been there to raise Mila, she would not be so fucked up.*

"Nigga-" Tina said, getting ready to pull out her own shit.

"Yes," Tessa said, cutting her off. "We can be paid. How much you got, and where is it at?" she asked.

"She must be fucking joking," Tina mumbled. She was utterly confused until she glanced over at Tessa who had her fingers crossed behind her back. *Bittttchhh,* Tina thought. They used to do that all the time when they were lying as kids.

"Alright, Sis," Tina said. "I will roll with you on this one."

Tina's Story

I can't wait to see what she has under her fucking sleeve, but I know one thing, these muthafuckers here about to get fucked up!! Tina thought.

Chapter 52

"So, let's go inside and talk about this situation," Tessa said. "I am always down to make some paper, and if the price is right. I am down."

"Alright," Joe said, raising his eyebrows. He was a smart ass nigga, and he planned to keep his eye on these two. He really wanted to settle shit amicably. He knew that he could be possibly putting his life on the line over this shit. He felt that he lived his life to the fullest already, though. He was not afraid of death. He did his dirt. He took many lives in his day. He hoped that he didn't have to add Tina and Tessa to that list. He would if that's what it came down to, though.

He kept his gun aimed at Tina and stepped to the side as the two girls walked back up the steps and into Lola's house.

Lola smiled as the girls walked into the door. She was blood thirsty. She enjoyed fucking people over. She was a shallow muthafucka just like she raised her daughter to be.

She remembered back when she taught Mila about death. At the time Mila was an innocent four-year-old child, but she needed her to understand the concept. She purchased Mila a pet gerbil with a large cage and all the accessories that she could find. She allowed Mila to take care of it and play with it, even though she hated the fucking rat, for six whole months.

Lola smiled eerily as she recalled waiting until Mila was attached to her new animal friend before she made her move. One summer day when Mila came in the house from playing, she sat on the floor next to the cage with the gerbil in her hand.

"Do you love it?" she asked Mila.

"Yes," Mila answered, looking down at the ground.

"In this world you cannot allow yourself to love anyone or anything. If you do, they will only break your small ass heart and fuck you over," Lola said, beginning to squeeze the squirming gerbil.

"Lola, what are you doing to it?" Mila asked, tears building up in her eyes.

"It doesn't love you, Mila. It has to die," Lola said over Mila's cries as she stuffed Mila's beloved gerbil in a plastic bag she had handy. She laughed wildly as she twisted the bag breaking the poor animal's bones and suffocating it to death.

"Why?" Mila asked as she cried her eyes out.

"Don't fucking ask me why. Go to your fucking room and think about what you have done to deserve this!" Lola yelled at Mila at the top of her lungs.

Lola remembered the defeated look on Mila's face as she headed up stairs. She knew that she would do as she was told. She would not dare talk back to her. That was a lesson she learned long ago.

"Why is she fucking staring off in space like that," Tina whispered to Tessa, as they headed back to the kitchen table.

"I don't know sis, she certified though," Tessa whispered to Tina. She looked at Lola standing there frozen in time, smiling and staring up at the ceiling. Her skin began to crawl. This woman had some of the worst energy she had ever felt in her life. She really could not wait to get out of this house.

Once everyone sat back down at Lola's table, Old School Joe sat his gun down in front of him.

"So, I am offering each of you one-hundred thousand dollars each to make this shit go away." he said.

"Nah I need one-fifty," Tessa said, sitting back in her chair. "She put me through hell."

"Alright," Old School Joe said, thinking that is only fair.

"Man, fuck these bitches," Lola said. "I would not give their ass a dam red cent."

"Lola, be quiet," Old School Joe said. "Look, the money is in my trunk." He said standing up, grabbing his gun and handing it to Lola.

"Don't make a move or she will shoot you. Give me ten seconds. Can we shake on this?" Old School Joe said thinking that the money was his only move in this chess game. If they took the money and still went after Mila, he would have to do something more drastic.

He reached his old hand over to shake Tessa's hand.

POW! POW!

"If anybody is going to get that money, it's me." Lola said as Old School Joe's body hit the table with a thud.

Tina and Tessa looked at each other in disbelief. She really just shot his ass.

"Alright, you two get up. Follow me out to the car to get this money, then I will hand y'all the keys and y'all drive off. Now, this ain't no fucking game. If I wanted to kill you both, I could just do it right now. I don't mind that you are after Mila, because she can take care of her damn self." She said, laughing that weird ass laugh again.

Lola thought it was time to teach Mila another life lesson she was about overdue.

****

Monty and Maybelle had talked for an hour about the baby and Mila. What was so crazy to Monty was that he started to recognize Maybelle. He had seen her walking around the hood before.

"Alright, so how do I sign my rights over to you? How do I even get the rights?" he asked Maybelle. He knew that since he was a nigga he might need to do DNA or some shit.

"Heaven will be in the hospital for a few weeks, so we will have time to work that out," Maybelle said with the biggest smile on her face. She would be able to take this sweet baby home and raise her legally like she was her own. *Ain't GOD good,* she thought, as she began to silently praise HIS name.

"Alright, sounds good." Monty said.

"I will have to be in the hospital for another day," she said, pointing to her wound. "But I will make this as easy as possible for you, I will find out everything we need to know."

Monty felt sorry for the lady. Mila had taken her on a wild ride. All the shit about the trash can and the blood and shit had his mind gone, but after what he heard about her over the last day, he believed every word of it. He began to think that the only way that he could get back in Dred's good graces was to find her and hand her over.

She was fucking up his money and his life. He didn't know how he would tell his mom about his daughter. A part of him was still hoping that it was not his, but the fact that the baby's feet looked so much like his said otherwise.

"Don't worry about anything, son. I mean that GOD will see us through. Just trust and believe, trust and believe." Maybelle said, clapping her hands together...

Chapter 53

Lola smacked Tessa on her ass as she walked out of the door.

Tessa looked back at her, mean mugging and ready to snap on that bitch. The way she just killed her baby daddy like that had them both thinking twice. She obviously didn't give a fuck about shit.

"It was a reflex. Bitch, you not all that," Lola said, wondering if she should have fucked with them a little while longer. Lola walked right up on Tessa's back, and put the gun between her butt cheeks.

"I will blow your ass away, literally," Lola said, laughing her ass off.

"Girl, get that shit out of my ass," Tessa said, unable to ignore the irritation anymore.

Lola cocked her gun and held it in place. She wanted this bitch to know that she was serious. With Joe's money in the trunk she would drop they ass dead right here on this side walk, and get missing.

Tina led the way. She tried to keep her eyes focused in front of her. She was pissed beyond anything. She had blood splatter on her clothes. She was kicking herself for not staying in the hotel until Dred came back. This crazy bitch was too unpredictable. She could pull the trigger at any time. She was pretty sure that what she said was right. Why kill them outside when she could just do it in her house?

With the key Lola handed her, she opened the trunk to see a briefcase. She grabbed the handle of it and handed it over to Lola, who was grinning like a Cheshire cat. As soon as she got her hands on the money she shoved Tessa and began to back up with the gun pointed at them until she got inside.

"Well, that was a fucking bust," Tina said, exhaling. "What the fuck was that?"

"Man, I don't know but let's just get the fuck out of here. Now we got crazy Sr and Jr to fucking deal with. This has been the longest couple weeks of my life," Tessa said.

"So, you just wanna go, you don't wanna fuck this bitch up really quick?" Tina asked, feeling some type of way.

"Yes, but we need to be smart about shit. We need to slow down and think this shit through. I mean, what if it had been one of us that she shot instead of Old School Joe?" Tessa said, showing her mature side. She didn't like how that shit just went down. She didn't like how they just got caught so off guard.

Tessa and Tina got into Old School Joe's car and headed toward the hotel, they both could not wait to see their men.

****

Lola opened the refrigerator and got her a beer. She sat down at the table with Joe's body still lying across it.

"Here nigga, you want a drink?" she said putting the neck of the beer up to his mouth. "Oh, you dead serious huh. Oh nigga I thought you would be dying of thirst," she said, laughing at her own corny ass jokes.

She plopped the heavy brief case on top of the table. Lola could not wait to throw the money in the air and running under it.

"You are the next contestant on the price is right," she said, humming the theme song. When the brief case opened it didn't contain money.

"Fucking rocks!" she said, screaming. Everybody on the whole block had to hear that shit.

"Rocks, ROCKS ROooCKKKS," she said in the most blood curling scream.

****

Souped reclined back on the couch at the hotel and dialed Old School Joe's number. It rang three times before Tina answered the phone.

"Souped!" she said.

"Babe, what's wrong" he asked, sitting up.

"I –" Tina started through the phone in the backseat as it went dead as she was talking. She put her pedal to the metal and sped off toward the hotel, she could not wait to tell him everything that happened.

****

"Hurry your fucking ass up and get dressed. Damn, you are taking longer than me!" Mila said, lying on Troy's bed.

"Bitch don't try to rush perfection. I am serving Picasso beat on this face." Troy said, vogueing.

Rinng! Rinnng!

"What up!" Mila said, rolling her eyes answering the phone.

"Hi, Mila, It's Tony. I really wanna talk to you soon." He said, into the receiver.

"Where did you disappear to last night" She said wondering what the fuck he was up to.

"Can we meet in person?" Tony asked.

"I have a couple other people to see, but I may be able to give you a couple of minutes." Mila said, rolling her eyes.

Tony rattled off a time and a place which Mila didn't even bother to write down. She didn't plan on meeting his ass. She had a whole other bad ass plan to take shit over.

She wanted beef between another boss ass team and Dred. There was no way that he will be able to get out of this shit, she said, *no fucking way*. Tony fidgety ass was not on the same level when she thought about it, and she didn't like scary ass niggas.

Chapter 54

Tina and Tessa pulled up to the hotel and valet in Old School Joe whip. Tina didn't waste any time. She knew that Souped had to be worried about her because the fucking phone went dead.

"Y'all ain't gonna believe this fuckery," Tina said, busting into the hotel room.

"Man," Tessa said, holding her hand on her head.

"You good babe?" Dred said, running over to her worried. "Who blood is this?" he said, getting ready to pat her down looking for a bullet wound.

"This Old School Joe blood," Tina said, feeling pissed off and pacing around.

Dred was still a little upset with Souped about letting them leave. After Souped received the call from Tina he was forced to tell Dred where they went.

"Did y'all fucking know this nigga was Mila's daddy? Key word was 'nigga.'" Tina went on to explain to them everything that happened while they were out. No one said a fucking word. They all sat there with their mouths open.

****

"Aye Aye, Twerk something," Mila said, slapping Troy's ass as he stepped out of the restroom. He decided to go full on female today.

"Dahzammm, lil mama what's yo name? Where you from," Mila said, fucking with Troy. He popped on one of his 1000.00 dollar flawless wet and wavy wigs on. He didn't just beat his face, he TKO'd that shit with the latest Mac line. He had on an olive boyfriend shirt dress with a blue jean jacket on. His ass was looking fat as hell in that shit. Mila knew for sure a muthafucka would have a hard time telling that this was a nigga. *Like there was no way they would know*, she thought.

"Ok, we going to do some fucking spy work, here is the plan. We are going to track down this one nigga daughter, kidnap the little bitch, and make it look like Dred did it." Mila said, feeling like fucking Einstein.

"Um bitch, this outfit is not reading kidnap," Troy said with his face screwed up. "Who daughter bitch?"

"NoNo's daughter," Mila said, hoping that Troy would not nut up.

"I live a peaceful life honey. If I am going to interrupt that shit, then I need to get paid. I know you loaded hoe, so I don't feel bad what so ever. That nigga NoNo don't fucking play. Why the fuck do y'all think they call him NoNo in the first fucking place?" he said, exhaling hard as hell. Troy then held his hand out.

"Alright, I got some paper for you. That's nothing. We get this nigga Dred killed then it's even more paper up for grabs!" Mila said. She could tell that Troy was down. "We gonna do this shit the right way. We need supplies and a spot. What you got on is fine for now. Mooo hoo ha ha ha," Mila said, trying to lighten the mood.

"Aiiight," Troy said. "But I need my paper first and foremost chica."

****

After hearing what just went down, Dred didn't know how to feel. *Now Mila's mom in on this shit.* He knew all about her and the things that she did to Mila. She was a sewer rat ass bitch. The fact that they had *her* involved was all bad.

Dred took stock of his mental shit list... *Mila, Tony, Lola and possibly Monty.* He decided that they all needed to get away for a little while and let nuthackers get comfortable.

"Aye y'all, we need to leave the city for a while." Dred said to everyone.

"I ain't running from no fucking body," Tina said, snapping back.

"This is not running." he shot back. "This is being smart about shit. I say we take a vacation and get some rest, and let a muthafucka get comfortable. Plan some shit, then come back bussing."

"Does this shit include a beach?" Tessa asked, stretching her arms. "This shit do sound kind of good."

"Alright, the shit is settled. Vacation on me," Dred said, thinking that he wanted to do more than plan. He wanted Tessa all to himself.

Chapter 55

Dred, Tessa, Souped, Tina, Rocko and Asha got out of the stretch hummer and walked toward the private jet Dred chartered to the Bahamas.

Tessa was so excited. She and Dred held hands as they walked toward the plane.

"Baby, I want you to clear your mind and not focus on anything but me," Dred said, kissing her hand.

"That should not be a problem," Tessa said, smiling at him.

"Your pretty ass," he said, looking at her pretty teeth gleaming in the sunlight.

"Aw, look at the love birds," Asha said, her blonde locks blowing in the light breeze.

"Aw, look at the fuck birds," Tina said, looking at Rocko and Asha. "Bitch, you just came up. You about to go on a free vacation and errrr thang. Turn up."

Asha hit her dab on their ass. They didn't even know she was that hip.

"OWWW," Rocko said, walking up behind her putting his dick on her ass and grinding.

Once everyone got settled on the plane the turn up continued. Tina got up on the jet speaker phone and start talking shit.

"Testicles one two. Testicles one two," Tina said in her best Snoop Dog Soul Plane impression.

Everybody got weak. Tessa threw a couple of courtesy nuts at her.

Tessa looked out the window as the clouds passed by. She could not help but think of how beautiful everything was. She was on a beautiful jet with a beautiful view and had a beautiful dark skinned sexual chocolate ass man sitting next to her. *Damn, why I am so blessed man? This is all so amazing.*

"I am tired," Dred said, laying his head on her shoulder.

"Me too," Tessa said as she began to rub his temples.

"It's a suite in here. You wanna go lay down?" Dred said, looking up at her, winking.

Tessa felt so happy and thought, *Damn could this shit get any better?*

"Hell yea, let's go stretch out," she said, giggling.

Dred stood up and directed Tessa to the back of the jet where behind a door was a small luxurious room that held a plush queen size bed. Dred locked the door behind them as he took off his shirt and grabbed the remote to the T.V.

Tessa looked down at him as she took off her shirt too, then her pants, until all she had on was a bra and boy shorts.

Dred was trying not to stare too hard at her fat pussy print. He wanted to nuzzle his face right in between her legs. *Her thick ass thighs,* he thought, *she didn't even have to turn around for a nigga to know that that ass was fat. Her perky breasts didn't even need a bra to sit in the position they were in.* He wanted to rip that shit off of her. It was not like they had not fucked before. It just had been a couple of weeks. He wanted her like it was the first time though.

They both flopped down on the bed. Dred laid on his side as Tessa scooted her ass right up on to his lap. If only she could see the look on his face. There was no way that he would be able to stop her from feeling his long ass dick starting to grow so he scooted back a little out of respect for her.

"You wanna play a game," Tessa asked, looking back at Dred.

"What kind of game? I'm down," Dred said, enjoying just looking at her.

"Pictionary," Tessa said, grabbing the paper and pen from the inn table.

She began to draw while he had to figure out what she was drawing without her saying a word.

"Road," Dred shouted, as she drew what looked like a street.

Tessa shook her head "no" as she drew a sign on the side of the road on her paper.

"Mile Marker," Dred said, liking this game. Tessa shook her head no and pointed again to the street.

"Mile?" Dred asked.

Tessa shook her head "yes" excitedly. Next, she drew an arrow pointing up.

He didn't even have to guess anymore. He happily solved her puzzle.

"Mile High Club," he said, getting off the bed, grabbing the pen and paper and throwing it across the room.

He slid his hands around her back, softly kissing her neck. She purred like a kitten. Each kiss sent shivers up her spine and made her pussy throb. As he knelt on the bed and she remained, he traced the kisses down to the top of her breast. Like a pro, he undid her bra and immediately caught one of her nipples in between his lips. He teased and nibbled it with his tongue, and she leaned her head back and enjoyed him.

His dick was rock hard. He could feel the precum on the tip of his dick rubbing against his boxers. In one swift motion he lifted her up by the waist and flung her on the bed. She giggled as he climbed over her. His wide shoulders and sexy chest turned her on to the max.

He pulled her panties down slowly as he lay in between her legs. The kisses trailed from her belly button all the way to the top of her shaved pussy. His heart beat faster as he approached her clit. He wanted it in his mouth badly, and could not believe that he was getting ready to taste it.

Tessa smiled wide and covered her eyes as she prepared to get some of his good ass head.

Dred inhaled and smelled her fresh pussy. His dick got so hard he had to adjust himself so that it was not pressing so hard against the bed. He slowly took his tongue and traced from the bottom of her clit to the top of it, slowly nudging it. He could already taste some of her wetness starting to seep out of her pussy. He wrapped his full lips around her clit and began to slowly suck as he held her legs down.

It felt so good that Tessa's body started to jerk with every suck.

"Don't you run from me," Dred said, his warm breath caressing her pussy as he began to lick and suck. He wanted to taste all of her. He could not wait until she came in his mouth.

Tessa peeked down at the top of Dred's head. His sexy strong chiseled back covered her thighs. The sight of him alone was enough to bring her into a screaming orgasm.

"Dreddd," Tessa moaned as she felt her pulsating pussy overflowing into Dred's mouth, while he thrust his tongue inside of her.

****

"What the fuck was that?" Tina said, as everyone in the front of the jet heard Tessa's moans.

"Oh hell nah," Souped said, laughing. "Shit, we gonna need a turn too."

Chapter 56

Dred tasted Tessa's sweet ass cum in his mouth. With all his weight he held her down as she came. Her clit was extremely sensitive and he knew that he could get another nut out of her. He took his sexy tongue out of her pussy hole and slowly moved it back up to her clit.

Tessa held his head as she squirmed around trying to get away from his tongue flicking against her swollen clit.

Dred was determined not to stop until she nutted again. He slurped and sucked her clit. It tasted so good to him. He planned on having her for breakfast tomorrow.

"I want the dick!" Tessa screamed, unable to hold back the urge to ride his thick ass dick.

"Oh, you want this dick?" Dred said, standing up. He pulled down his pants and boxers to reveal that big ass dick standing at full attention.

"I wanna ride you baby." Tessa said, legs still shaking.

"You gonna ride this fucking roller coaster first," he said, grabbing her legs and pulling her to the edge of the bed. He gripped her ankles and held her legs straight up in the air as he slowly inched his dick into her wet pussy.

Dred felt the warmness of her tight ass pussy wrapped around his dick, hugging it. That pussy was telling him that she never wanted to let him go. He slid his dick half way in her and slowly began to pump as he licked her ankles and her legs.

The sensation of looking at him, being fucked, and feeling his tongue was sending Tessa over the edge. She felt like she was about to come again.

"Yes Daddy. Give me that hard ass dick." Tessa moaned.

"Oh, you want this shit? You are about to get it. You ready to ride this roller coaster," he said as he gripped her ankles and pulled them together. As he pumped he began to move her legs in a circular motion.

"Oh, damn… Right there, right fucking there," Tessa screamed, not caring who heard her.

"Mmmmm Hmmm, you want all this dick?" he asked, biting his bottom lip.

"Yes, daddy," Tessa said, throwing her head back in ecstasy.

"This my fucking pussy," he said, throwing his dick in her with a motion that she had never felt from another man. His whole stroke was different, the rhythm of it.

"Yes, all yours," Tessa said, her eyes rolling into the back of her head.

"Forever," Dred said, breathing hard and still keeping his tempo in that pussy. His dick was covered in her juices.

"I'm cuming!" Tessa screamed as her body convulsed. The feeling of her nut and his dick touching every part of her pussy was the stuff that dreams were made of.

Dred continued to pound her. He moved his hands down to grip her thick thighs and ass. Wanting to be closer to her, he laid his body right on top of hers and began kissing her passionately as he slowed his stoke down to a grind.

His mouth tasted of mint and his body smelled so good. She wished that he could stay inside of her forever. She explored his shoulders and back. She was completely lost in his kisses. It was like nothing else existed.

Dred began to sing in her ear, "forever my lady, it's like a dreeamm... I'm holding you close, keeping you warm, this is extacyyy..."

Damn, Tessa thought. *He sounded better than Jodeci, singing that song.*

She joined in with him, and the sound of her sweet voice caused his dick to feel like it was getting ready to explode.

Just when he thought that he could not wait any longer, while still covering her body with his, he pulled his dick out and nutted all over her pussy lips.

His body shuttered in her arms as she rubbed his neck and kissed the top of his head.

"You're the fucking best," he said under his breath.

Chapter 57

"Mannn they back there cutting the fuck up!" Tina said, flopping in her seat.

"Damn did y'all feel that," Souped said, cracking up.

"Hellll yea, they back there going so hard they literally shaking the back of this shit" Tina said, getting weak.

****

Maybelle rolled her chair up to Heaven's incubator and looked in on her. *She's so beautiful,* she thought. *What a good thing she ended up here getting the care she needed.*

"I am going to give you a happy life," Maybelle said, rolling away in her chair, feeling like a miracle was occurring.

****

Lola slid on her Pink jogging suit from Victoria's Secret and laced up her Jordans. As she headed toward the front door she shook out her fresh wrap and combed it down with the rat-tail comb. She was pissed off that money was not in that brief case. *Was this nigga serious?* She thought.

Lola was having a bad day, she thought again and again. *When Lola has a bad day, every fucking body gonna have a bad day around this bitch.*

Lola was the type of bitch that would bump your car in the parking lot with her door and scratch your shit up, on purpose. Lola enjoyed doing shit like cutting the wire near the port and fucking up your phone charger.

Her favorite type of weather had become rain. *You can piss some people off in the rain,* she thought, locking her door and smiling.

She had become tamer over the years, settling for irritating people frequently for her fuck you fix.

Last night she put on red lip stick and headed out for a night in the city. She dressed to the nines, and she looked good. Lola made forty look brand new.

Lola left her lipstick print boldly on the collar of over 50 married men just to start shit. Like James Brown was the godfather of soul, she was the original Petty Betty.

She was such a pretty older lady though, almost regal in her appearance once you really took the time to look at her. *People would shit bricks to know what I am really am,* Lola thought.

As Lola started her car, she knew her first stop was her daughter's house. *I am about to go check on her ass, she not handling business.*

As Lola knocked on what she thought was Mila's door, no one answered. She decided to sit on the porch for a while and play on her phone to see if anyone came home.

It had been only eight minutes before Lola started to say fuck this shit. No sooner than she said that did a car pulled into the driveway. A woman got out in a maid's outfit and headed up towards the front door.

"Yes," Lola said. "I am Mila's mother. I will wait inside for them to come home. If her bitch work here, she damn sure know my daughter," she said, laughing.

"Ma'am" the housekeeper said. "Mila does not live here anymore. I don't have permission to let you in."

The housekeeper attempted to close the door behind her, but Mila's mom slid inside knocking the poor girl out of the way.

"Bitch, I will wait inside. Go fix me a fucking sandwich," she said, pulling out her pistol. *Mila has lost control of her fucking castle, I knew something was off. Here I am, still gotta teach this bitch lessons.*

****

"Oh, she is such a blessing," Maybelle said, smiling widely as she lay back on her hospital bed. She saw herself braiding Heaven's natural hair and dressing her cute in her mind. She could not wait to get home, she said, waving her hands again, praising the lord's name.

Chapter 58

"Put your head down dumb ass," Mila said to Troy. They were parked across the street from a private school that NoNo's fifteen-year-old daughter attended. They were scoping the scene to see what her routine was. Mila was wondering who picked her up and what she normally did with her time after school.

"You childish," Troy said. "I am ducking my ass down as best as possible hoe. I'm out here kidnapping people and shit with your ass and you got the nerve to be talking shit, bitch swerve."

Mila laughed out loud at Troy talking shit. He had rolled his eyes and his head every way possible getting that point across.

Mila slid her seat back in the rented all black Navigator truck. The school would be getting out in a few minutes and she hoped that she would see the lil bitch coming out. NoNo's house was not the place to stake out at, his niggas would peep some shit like that and fuck around and light the whole truck up. Mila liked to take chances, so for real, she didn't really give a fuck. She was just trying to water her shit down for Troy.

All the way outside they could hear the bell for dismissal ring in the small, exclusive private school. As the students poured out of the high school for the privileged, it was apparent that most of them had their own cars. From the ruckus you could tell that all of the students were happy as hell it was the weekend. Mila looked out her window wondering to herself what life had been like if she had a normal mother. By the time she figured out what she was going through at home was not normal she was already a teenager. Her jealousy began to build towards NoNo's daughter. *Lil bitches like that don't even know what they got going for them, this lil bitch gonna learn today. If she makes it out of this shit alive,* she thought, laughing.

"Bitch, what is funny and do you see her ass? I am tired of sitting out here." Troy said with his hand over his eyes blocking out the sun that was beating down on him through the windshield.

"Ahhh nothing. We about to go in a sec." Mila said, thinking that she would have to find her soon.

Up ahead a teenage boy walked from car to car passing out a flyer. He walked up to Mila next smelling like straight weed and handed her a flyer.

"When is this?" Mila asked.

"This shit is tonight, we gonna turn up," he said smiling at Mila. He was wondering how old she was. He had to admit, though, she was sexy as fuck. He thought about offering her VIP.

"You got some more of that weed?" Mila asked, smiling and looking forward. "That's kush you smoking, what you know about that youngster?"

"I am grown as fuck, I just turned eighteen," he said reaching into his backpack and handing Mila a half ounce of dank. "Make sure you and your girl show y'all pretty faces tonight, everyone will be there."

"We willlll," Troy said in his high pitched, female voice.

"Ok boo. Give me your number," Mila said, smacking her bubble gum. She was sure she could still pass for around 22 with the right outfit.

The young boy gave Mila his number and walked off with pep in his step. *Damn,* he thought. *I got the juice, those hoes were bad as fuck. Imma hook her girl up with my nigga. He loved him some fine ass black girls he thought.*

"Got her ass nigga, her lil ass most definitely gonna be at this fucking party," Mila said, waving the flyer in the air. "We got her ass!"

Chapter 59

Lola smacked fire out of the maid at Dred's house.

"I'll go make the sandwich," the maid said with her head down, heading toward the kitchen.

Lola walked behind her laughing, "Hurry your ass up," she screamed as she kicked her in her ass.

The kick caused the maid to stumble forward, and the soft cries from the maid were starting to piss Lola off.

"Bitch, two tears in a fucking bucket. I don't give a fuckity fuck about your tears," Lola said, sounding like a complete asshole.

"You're gonna make that damn sandwich and tell me everything that's been going on around this house. I wanna know everything. Bitch, if the fucking toilet was stopped up last week I wanna know how many times you pumped the plunger. You get my drift bitch?" Lola said, pointing her finger at the maid as she sat at the island in Dred's enormous kitchen.

"I have only been working here for a couple of days. I have no clue what's going on here. Nobody has been home the whole time!" the maid said, crying as she spread mayo on Lola's sandwich.

"Did you just fucking scream at me? You better check that shit in bitch!" Lola said, hopping up from the table and running full speed toward the stove near the maid and grabbed a frying pan lying on the burner.

Lola laughed as the maid screamed and attempted to run.

Whack! Whack! Whack!

"Take that, you smart mouth ass bitch." Lola said maniacally.

Lola hit the maid until she lost consciousness then washed her hands and picked up her sandwich.

"Hmm this bitch makes a pretty good sandwich," she said with a mouth full of food. Lola finished her lunch happily, just chilling like she was not in someone else's house.

Lola grabbed the maid by her hair.

"I'm gonna make this less painful for you," Lola said eerily to the knocked out maid, "since that sandwich was so fucking good."

Lola dragged the petite maid by her hair down the hallway to Dred's laundry room.

"This rich muthafucka," she screamed, knocking pictures off of Dred's wall with her free hand.

Once Lola got to Dred's Landry room she opened the door to the large industrial dryer that was used by Dred's staff. Lola looked around the room, *this shit look like a fucking brand new dry cleaners.*

Void of emotion, Lola stuffed the maid into the dryer. Her body was just small enough to fit.

"This is the shit," Lola said, starting to get a rush. She had discovered long ago that she was somewhat of a serial killer. If everyone knew all of the things she did in her lifetime, she would go down a legend.

Lola tapped on the circular window of the closed dryer door. She stood there tapping until the maid began to regain consciousness.

Tap Tap Tap....

The maids muffled screams and look of horror caused Lola much satisfaction as she smiled and waved at the girl beating against the window.

Lola pressed the start button on the dryer and watched as the body inside began to slowly spin around. The motor of the dryer gave a little resistance, but it looked so expensive Lola knew it would do the job.

She stood there and watched as blood began to splash and the girl's body was distorted beyond recognition.

"Ha Ha Ha Haaa!" Lola screamed. "I'm back!"

Chapter 60

Dred and Tessa hogged the private room in the jet, fucking for hours on end. Tina and Souped both knocked on the door at different times trying to get their turn in the bed.

Dred and Tessa swerved their ass and acted as if they didn't hear anyone knocking. They laughed every time too. Dred thought that shit was hilarious. "Ain't no fucking way I am giving up this room, they cool." Dred said as he continued to blast Tessa's back out.

By the time the jet landed, Tina and Souped were pissed and very horny.

"Damn," Tina said to Souped under her breath. "That was not just any type of sex we missed out on. That was jet sex, mile high club type shit!"

"Don't trip," he said. "We about to have a lot of firsts around this bitch." Souped said. "Did you forget your man rich too? On the way back we getting our own shit and we running around that muthafucka butt booty ass naked!"

"Ayyyyeee," Tina said, dropping it low for a second. "And Imma keep that ass dropping, keep that ass dropping."

Souped smiled and looked at Tina's dangerously sexy ass. She was the total package, a straight bad ass bitch.

He didn't know why, but he wanted to do shit for her that he had never done for the most part for anyone else. He was going to make this a trip she would never forget. Nothing was off limits. He was a fucking rock star in the rap game and he wanted to show her the type of royalty she had just become.

He liked that she didn't focus on the fact that he was a rapper. She didn't even ask much about it. She just went with the flow. Most women would start off attractive then lose themselves in him. He could tell that Tina put herself first and that shit was sexy to him. It was not about how good she was going to treat him, but the other way around. He knew that she had standards and he would always have to work to please her. That made him happy, she made him happy.

Souped snapped out of his thoughts as he shut the door to the limo that was waiting for them at yet another private landing strip. He was happy they didn't fly mainstream, with the shooting, all the paparazzi was sure to be looking for his ass.

Dred booked the most expensive vacation home in Nassau, Bahamas. It was a beautiful beach side estate with all of the luxury the ladies could ask for.

Tina burst through the front door of the mansion excited as fuck. She grabbed Souped's hand and dragged him through the house straight out the back glass patio door and down to the beach.

It was a private beach most likely owned by the owner of the vacation home. The sun was setting and in a few minutes the colorful sky would be completely dark. The water was calm and beautiful. There was a faint reflection of the sky cast down on the water. *It's beautiful,* Tina thought with the biggest smile. She stretched out her arms and closed her eyes as she let the cool breeze caress her body. *This was heaven on earth,* she thought.

Souped walked up behind her, put his arms around her and began to kiss her neck with his soft and sexy lips.

Tina playfully walked forward, and away from his embrace as she began to take off her clothes, putting on a sexy little show that had Souped's dick rock hard.

Chapter 61

Tina stripped down to her underwear and started to put on a full show for Souped who began to get undressed as well. She was twerking and moving her body around to the beat in her head.

"Damn," Souped said, gripping his throbbing hard long black dick. The way she was throwing her ass around all he could do was stand there and watch. He didn't want it to stop. Her sexy thick ass cheeks clapped together on tempo. He could tell she was wet as fuck. Her panties were starting to show it. He wanted to put his face right in between that tasty ass pussy like he had before.

Tina laughed as she had a great time dancing for him. She had a smile on her face for so long now her cheeks were starting to hurt. *This shit is truly amazing,* she thought. *I could not paint a more perfect picture.*

She slid off her panties, bending all the way over and shaking her ass slowly from side to side, teasing Souped.

"We be all night," Tina sung. She sounded like a damn good singer. Souped was impressed, *was there anything that she could not do? She is a jack of all trades.*

He watched her walk towards the water, taking off her bra on the way. She was completely naked when she stepped her foot in the cool water. She turned around as she let her long natural hair fly free from her bun. The soft coils surrounded her beautiful face like a crown of glory. The fading light filtered through the outline of her hair, giving the illusion of a large golden halo.

"She dope as fuck," Souped said and he stood in awe of the powerful sight of her standing on the ocean's edge, completely bare. He pulled out his phone and snapped a quick picture of her. He hoped she didn't mind. He was not trying to be disrespectful. He just wanted to make sure this memory was one that he would always be able to look back on.

Tina gracefully pointed at him and motioned for him to come here. He kicked off his shoes and tore the rest of his clothes away, and then jogged down to her.

He scooped her in his arms as they embraced and shared a kiss that felt like nothing less than pure ecstasy. Playfully, Souped picked Tina up pretending to throw her in the water. He must have forgotten for a split second how gangster she was. In the blink of an eye she clipped his leg causing him to fall backwards where the sand met the water.

"Ah shit," he laughed as Tina straddled him, looking him dead in his eyes. His laughter stopped when she grabbed his long dick and slowly slid it in her pussy.

"Surf Board, Surf Board," Tina joked as she said fuck romance, and started to pop and tick on his dick.

The waves began to slowly roll in as the water went from inches to a foot deep. Souped lifted up and wrapped his arms around Tina as he slowly grinded in and out of her. He made damn sure to rub the head of his dick against her g-spot with each stroke. Tina's body felt so good. She looked down at him, her eyes watering. She was lost in passion.

They wanted each other so bad, Souped could not hold back. Everything he did was on instinct. They crashed their bodies into each other, mimicking the pattern of the water. The sky had become completely black, and the dim light was just enough for them.

Souped stood up out of the water with Tina's legs wrapped around his waist. He gripped her ass and thrust her on to his waiting dick. He hit the back of her pussy so hard and she loved it.

"Oh baby, you love me?" he whispered into Tina ear as he nibbled on her earlobe and lightly smacked her ass.

"Yes, I love you," Tina said, releasing the words in his ear, and her warm cum on his dick at the same time.

Chapter 62

"It's turn up time bitchhh," Troy said, adjusting his red body con dress. He had on his favorite body wave wig. He had his long dick tucked as best as he could with the nude spanks.

"You are a straight up dick sucking ho bag. This is a fucking high school party. You tryna catch a case?" Mila said, laughing at his ass.

"Hell nah bitch, you know how this shit go, somebody 18 in that there with a nice trust fund," Troy said, batting his eyes.

"You are a fucking hot ass mess," Mila said laughing at him. She had to admit though, he looked damn good.

"Um shade, since when do I ever not look good, this sexy shit comes standard," Troy said while applying eyeliner in the bathroom mirror. The party had already started but Mila wanted to be fashionably late. *Let they ass be drunk by the time we get there,* she reasoned to herself.

In an attempt to look younger than she appears she had put two crispy ass French braids in her hair. She had on a mini skirt and a collar shirt on her Brittany Spears shit.

"Girrll, did you really just go all out school girl like that," Troy said, getting weak when he saw her outfit. "Hit me baby one more time," he said as he danced around.

"Shut yo duct tape dick ass up," Mila said, tapping him in his stomach.

****

Maybelle sat in her bed in her room and prayed with all her might. She knew the lord had a plan for her, and all she had to do was stay faithful.

"Ok hun, you ready to get out of here?" The nurse asked her.

Maybelle was so happy to hear those words, she had been in the hospital for two days by now and she was ready to go back home. She didn't know what kind of mess it would be in. She wondered about her couch. It had to be covered with her blood.

While she was in the hospital the police had come to see her twice to ask her about the night in question. She didn't want to complicate things further so she simply told them that she did not remember what happened to her.

Her only concern at this point was baby Heaven.

The nurse accompanied Maybelle to the front door and wished her well on her recovery.

Monty got out of the driver's seat to open the door for Maybelle. Over the last couple days they had gotten to know each other. He was feeling less guilty about turning the baby over to her. Because Mila left the baby in the hospital, child protective services were involved. Maybelle and Monty had spoken to them twice already.

"You doing O.K. Miss Belle?" Monty said, looking at her.

"Yes, sore still but I will be fine," She said as she got in his car, feeling comfortable in his presence.

****

Mila and Troy pulled up to the party, like dammmmn. This shit was all the way gone. There were so many people there they were spilling onto the street. Red cups and weed smoke seemed to be a common theme.

Mila rubbed her hands together, thinking to herself, *I am about to have some muthafucking fun!*

Chapter 63

"Yass, the turn up is authentic off up in dis shit!" Troy said, stepping out of the truck.

These rich ass little kids had a whole mansion lit the fuck up. The large U-shaped driveway was cluttered with cars. Benz's, Range Rovers, all type of hot shit. *Troy was right. It was definitely some grown ass muthafuckers in this party.*

Mila saw a whole group of college kids hanging over to the side. She was starting to wonder if this was really a college party and some dude had just decided to pass out flyers to the high school peeps. This shit was popping that one way. The crowd was mixed and full of trendy ass college kids. She saw a sorority over to the side stepping and everything.

"Oooo bitch, this is why I love hanging with your ass. Can we party before we start snatching bitches up and shit? I am ready to mingle in this bitch, these balling ass lil muthafuckers." Troy said, applying more lip gloss on his lips.

"Yes, we can kick it," Mila was salty as hell she was still bleeding and she could not be the thot that she wanted to be. She wanted some dick bad though. She had not fucked in a second.

Mila rubbed her hand down her flat ass stomach, *I got that fucking snap back,* she thought. *Pooty tang off in this bitch, shit soon as this flow stop I am going be out there smoking the biggest riches dick I can find.*

Troy pulled out his phone and checked his Instagram. He had 85 thousand followers and he could not wait to show them this shit. He took a short video with him and Mila talking shit.

"Your ass is crazy," Troy said, laughing. "Her bad ass needed an account she on fleek," he said, looking at her smooth ass skin. He didn't like bitches, but on a drunk night he might slide that dick off in Mila he said, laughing to himself.

"Oh shit, she here nigga, she here, her lil ass!!!" Mila said, talking shit. "Let's go see what's popping in the back yard, this ill bitch knows who I am. Aye yo this is what we are gonna d--"

"Unt uh hold up bih you said we handing fun first. Cut your diabolical ass brain off for a second bitch and just kick it. I know you can't fuck but you can still flirt your ass off. Come on, fun please!" Troy said, stomping his feet like a little ass kid.

"Alright, one-hour nigga," Mila said, giving in.

Chapter 64

"Ohh shit! Look at his fine ass," Troy said, pointing to a tall caramel dude who kind of resembled August Alsina.

"Um if that's your type, he ain't really all that to me," Mila said, scanning the room. *He was cute,* she thought. *I'm just hating.*

"You know damn well he cute and he about to be mine," Troy said, getting ready to walk over to the dude.

"Ok, well be careful because you still got a dick down there and you know how niggas is," Mila said.

"I will beat his ass," Troy said, getting weak and temporarily putting bass in his voice.

"Alright, well I am going to sit here and get a drink." Mila said while heading over to the makeshift bar they set up in the huge back yard. She could feel eyes on her. She was looking sexy as fuck. As she walked, the breeze carried her sweet scent to the nose of every nigga in the vicinity.

"Dammmmn baby," A shitty ass dude said, walking over to Mila putting his arm around her.

"Don't fucking touch me," Mila said, brushing his hand off of her shoulder. *This muthafucker better get a got damn clue. I'm the last bitch in here he wanna fuck with.*

"Fuck you, you thot ass hoe," he said, salty that he was not getting any play.

"Whatever you say nigga," Mila said, waving her hand away to go sit at the bar.

The young boy pulled out his phone and began recording Mila saying, "Hoes be like, 'I got a man, but be lonely as fuck.'" He stammered and Mila realized that he was obviously drunk or on coke. "Hoes be like, 'give me that dick in a box.'"

"Are you going to keep bothering me?" Mila said, nicely trying not to snap. NoNo's daughter was at the party and she knew what she looked like. She was trying to keep a low profile but this nigga was testing her patience.

"Hoes be like, 'why you bothering me?'" the guy said, mocking Mila, still recording on his phone.

"Haha ha ha," Mila said, laughing sweetly. "You know, what you are too funny. You're right, maybe I do want you. Can we go somewhere more private?"

"Damn, Ok," the guy said. He could not have been older than 21 years old. "Come on, follow your leader," he said, burping.

Laughing, Mila followed behind him as he led her into the master bathroom on the second floor of the huge house. *The loud music damn near shaking the walls,* Mila thought. She was happy it was so loud.

"So baby," Mila said. "Give me your phone, let's make a movie."

"OH, that's dirty." He said, handing her his phone. "You going to be my little hoe."

Mila turned around to the counter with her back to him as she quickly deleted the video of her off of his phone. *Why did he have to fuck with me,* she thought. *This shit be they fault; they ask for this shit to happen to them.*

"Oh damn, look at that ass." He said, standing behind Mila watching every jiggle her ass made.

"You ready to get this shit lit!" Mila said, fumbling around with something on the counter.

"Yes, turn up then, girl" he said about to reach his hands out and touch Mila's ass.

Quickly Mila grabbed her lighter from her bra and turned around with a can of hair spray. Before he knew what hit him she flicked her lighter and the hairspray at the same time engulfing his face in flames.

"AHHHHAHHHH," he screamed.

"No one can hear you," Mila laughed as she shot the flames at him, burning his skin. "Lames be like, 'ahhh I'm on fire!'"

As he ran to the door she quickly took off one of her high heeled shoes. With the speed of a fucking ninja Mila raced over to the unlucky young man, reached around him and stabbed him in his neck with the heel of her shoes.

Haha, Mila thought. *Nigga want to talk shit to me. We need to get ol girl and get the fuck out of her now. The fuck Troy talking about we can part later. Dred ass got to die. He won't catch me slipping out here.*

She exited the bathroom locking the door from the inside hoping to delay anyone from entering there.

"This a dude." someone said.

"What the fuck?" another one said.

"Ahh nigga, this crazy." said a guy.

Mila walked toward a circle of people out back where she left Troy.

"Oh Fuck," Mila said under her breath as she got close enough to see what was going on. "They got Troy ass hemmed up! Fuck!"

Chapter 65

Tina and Souped joined the crew back in the house after about an hour of sex on the beach.

"Haha, we broke that beach in first." Tina said, pointing at Tessa talking shit.

"You petty," Tessa said, laughing. "We still gonna fuck on it too," she said, laughing.

"Not tonight though, y'all better let all that nut out there get washed away first," Tina said through her laughs.

Souped started laughing so hard when he heard Tina say that. She was so unpredictable and he loved it. He could still see her on top of him, titties bouncing, looking down at him with the sexiest fuck face ever.

"Tell 'em Bae," Souped said.

"Y'all fooling," Dred said, walking into the room thinking how glad he was now that everyone was enjoying themselves.

****

Lola walked around Dred's house smoking a joint and snooping into everything she could.

"This stupid bitch, she really fucked up. She had everything at her fingertips!" Lola said, walking into Mila's closet which was as big as a studio apartment.

She was disappointed in her daughter. She taught her better than to not destroy a nigga properly. *Mila could have fucked Dred's life up, but instead it looked like she was fucking up hers,* she thought.

Lola grabbed the keys to Dred's house that belonged to the maid and stormed out. Mila had her fucked up. She was a waste of fucking space. *All those years of lessons got her nowhere. She still out here wet behind the ears.*

"I know exactly where you are bitch and I am coming to let your ass have it," Lola exclaimed, talking to herself. "That damn Troy house."

Lola could not wait to give Mila a piece of her mind. *She better get at those two bitches,* she thought while laughing.

Lola stopped by the gas station on her way to Troy's house. She was hoping he lived in the same place. She reached in her glove box and got a small zip lock bad full of rat droppings. She kept a whole glove box full of weird shit. Fucking other people's day up always made her feel better.

Lola went to the back of the store and opened up a two liter of coke real slick. She took a couple of hard rat droppings and dropped them in the bottle.

"Blop," she said, and then she put the cap on as tight as she could.

Next, she walked over to the coffee pot, and as soon as the clerk turned his head she dropped a few rat droppings in the coffee pot.

"Blop, blop," Lola said, giggling.

Tina's Story

Fuck it, it's night time, but muthafucka is still drinking this coffee, she thought mad. Usually, she liked to fuck up the morning coffee. But as she walked out the door she exhaled, "the best part of waking up is rat shit in yo guts," she sung, laughing.

****

Mila had a couple of seconds to size the situation up. Troy was getting cussed out. *I just fucking told his ass. I should leave his ass, that would teach him,* Mila thought.

Chapter 66

"Oh shit," Mila said as she stood on her tippy toes to try and get a glimpse of the middle of the crowd. "This some bullshit, fuck this," Mila said, turning around to walk back to her car.

"I told his ass before we got here," she reasoned to herself, "But noooo, he just had to get some dick."

On her way back to the car she saw two girls over by a bush. One girl, who was obviously intoxicated, was bent over hurling in the bushes and what looked to be her best friend was holding her hair and rubbing her back.

"Aww, now that's true friendship," Mila said, under her breath.

"Arrgggggg," she moaned, stomping the ground. There was no way she could leave him. Mila pulled her pistol out of her bra and headed back to the back yard where she ducked off behind a couple trees lining it.

POW! POW! POW!

Mila let off three rounds into the air real smooth then ran from behind the tree screaming.

"They shooting! They shooting!" waving her hands in the air, "Run for your lives."

No sooner than Mila pulled the trigger the crowd started to disperse. The ring leader that had tried to hem Troy up threw him to the ground.

"No the fuck you won't" Troy said, quickly getting up, putting up his dukes.

Without the hype of the crowd this lil dude was not about shit, Troy thought. Too pissed to control himself Troy began welling on him with his fists, tears streaming down his face. How dare he embarrass him like that in front of all those people?

Mila ran over to Troy where he had him on the ground.

"Oh, really though you tried to shit on me though, but you the shitty one, that ain't how this works hun," Troy said in his Nicki voice.

"Shit, let me get my licks in," Mila said, kicking him in the gut, and he lay there balled up.

"Hahaha, bitch you crazy," Troy said. "I knew you would do the right thing. I saw your ass about to leave me," Troy said, getting weak.

Mila looked down at the ground, she was about to lie, but she decided against it.

"Yeah, I was about to leave your ass but I couldn't, so you should feel hella special." Mila said, smiling at him.

"Damn! Look who we have here," Mila said, pointing. "That's his fucking daughter right there!"

"Let's do this shit then, fuck this party and everybody in it," Troy said, looking at the young dude who ass he just whopped, limping away.

"Why you letting him go?" Mila asked

"He learned his lesson," Troy said.

That word alone still to this day sent shivers up Mila's spine. Her mother loved to teach "lessons."

Chapter 67

Mila looked over at NoNo's daughter. She could not even remember the lil hoe's name. *This is the key to my way out of this shit,* she thought.

"How we going to grab her?" Troy said. "I don't know about this part of the game."

"We not grabbing her here. It's too much going on, we gonna follow her ass. The night just started and she definitely not going home yet. I know I wouldn't be." Mila said like she was talking about the weather or some shit. Like kidnapping is just some everyday shit.

"Shit, all of the hoes wanna be my friend," Troy said, flicking his hair. "Should I go over and get cool with they ass?"

"Hell nah, I am not on that. We just gonna keep watching her. She gonna separate from her friend's sooner or later." Mila said, leaning against the side of the house.

It seemed like half of the kids left the party and the other half were still there drinking and chilling. *Maybe they thought it was some asshole at the party was shooting and shit for no reason,* Mila thought.

NoNo's daughter was on the other side of the yard with her friend being a little fast ass. Mila watched her every move like a hawk, all the while thinking about how Dred was going to get what he deserved.

"AhHHHHHAAHH! Call 911! Call 911! Somebody up in that bathroom dead," Somebody yelled, running out the back door of the house.

"Damn" Troy said, looking at Mila. "You can't go no fucking where without killing somebody. That's a damn shame."

"He asked for it. They scattering like roaches for real this time." Mila laughed, she was enjoying this whole shit. "Look at them so scared of a dead body. Hell naa," she said under her breath.

"She on the move," Troy snapped, as he and Mila walked as fast the high heels and grass would allow. Mila dashed ahead of Troy. She was passionate about this shit. She took off her heels so that she could walk faster.

"Ugh, you walking on this ground with no shoes on" Troy said, rolling his eyes. "What the fuck is that on your shoe is that fucking blood bitch?"

"You know it, these some real red bottoms now," Mila said, laughing.

"Alright, I see her," Mila said, out of breath, while hitting Troy on his shoulder. A sense of victory washed over her when she saw NoNo's daughter hop in the front seat of the car right next to hers.

"Got that ass bitch!" Mila said, rubbing her hands together.

Chapter 68

Mila and Troy rushed over to the whip and hopped inside. They pulled off just in time to get behind the black Benz Coupe that NoNo's daughter was in.

"Fuck yeah," Mila thought, grabbing the ski-masks out of the center console and handed one to Troy.

In the passenger side Troy was taking off his dress and putting on a fitted white tee and some jogging pants and gym shoes. He tore the wig off of his head. He wanted to be comfortable. He was going to be the one to grab her and throw her in the car. His heart was beating and his palms were sweating. He was starting to feel his nerves getting bad.

"What do you got me into?" Troy asked Mila.

"Unless you plan on getting out the car right now, don't blame me for shit! I don't have time to baby your ass. This shit is about to happen so step up or step down!" she responded.

"Na, I'm cool. I'm just saying. Where are we going to take her, back to my house?" Troy said.

"Are you dumb? Hell no. We taking her to that bitch Tessa's house. I know exactly where she lives." Mila said. "Dred would not let her go back to that regular ass house. We good there, and it's not that far away!"

"So we breaking into somebody house too, great just great!" Troy said, throwing his wig in the back seat.

"So now you getting cold feet, fuck that!" Mila said still trailing the BMW. They had been driving for about ten minutes now. Mila's patience was running super thin with Troy's nagging in her ear. As the street they were on turned into a dark curving hill lined by trees Mila saw the perfect opportunity.

"Put on your seat belt," Mila screamed at Troy as she put on hers.

"Why, what you about to do?" Troy asked, looking at Mila, and starting to get pissed himself.

"You got three seconds put it on now or be fucked!" Mila said, looking straight ahead with a deadly look in her eye.

Troy scrambled to grab his seat belt and lock it in as Mila hit the gas on the Truck and slammed into the back of the BMW. Mila tasted the blood on her lip as the force had caused her to be slightly thrown into the steering wheel.

"AHHHHAHAHhhh," Troy was still screaming almost as if he was in shock.

"Get out and get her" Mila said calmly, looking at the BMW that had swerved off the road and smacked right into a tree.

"What did you just do!" Troy said. "I don't want to be a part of a murder!"

Mila pointed her pistol at Troy as she repeated herself. She was in the "I don't give a fuck mode" and there was nothing a muthafucker could say to her. She wanted this lil bitch and she wanted her now.

"Damn, a gun, though, bitch? You got the worst friend of the year award for that shit bitch!" Troy said, putting on his ski mask and getting out of the car, and hoping that everyone in the totaled car was still alive.

Chapter 69

Troy walked over to the car and he could hear the moans of the people inside.

"UGH," he said, retching from the sight inside the car. The driver didn't have her seat belt on and she went right through the window. Her neck was cut to the white meat. He wondered why the air bags didn't deploy.

"Help us" said the girl in the front seat looking up towards Troy.

Once she noticed Troy had a ski mask on, she began to scream for dear life.

"Noooooooooo, Get away from us! Do you know who my father is?" the teenager screamed at the top of her lungs.

"We know, but we don't give a fuck," Troy said, reaching through the window and unbuckling the girl.

Damn she strong, he thought as he withstood her kicking and punching. He tried to be patient with her as he pulled her out of the car, but when she bit him on his back he was good no more. His body was his money and he took very good care of his skin. He was pissed and he could tell that she drew blood and there might be a scar.

Pow!

Troy punched the young girl in her face like she was a man. *Oh shit,* he thought. *I really didn't mean to hit her that hard, it was a reflex.*

Quickly, he pulled her limp body out through the window and threw her over his shoulder. He could see Mila in the car, giving the thumbs up and clapping. *She looked dangerously beautiful,* he thought. All this time he had stayed her friend hoping that she would change. *Would she?* He thought. "I'm not doing life in jail for no fucking body," he said under his breath.

He placed the girl in the back seat and then got in himself.

"Ugh, you not happy? Why you got the do-do face?" Mila asked.

"Happy? People are dead… KIDS are dead! I am trying, but I am just not like you. I care about people," he said, tears streaming down his cheek.

Mila started to drive away from the scene. Troy could not even read her. Her face had gone stone cold.

"I will take you home now," Mila said in a flat, emotionless voice.

Troy felt like he was in the car with a whole different person. He was starting to think she was too unpredictable; *would she ever kill me?* he asked himself. His palms started to sweat and a thick, eerie, feeling swept over him when he realized he didn't know.

Chapter 70

Mila dropped Troy off at home with mixed feelings. He didn't know how close he was to getting shot in his head. As she drove she thought back to her childhood. *NoNo's daughter was such a lucky bitch,* she thought. *She didn't have a care in the world. When I was her age I had to deal with all type of shit.*

Mila pulled up outside of Tessa's small home in a new development on the outskirts of town. Prior to the kidnapping Mila stalked Tessa for weeks, so she had the key to her house and knew the alarm code. "Money can buy you anything these days," Mila said, closing the car door.

****

Souped was happy to be out with everyone but his arm was hurting so damn bad. He would rather be laid up with Tina, he thought, as he sat at the table in VIP. It would not be long before someone recognized him. He was at the top of the blogs.

Tina looked over at Souped with his strong, handsome face. She frowned when she saw his eyes furrowed.

"What's the matter, bae," Tina asked softly.

"My arm hurting," Souped said. "Don't worry about it though, I will be fine."

****

Monty pulled up to Maybelle's front door. He was happy to be dropping her off at home. She had done so much for him. He thought about how Maybelle was such a beautiful person. He looked over at her and thought that she really was not that bad looking. She was in her thirties and it was more of her demeanor that made her seem older. *She had what they called an "old soul,"* he thought.

"Damn," he said as Maybelle got out of the car. "She got ass too," he laughed.

Maybelle could feel Monty's eyes on her. She heard the soft moan escape from his lips. She knew he was staring at her rear end.

He better keep his hands to himself, I am God's property. Won't be no bumping and grinding or knocking down of these walls.

Maybelle knew that she would never get romantic with him, but even still she was very flattered. With that bandage on her face, she had started to feel a little down about her appearance.

I wanna really start eating right and get this extra weight off me, she thought. *I have been given a second chance and I want to live the right way all the way around. Thank you Lord,* she praised to herself as she opened the hallway door to her building.

"Hold up," Monty said, jogging up the walk way, "I'll get the door for you."

"Why thank you young man," Belle replied, with the emphasis on "young."

"Still a man, none-the-less," Monty replied, winking at Maybelle.

She decided not to respond to his comment and headed up the narrow, musty stairway.

Maybelle could never call what this hallway would smell like each day. One day it smelled like feet the next day it would smell like noodles. She could not wait to get inside her apartment. She knew that it would not stink in there. There would be a lot for her to clean but she was more than happy to do the cleaning. Cleaning was her escape, it kept her mind occupied.

Maybelle stuck her key in the door and turned the knob. When she did she was surprised to see that her living room was spotless.

"What in the world," Maybelle said, looking around.

"I hope you don't mind. I took your key from the hospital and came here to clean up. I didn't want you to have to see your own blood," Monty said with his eyes raised, searching her face for a reaction.

"Well," Maybelle replied, thinking to herself, who was she not to accept a kind gesture. She would have to let him know for future references that he should not be entering her apartment unauthorized.

"Thank you," Maybelle said to Monty, kindly.

"I won't invade your space, I promise. I am just so grateful to you" Monty said, smiling.

"Yes, well you are helping me too," Maybelle said, fidgeting. *Is he getting ready to leave?* She thought, *why is he still just standing here?*

"Do you mind if I hang out for a while," Monty asked, looking around her apartment already seeing that it was a nice spot and it was still in the hood. He was seriously sizing Maybelle up for takeover.

"Um, well, for a little while," Mabelle said, *but don't get too comfortable she,* thought but didn't dare say it out loud.

****

Mila pulled into Tessa's driveway.

"This cheap ass house!" she said, laughing, "I bet she enjoying my leftovers!" She lowered the driveway door slowly as she looked toward the back seat to see NoNo's daughter still passed out.

I did this shit, she thought, sending a wave of excitement over her body. *I cannot be fucked with. I am the fucking best at this shit. Look at her ass looking all innocent and shit, I give no fucks. She will be used to get what I want, and used well. I will probably have to kill her ass.* Mila's mind continued to wander as she sat in the car with the radio off. She was starting to doze off and decided that she better get the girl tied up so she can get some rest.

Inside Tessa's house Mila carried the girl's body to Tessa's bedroom and lay her on the bed. She tied her arms to the head of the bed. "That should keep you put," she said, admiring her handy work. Mila grabbed a pillow and a blanket then made a pallet on the floor.

"I am not letting her ass out of my sight. I will let NoNo sweat wondering why his daughter didn't come home," she said, thinking out loud. "That should fuck his head up."

****

Lola pulled up outside of Troy's house a couple of minutes after he went inside.

She got out her car with splatters of blood still on her shirt, looking crazy, sexy and cool. Lola looked like she was the costar in a new horror film.

Knock! Knock! Knock!

Troy sat on his couch trembling, *what the fuck now?* he thought. He wished he had never opened the door for Mila now. He didn't want to be involved in this sick shit right now. Troy was starting to feel bad for the girl and her dead friend. He had turned on the news as soon as he got home, and he was expecting that to be breaking news any minute. Troy got up from his seat as the knocks on the hallway door continued. He hoped that was a visitor knocking for another resident to come out and open the hallway door.

Slowly, he crept over to his window and took a peak. He was not prepared to see Lola ass out there. At least with Mila he knew that she had some love for him. Lola just didn't give a fuck and there was no fucking way he was answering that door. Just as he thought that he saw his next door neighbor open the hallway door and let her in.

"Yea, I just heard him come in a minute ago," the preppy neighbor said to Lola. Troy could hear the whole conversation through the paper thin walls.

"Oh this dumb bitch gonna open the door," he said under his breath. He was feeling like Jason was standing outside his of door. He knew Lola was the thing that nightmares were made of.

"I know she better carry her ass on," Troy said, heading to grab a knife from his kitchen.

Troy paced the floor tapping the knife on his palm as Lola relentlessly knocked on his door. She knew that he was home. Hell, the girl had just told her... He placed his hand on his heart. It was beating fast. He took deep breaths just to try and slow down the pounding.

"Pull it together bish!" he said as he walked over to the door.

"Who is it?" he asked, trying to make his voice sound sleepy.

"Lola, I am here to see my daughter." he responded.

"Hey Lola, Mila is not here and I have company." he said, trying to stop his voice from shaking. He didn't know why she was looking for Mila. There was no telling what was going on between these two.

"Okay, tell her I stopped by!" she said.

Troy watched as Lola turned and walked towards the hallway door. He breathed a sigh of relief, happy he had gotten out of that situation not even having to open his door.

"I am smart is fiz nuk," Troy said under his breath as he plopped down on his couch.

"This fool," Lola said as she walked out the hallway door to the front porch, slowly closing the front door so that she could leave it gently cracked... "Her ass defiantly in there and if she not, he knows something," Lola said. She hated a muthafucka tryna think they on some slick shit. *I don't give a fuck about company I am going in that apartment one way or another. I will set this whole fucking building on fire.* Lola sat outside in her car staring hatefully at Troy's apartment window.

Chapter 71

Dred and Tessa danced the night away. The beach front club had just the right scenery. They took drink after drink and now they were definitely feeling it. The liquor had completely taken over Tessa, and Dred was happy to see her so uninhibited. The way she danced and looked into his eyes had him ready to take her right there on the dance floor. Dred was thinking about the wild drunken sex they would have later tonight. He could not fucking wait!

Over in VIP Souped and Rocko sat with Tina and Asha, talking and having a good time. Souped was still complaining about his arm, but the alcohol had slowly made him start to forget how much it hurt. Tina's smile and sense of humor had set the whole mood. He loved everything thing about her. She was everything that he had been looking for in a woman. He had vowed to himself to treat her right. *Fuck the groupies*, he thought.

****

Above her in the bed, Mila could hear NoNo's daughter stirring. *Oh fuck, this little bitch about to wake up.* Mila sat up on the floor and grabbed her ski mask. As she put it on she smiled, *shit was going to smooth.* She had her, the sun was starting rise outside and she was sure that by now NoNo was looking for her spoiled ass.

Mila stood up and carefully searched the girl's pockets looking for her cell phone.

"Yep, I knew it." Mila said, giggling when she pulled out the girl's bedazzled iPhone. It was locked and Mila was pissed. *Fuck it*, she thought it's time to wake this bitch up. Mila went to Tessa's kitchen, and grabbed a few things.

"This basic bitch ass kitchen," Mila said, kicking Tessa's trash can. This shit was starting to piss her off.

"Cold World!" she screamed as she poured a cup of cold water on the girl's face.

"Huh," the girl mumbled as she woke up. Her vision was blurry and it took her a couple of seconds to realize that she was not dreaming.

"Wakie, wakie," Mila said, trying to disguise her voice. "This is real fucking life!"

"Ahhhhhh!" the girl began to scream at the top of her lungs.

"Shhh," Mila said, as she put the gun up to the girl's temple. "How you handle this situation will determine if you live or die. Do you understand?" Mila stroked the girl's terrified face as the girl pulled away from her shaking and crying.

"WH-Where are my friends?" the girl asked.

"Dead!" Mila yelled, doing jazz fingers and smiling. The teenager whimpered and whispered "no" through her tears that fell like waterfalls down her cheek. She didn't want to cause a commotion, because she knew that her daddy, somehow, would find her.

"What's the unlock code to your phone?" Mila asked.

"Tashabish," she replied.

"Bish is a cuss word and I fucking hope you know that shit. Fast ass little girl," Mila said, dropping her twisted words of wisdom as she unlocked her phone.

"So your name is Tasha? "Mila asked as she began to search her phone.

"Yeah," Tasha replied, trying her best to do as her father taught her and keep her cool.

"Oh, look, Daddy's looking for you!" Mila exclaimed, laughing as she scrolled through the numerous missed calls and text messages from "Daddy".

BUZZ BUZZZ

"Oh that's your Dad now! Perfect timing!" Mila causally answered the phone as she covered the girl's mouth.

****

Lola beat her head against her hands as they gripped the steering wheel. Her knuckles where white, she was squeezing it so hard. Her problem had always been she never knew how to control her anger. Even since she was a child she could remember being completely out of control. Lola looked in the rear view mirror. Her eyes were red and he cheeks flushed. She absolutely hated things not going her way. *I took time out of my day to come see this girl and she wanna pretend not to be in there. Who does she think she's fucking with? I will take my belt off and whip her grown ass.*

Lola thought back to when she first had given birth to Mila. There was no one else in the hospital room. She was young and she had no friends and family. No one loved her and she loved no one. Looking over at Troy's window she kept thinking how ungrateful and disobedient Mila was being. It completely pissed her off. She patted her pocket to be sure that her lighter was there before getting out the car and dashing across the street.

Beep!

A car swerved, nearly hitting Lola, as she threw up her middle finger to the shocked driver.

"Get the fuck outta here!" She screamed at the car as it beeped its horn again and sped off.

She crept around the building like a true stalker and right over to where she guessed Troy's bedroom window would be. Lola grabbed loose twigs and after a few minutes started a small camp like fire right under Troy's window. The breeze fanned the flames which after 20 minutes gave birth to a full on fire creeping up the side of Troy's building.

Satisfied with her work, she took out her cell phone and took a picture.

"Ha ha!" she laughed, clapping her hands together then walking back calmly toward her car. "The roof, the roof, the roof is on fire! We don't need no water let the muthafucka burn," Lola sung, laughing. Inside the apartment Troy lay on the couch, sprawled out sleeping, oblivious to what was going on.

Lola sat in her car watching the smoke start to rise higher into the night sky. She wished that she could stand closer to the house and watch the flames grow, she loved a good fire. Right now, her focus was on seeing Mila's face as she ran out of the burning house.

"Mmmm Hmmm, and I will not be saving her ass! If she dies then it was fucking meant to be," Lola mumbled to herself. It took a few minutes for the glow of the flame to peek around the corner of Troy's building. Lola clapped her hands excitedly. It would not be much longer before Troy's bedroom was as hot as a cheap prostitute's pussy.

When the smoke alarm started to beep it was music to Lola's ears she could hear it all the way outside. Lola tapped her knuckles on her steering wheel making a beat along with the sound of the smoke detectors.

"Mila, bring yo ass out! Mila, bring your ass out!" she sung through her laugher.

****

Troy sat straight up on the couch choking on the thick smoke that was pouring in from his bedroom.

"That crazy ass bitch!" he got up running to try and grab his purse. He briefly thought of the expensive clothes, shoes and purses that he had accumulated this year. Troy wished that he could grab some of his things. He wanted to save his favorite Chanel bag like it was a real person.

"Oh Lawd! She tryna kill me," he said, grabbing his coat out of the closet. Lola knocked on his door earlier and there was not a fucking doubt in his mind that this shit had her name written all over it.

As soon as Troy opened his door the smoke poured into the hallway of the small building.

"Fire, Fire!" Troy screamed in the hallway sounding one hundred percent female. He threw the hallway door open and stepped on the front porch choking. Troy had breathed in some of the smoke when he yelled fire. Once he caught his breath he had to address the fact that his eyes were burning. He rubbed them with the bottom of his shirt as the other residents nearly ran him over rushing to exit the building. The first thing Troy saw when he took his hands away from his eyes and looked up was Mila's mama sitting across the street grinning at him.

"Oh Helllllllllll the Fuck NO!" he yelled, snapping his head around heading straight towards her car.

****

"Listen to me very carefully," Mila said, changing her voice in the receiver.

"We have your daughter. We will kill her if you don't do as we say!" Mila continued, "You will never see her ass again. I will be in touch." Mila hung up on NoNo as she zoned out on Tasha's screams in the background.

She found a pen on the bedside table and jotted NoNo's number on the palm of her hand. As Tasha's cell phone began to ring off the hook, Mila walked to the kitchen. She grabbed a pot, filled it with water and sat it on the stove. Once the water started to boil she dropped Tasha's cell phone in it.

"Try and track that shit," Mila said, laughing. As Mila walked into Tessa's bedroom and saw Tasha she had a brief flash back of once being tied to her bed as a teenager. She felt an eerie feeling in her stomach. Something didn't feel right but she could not call what it was. Shaking it off, she snapped back to reality only to still hear Tasha screaming.

"Shut the fuck up, I am the last person you want to piss off right now!" Mila yelled, shutting her ass right up.

Chapter 72

Maybelle took a pain pill and dozed off shortly after they arrived at her house. When she woke up it was dark outside.

"What time is it?" she mumbled, reaching over for her alarm clock. Is it really that late? Maybelle rubbed the sleep out of her eyes and threw the covers off of her. *Thank you LORD,* she thought. Standing up, she was relieved to be home in her comfy corner of the world. Sliding on her house shoes she thought once again about baby Heaven. She wanted to go visit her in the morning. She missed her already. When Maybelle walked in her living room she was startled to see Monty lying under her sink.

"Hey sleepy head," Monty said, sitting up. "Your pipes were leaking, so I ran out and got the supplies to fix it, I hope you don't mind."

"No, I don't mind," Maybelle said bashfully, looking down at the ground.

These are not the only pipes that need to be fixed, Monty thought.

****

Troy's head was throbbing as he crossed the street as fast as he could. His ears were ringing. He didn't know if it was the smoke alarm or the shear anger. He usually didn't hit bitches but this was not your average bitch. What the fuck was he supposed to do, he reasoned. Lola had just set his house on fire.

"Oh shit!" Lola said, "I guess he was telling the truth and she is not in there. Well whoopedy-fucking-do!" She found it very amusing that Troy was running full speed ahead toward her.

Without blinking she threw her car in reverse, pulled back then hit the gas full speed ahead towards Troy.

When the car hit Troy he was not surprised. As his body rolled over the car he came, for a slit second, eye to eye with Lola through her windshield and it sent shivers down his spine. Troy laid on the ground watching Lola's car swerve as she sped away up the street. He was banged up and he knew he was lucky that she did not have enough speed to hit him harder. Lying on the ground, he felt like a damn fool. Every time he was around Mila something bad happened. He was tired of her energy coming in and destroying shit. He could not explain to himself why he was so drawn to her. She was like a movie come to life. He could hear the gasps of his neighbors as he started to pay more attention to his surroundings.

Troy was still lying in the middle of the street, and his home was still on fire. *All my hard work earning my possessions, you know how many niggas I had to fuck for that shit?* he thought. Troy could hear everyone around him screaming as he began to lift himself up.

"GET UP!" someone yelled.

"Ahhhh!" another person screamed.

Troy looked up to see Lola's car speeding full force up the street towards him, she had come back to finish him off. His life flashed before his eyes. One of his neighbors, someone he didn't even know liked him, grabbed him by his arms and dragged him toward the side walk. He was inches away from being run over. Lola was not done with Troy yet. She threw her car in reverse.

****

Maybelle looked at Monty as he worked under her sink. His muscles flexed and tightened as he removed the pipe under her sink.

"Lord," she said under her breath turning her back to him. She could not stand to look at him anymore. Maybelle didn't want to be tempted. She was rebuking it with everything in her.

Monty was happy she turned her back to him. He was staring at her ass like no tomorrow. *Damn, she keeps her house clean as fuck*, he thought. *I know she know how to cook. She got the same seasonings my grandma used to use. I don't mind a sexy ass older woman.*

Maybelle fidgeted. *It's late at night does he plan to spend the night or something? What in the world is going on in his head?* Monty liked that Maybelle seemed so wholesome and submissive. He felt like he could get his way with her.

I mean my intentions are good, he thought. *I just need to make sure the end result is good*, he laughed to himself. It was oblivious to him that he tended to make the wrong choices when it comes to women.

He is just a boy that is trying hard to be a man, Maybelle thought, shaking her head, *the world is too fast these days.* Maybelle could not ignore the chemistry in the air.

She refused to fall victim to it though. The temptation was there for sure. Maybelle turned to face Monty. When she did her eyes almost popped out of her head. She had not had sex in a while, but she still knew a big dick when she saw one. Monty's pants had shifted and through his exposed boxers she could see the outline of his penis. She closed her eyes hoping to escape from the sight of it. It did not work. The image was burned into her mind.

"Uh uh, it's time for you to go," Maybelle said as nice as she could. Monty dropped his tool and stood up not saying a word. He walked right up to her face and looked her in her eyes.

"Why, what are you afraid of?" Monty asked.

"I don't even know you," she said, frozen in place.

"Ok, solve that problem and get to know me," Monty replied, taking one step closer to her. He reached out and touched the bandage on her face.

Maybelle was starting to feel insecure. She knew that she would have a scar there. She also felt too big. She had been trying to lose weight forever. She figured if she could lose about fifty pounds she would be a strong eight.

"I serve the Lord. I don't want to live in Sin!" Maybelle said, putting her hands up.

"Did he tell you that you were not allowed to be loved," Monty said, looking at her. *I know every type of women there is to know and I know for sure that she falls into the wife category. I don't know if I can do this and I may hurt her, but pain is a part of life,* he thought.

Chapter 73

Once the crew got back from the club Dred and Tessa immediately ran upstairs to the master suite. Dred laughed as he watched her ass jiggle running up the stairs.

POP!

Dred smacked her on her ass playfully. Tessa felt a jolt of electricity pulse through her body. She liked to make love but tonight she wanted that ruff hair pulling, ass smacking, sex. She bit down on her lip hard, thinking of Dred touching her body. The alcohol had her loose and she was sure that this was going to be one wild night.

"Twerk that ass for me," Dred said. He was upstairs in the hallway.

"O.K. Den bae, you like to watch, huh?" she said, biting the tip of her nail as she turned around and looked at him over her shoulder. Tessa bent over and grabbed her ankles while rocking her ass from side to side.

The muffled sound of ass clapping was music to Dred's ears. He loved it. His eyes burned a hole through her soft, round ass as he watched her rub her pussy over her clothes. "Take it off, now!" he said, forcefully rubbing his chin. His hard dick pressed against his shorts. It definitely was starting to need more room. *My dick got claustrophobia*, he thought, adjusting it.

Tessa took off all her clothes as fast as she could. Dred let out a sexy chuckle when she stumbled forward. They were both drunk so he thought she looked super cute.

"You need some help?" he asked, stepping forward.

"Na, you stay right there and watch," she said, laying down on her back and spreading her legs wide open.

"Damn, alright!" Dred said, stepping back. "Right here in the hallway?"

Dred could hear the rest of the group talking and playing music downstairs.

"Man, fuck them they ain't thinking about us," Tessa replied, licking her two fingers.

"Okay Boss!" Dred said, smiling. He truthfully didn't give a fuck either. He loved a freaky ass woman. Tessa began to rub circles around her clit as Dred watched intently. He did not want to miss a moment of this.

"Fuck blinking," he said. Tessa thrust her hips up, raising her ass off of the floor, as she inserted her fingers into her pussy. Her pussy juices were covering her fingers as the combination of alcohol and Dred had her pussy gushing.

****

Rocko and Asha walked into the home office of the beautiful estate. They slipped away from Tina and Souped to get some privacy. Rocko was hoping to get some head. "Damn, what's this?" Asha said grabbing the remote and hitting the power button. In front of them was a huge wall of T.V.'s. Her mouth flung open. She was still in shock at the extravagance of everything. Just days ago she was working at the hospital. Now, here she is with Rocko on an island in a dope ass beach-side estate. It's crazy how life works. When the T.V.'s came on, Rocko and Asha could not believe their fucking eyes.

Chapter 74

Lola tuned her car around and headed back into Troy's direction. His whole body felt like it was on fire, just like his apartment he was watching burn to the ground. Troy was in semi shock, he had been hit by a lot of things, but a car was not one of them. Nothing appeared to be broken. He wiggled his toes, like the girl in Kill Bill. The only difference was his moved immediately. He was grateful to the man who pulled him out the way. He could be dead right now and that was a hard pill to swallow.

"On your feet," one of the men said, tugging on his arm.

"Up now!" another said frantically.

"Oh fuck!" Troy yelled. Lola was coming back towards him again. The people standing around could not believe their eyes. Someone was purposely being run down, outside, in crowd full of people. This was newsworthy. The phones were out and pointed at Troy. He pushed through his pain and got up on his feet as fast as he could. He thought he was out of the way, but a curb didn't mean shit to Lola. She never gave two fucks about rules, especially man made ones.

Screeeeechhh!

Lola's tires squealed as she cut her wheel and went up on the curb in-between two parked cars. Lola was in her happy place. She was terrorizing not only

Troy, but every single person watching. The screams and gasps only made things worse. This was like her crack. The belt was wrapped around her arm and the people were unknowingly pushing the needle in.

"Run, bitch!" Lola yelled out of her car window.

The men who were helping Troy scattered, it was every man for himself now. They already risked their lives for him once, what more did he expect? Troy ran in between two houses as he finally heard sirens. *About fucking time*, he thought. He kept going because he knew for a fact that she would get out of that car and chase his ass. He didn't know how much farther he could run. When he made it to the far end of the back yard he ran out of gas. His knees buckled and his body crumbled to the ground.

Everything spun around him as he struggled to regain his strength.

"I'm not ready to die!" he exclaimed softly.

The sweat poured down Troy's pretty face as his breathing intensified. Gathering all of his strength he crawled over to a nearby tree.

"Please!" he silently cried, "Not yet!"

****

Mila was in cruise control; this type of shit came easy for her. The girl's tears were non-existent to her, a worthless waste of time. Mila no longer believed that crying was useful. For as long as she can remember she was trained to be emotionless.

Mila closed her eyes and sat back in Tessa's chair. Her eyes were heavy and she was exhausted. *I just need a couple of hours*, she thought.

"Hey, I am about to take a nap. Girl, don't try to fucking escape, it won't work. I am a light sleeper. If I catch you I will cut off your baby toe. Word of advice honey, men hate ugly feet!" Mila laughed, taunting Tasha.

The girl's whimpers were really starting to irk Mila. *I know it's a belt around here somewhere, if she doesn't shut the fuck up right now. I know something.* Mila got up from the chair and raced over to Tessa's closet. When she opened the small as closet, she laughed her ass off.

"Bum ass bitch. I am still gonna get your ass honey, just watch!" Mila squealed, dead fucking serious. Searching in the closet she found what she was looking for.

POP!

Mila put the belt together and snapped it, just like she had seen her mother do.

"Tighten up!" Mila said, leaning over in her face.

All Tasha could do was wonder what happened to her. What was it that had made her so cold?

Chapter 75

"Got damn!" Rocky said, looking at Tessa and Dred going at it on the TV screens.

Asha could not believe her eyes that Dred was one sexy ass dude. He had Tessa's leg wrapped around his neck and he was slamming his body down on her. It did not take her to long to see that he knew just what he was doing.

Both of them stood there in silence. The tension was building in the room; they knew they were wrong but they could not peel their eyes off of the screen. This was one of the best pornos they had ever seen in their lives.

Asha started to squirm. It was dick in this room with her and there was no reason why she should not get her some. *I know everyone thinks that I already fucked him, but that's cool. I am not that easy, we cuddled and that shit felt so good.* With Rocko's strong ass arms wrapped around her, she fell fast asleep the other night. That was an unusual occurrence for her. Usually it took a lot for her to fall asleep. Asha had been suffering from mild insomnia.

"Damn, all this time a sexy ass boo thang was the cure," she mumbled.

Rocko was staring intently at Tessa. "Damn, look at those thick ass thighs," he mumbled. His dick was starting to rock up. "I know that pussy good, look at her fuck faces. She bad as fuck."

He looked over at Asha and sized her up. *I wonder what that pussy do*, he thought winking at her.

Asha licked her lips. Rocko was about to get fucked. She didn't know if she would ever get the chance to see Dred naked again so she continued to watch. The muscles in his back were flexing as he moved. *Let me see it, let me see it.* She was hoping he would just pull that dick out for a quick second. There was no doubt in her mind it was huge.

"Oh, shit!" Asha said. When Dred and Tessa finally switched positions she caught a glimpse of his dick. "Wow!"

Asha did not mean to say that out loud. She was sure that Rocko had heard her.

"Oh, you liked that?" Rocko said, chuckling.

"Um, it just caught me off guard," she said, clearing her throat.

"I bet!" Rocko said, her cheeks were flushed, and he could tell she was embarrassed. He did not give a damn. Shit was just about to get real.

"You want to know why they call me Rocko?" he said, bull shitting around with her.

He unzipped his own pants slowly. He wanted to tease her. He wanted to get that pussy wet without even touching her. He bit his lip hard, his white teeth peeking out.

He was ready to fuck, no questions about it. After being so close to her the other night, he thought his dick was going to explode. He had pressed it against her ass for a split second and she had nudged away. Rocko was tired but he didn't feel like pressing the issue. Once his man calmed down he got real close to her and gave her that affection women loved to get. In no time she was fast asleep.

"Let me," Asha said, walking towards him.

Trying to look as sexy as she could she slowly walked over to him. Asha was intimidated by the image of Tessa on the screens. Her body was way better. One thing she knew from being a nurse was not all pussy was built the same. She didn't know about Tessa but her pussy was as tight and wet as they come. In fact, if she fucked him he would definitely need a raincoat, she thought. Not a condom but a real live rain coat.

Slowly, she unzipped the rest of his zipper and slid her hand through the hole in his boxers. Asha gasped as she felt a thick piece of meat in her hands. It bent in half as she pulled it through.

"Oh, you damn sure about to get this pussy, you know that right?" Asha said, taking off her shirt.

"Sit down, daddy," Asha instructed as she motioned towards the desk. Her soft perky breasts hung beneath her and brushed against the inside of Rocko's thighs as she took his tasty dick all the way in her mouth.

"Mmmmmmmm..." she moaned sending vibrations up the sides of his dick.

She looked up into his eyes and told him how much she loved his dick.

"This dick tastes so fucking good. It's so fat and hard," she said softly, with the head of his dick still touching her lips.

Asha sucked and pressed his dick on the inside of her cheeks. She closed her eyes and put her face straight down as she began bobbing up and down on his dick.

Rocko's dick was rock hard and he had to give her a round of fucking applause. She was doing her damn thing!

His dick slid into her mouth... in... and out... in... and out. The taste of his dick was sending her over the edge. She could feel her pussy juices dripping.

The grip around the base of his cock tightened as my head bobs down... and up your cock... down... and up... in... and out... in... and out...

Coming up for air Asha licked his sensitive head as she tilted her head back so that her neck straightened out. Slowly, she leaned forward as his dick entered her mouth. Her throat opened as she stuffed his entire dick down her hungry throat.

Rocko's neatly trimmed hair tickled her cheeks as she felt entire length of his dick in her mouth. She felt the head touching her tonsils. She held it back there, expanding her mouth so she that she could pull in some air through her nose. Asha was hype. She had her doctorate in dick sucking.

Rocko could only stand there in awe as he wondered how the fuck she was doing this shit. His nut was building and when she started to caress his balls he could not hold it any more. Without warning, he shot a thick load of cum down her throat.

Umm damn, he thought when he saw her swallow it whole.

"Go over there and sit down!" Rocko commanded, her pointing toward the couch in the large office.

Asha happily stood and did as she was told. When she sat down he came over and kneeled down in front of her, all the while seducing her with his pretty eyes.

Rocko gently grabbed her breasts and put her firm nipple between his lips into his mouth. Sucking gently, he sent waves of pleasure through Asha. She closes her eyes and arched her back as she enjoyed the sensation of his sexy lips on her body

Undoing the snap of her jeans Rocko slide her panties off, all the while kissing her on her neck. Asha spread her legs wanting Rocko to take a good look at her pussy. Asha grabbed her breasts and started to pinch and pull on them. She got wetter and wetter as he touched her pussy, teasing her. He rubbed the wetness escaping from her tight hole all over her clit.

As Rocko rubbed her clit so good it sent quivers all over her body. He was enjoying watching and teasing her. He slid his finger slowly across her very sensitive love button, preparing her for his tongue.

Barely able to catch her breath, Asha grabbed for him and kissed him as her fingers explore his strong body.

He pushed her further down into the couch and raised her legs to bend her knees. She looked down at his sexy grin as he buried his face in her pussy. He flicked her clit with his tongue and took it between his lips to gently suck on it.

Asha moaned loudly and bucked her pussy into his face. She moaned and told him how good his head was. She wrapped her legs around his legs and rode her orgasm through to the end with Rocko continuing to lick and tease.

When Rocko finally slide into her he could feel his dick stretching her pussy out. They moaned simultaneously, each feeling overwhelmed with pleasure. He pulled back and thrust back in again over and over.

"Daddy, fuck me!" Asha moaned.

Needing no invitation, he thrust his dick in harder and harder as they both moaned and struggled to catch their breath. Her orgasm consumed her body when it released. She felt his heart beating faster followed by spurt after spurt of nut flooding her pussy.

<u>Chapter 76</u>

With Mila dosed off in the chair Tasha knew that she had no choice but to try and escape. Her father raised her to be a fighter and there was no way that she would not go out swinging.

Tasha was no regular teenage girl. NoNo was a King Pin and to her that meant she was a princess. "This lowlife thot," she said under her breath as she wiggled her small hands trying to get free.

***

Lola heard the sirens approaching. She did not feel like going to jail that night. She did a U-turn, fucking up somebody's lawn and took off in the opposite direction.

"Ha, ha, he on my shit list!" Lola said, making a mental note. She did not know why he was on there, but he was and that meant that he was good as dead.

"Where can I find you!" she said, tapping her index finger on her chin.

Lola was an adrenalin junkie. Her high was through the roof. She needed something, anything to tide her over until she found her daughter. She knew exactly what she would do.

****

"So you still want me to leave?" Monty asked. "I will respect your boundaries. I just think that you need somebody here with you. I don't think it's safe here yet."

"Need somebody?" Maybelle asked. "Now you just tried it, because I can tell you right here and now all I need is the LORD!"

"I did not mean to offend you." Monty replied, looking into her eyes, "Maybe I am coming on a little strong." He admitted. "Can you blame me though? When you look in the mirror do you see what I see?"

"Well," Maybelle hesitated, trying to figure out how she could answer the question. "Since we have to handle business in the morning anyway, I guess it's ok if you stay the night. You will be sleeping on the couch."

"I have no problem with that. Are you hungry, can I get you something?" Monty asked sincerely.

"Sure," She said softly, wondering if this was all a part of a bigger design.

****

Tear after tear fell down Tasha's face. She wanted her dad. This whole situation was an eye opener for her. She lay the whole time thinking what she did to deserve this. All of the answers were coming to her. She was a bully in school. She at times liked to disrespect her mother. Now, she could only think what she would not give to be in her mother's arms. Life was a bitch.

Her best friend was dead. She would never in life be able to get the image of her being thrown through that car window out of her. It was embedded there for life. She hoped that she would not see it in her dreams at night.

"Ahhh," she winced as she finally released one of her arms. It had taken hours and her wrists were bloody, but it was worth it.

It took her another fifteen minutes or so to undo her other hand. Tasha was scared to make a sound; her hand was trembling. This lady is certified crazy. *She trying to change her voice but I know exactly who she is,* Tasha resolved.

Quickly, with her heart beating out her chest she inched her way off the bed. When her feet touched the floor she felt like she had been reborn. Even though she was not out of the woods yet, she felt free as a bird.

Tasha crept her way to the front door, once her hand touched the knob she dashed out the door and ran like there was no tomorrow.

After about a half of block Tasha saw a young couple outside smoking and talking on their front porch.

"What's going on!" the man said, squinting his eyes as Tasha rushed toward them. Her appearance told the story of a teenager who had just had a hell of a day.

"She- she," Tasha started to hyperventilate.

"Call the police!" the woman said.

"No-call-m-m-my father!" she said, fighting to calm down and catch her breath.

The man handed her his phone and she dialed her daddy's number.

"Dad! I'm out, I'm out!" She screamed into the phone crying.

"Baby! Where are you?" NoNo said.

"I don't know, I ran and I am using someone's phone!" Tasha replied, relieved to hear his voice again.

"Give them the phone." The man said.

Tasha watched the man talk to her father, shaking and looking around thinking that at any minute that lady would jump out the bushes and grab her.

"He said to take her in our house and he would pay us when he gets here!" the man said.

"How much?" the lady asked, smiling from ear to ear.

"A whole fucking lot. Something is up. Let's get the fuck in the house before whoever did this to her comes back!" the man said, rushing Tasha into their home.

****

Lola pulled up outside of the lavish retirement home.

"Wow, he really set her up nice!" Lola said, looking around. There were beautiful condos lining the property with a huge pond right in the center.

"Whelp, her last days have been nice." Lola laughed.

Dred had no business with that other girl and she was pissed about it. *Well, not really,* she thought. *I just need a reason to fuck some shit up.*

Before she came here she dropped back by Dred's house and snooped around some more. In his kitchen drawer there was a folder with all of his mother's information it in.

"Hehehee!" she laughed a deep hearty laugh as she got out the car. Lola also changed into one of Mila's little black dresses. She pulled her hair up into a sleek chignon. She knew that she was still beautiful, and if she wanted, she could at least fuck any man she wanted.

Something had awoken in her, something that she had allowed to lay dormant. This time around she was fucking up any and everything in her path.

The elderly men in the upscale community watched Lola as she walked by looking like a movie star.

"Oww!" one of them catcalled.

"Not today boys!" Lola said, waving her finger. "I like my men young," she laughed.

"I am not putting in all that work to get y'all dick hard," she laughed, to herself.

She walked, turning heads until she finally got to her destination. Lola stood outside Dred's mother's building feeling excited.

"This bitch gotta go!" she exclaimed

Chapter 77

Everyone had a wild night and they were off to a late start. Asha and Rocko had fucked all night long and she was feeling like they "go together."

Dred sat in the entertainment room nestled up to Tessa watching in movie. He pulled out his phone and clicked on his smart home app.

He had cameras installed all over his crib when he hired the new maid. He was trying to lock down his spot but somewhere along the lines recently he decided for sure that he would be selling that house. He just kept thinking it would be wrong to expect Tessa to start a life in Mila's old space.

Dred pulled up the security cams and took a peek. Everything seemed to be normal until he caught a glimpse of something moving in the corner of the screen.

He clicked on a new camera view. He could not fucking believe that Mila's mom was in his fucking house. He had to admit that she was a dangerous ass bitch, even more so than Mila.

"Wow!" he said, drawing Tina's attention.

"Bro what's that fucked up look on your face about?" Tina asked.

"Man, I got a fucked up feeling. I think we need to go back." he said.

"Go back!?" Asha and Rocko said at the same time. They were not feeling that shit. Why the fuck would they go back now? They just set it off and shit they wanted to fuck on the beach too.

"For real, if y'all two want y'all can just stay here," Dred said, dead serious.

"Yea that's probably what we will do," Rocko said, winking at Asha.

"But fuck that though. What are you saying? What is going on?" Tina asked, still sitting there puzzled. Where this came from, something must have happened.

"Mila's crazy ass momma is at my crib snooping around, this shit is ill." Dred said, draping his hand over his forehead. "What if I would have had a baby by that bitch?"

Shit is crazy, I am one lucky ass nigga main. I can't believe I got out of that shit intact!

"So damn. Shit, I'm down. I was never with that sit and rest shit. I am down as fuck to merk that silly ass hoe." Tina still was trying to wrap her head around how Lola just shot her baby daddy in the head like that.

"Yeah, I'm ready to go back. I would feel better on vacation if shit was settled. I been kinda of worried about my peoples. You think Mila would try to fuck with some of them?" Tessa asked, already knowing the answer to that question.

"Hell, yea she would," Tina said, sitting up straight. She had not thought about that. "Oh, we need to go right fucking now!"

They were all thinking the same thing. Dred hopped on his cell ASAP and called his travel agent. He needed to get back home right this fucking minute.

Rocko and Asha looked at each other relieved that they didn't have to deal with any more of the drama. He was sore as fuck. His bullet wound was worse than Souped. Souped was shot in the arm, he was shot in the back. He rode for Dred, but shit, he had to look out for self too. Plus, this pretty as bitch had him wanting to kick it for a second.

****

In few hours Dred, Tessa, Tina and Souped were packed and ready to head back to the states. At the landing strip Tina and Souped raced ahead of Tessa and Dred.

"What the fuck y'all doing!" Dred asked, getting weak.

"Dibs!" Souped said, running to the private bedroom of the jet, Tina dramatically dove inside and Souped closed the door.

"Ha Haaaa!!" Tina said, doing the dougie.

"Yea Boyyy!" Souped said, doing a Flavor Flav impression.

"Ahh, you cracked nigga!" she said.

"I am about to crack that ass!" Souped said inching closer to her.

"Oh, is that right?" Tina asked, feeling like a million bucks.

When Souped reached out to grab Tina he felt a sharp pain shoot up through his arm. The sensation caused him to wince in pain.

"Bae what's wrong!" Tina said, feeling worried. "You need a fucking Doctor!"

"I know," he said, sitting down on the bed as the plane took off.

Now that she looked closely at him, he looked off. He had the faint appearance of bags around his eyes. Tina could not tell if he was just exhausted or if she should really be worried.

****

Mila woke up in the chair stretching her body out, that shit felt so swell. She felt rejuvenated. She did not know how long she had slept, but it had to be a long ass time.

When she finally cleared her eyes and looked up she was shocked to see that the little bitch was not in the bed.

"Ohhhhhhh shit!" She said, hitting herself upside the head. Mila's head felt like it was about to explode.

Chapter 78

"Every fucking thing is ruined!" she screamed. Mila was no dummy she knew that she had to get the fuck out of dodge. If Tasha made it back to her father it was not doubt in her mind that they were on their way here.

Mila grabbed the comfort off Tessa bed and in one big ole fuck you she put the whole cover on top of the stove and turned on all of the burners.

"If that don't burn this bitch down, I don't know what will" she said, grabbing her keys.

Mila was a page out of her mother's book and she knew it. What she did not know and maybe would never know was if she was born this way or raised this way.

Either way, it was too late to even give a fuck. She walked into the cold, plain garage and shuttered. Every now and then the realization that she was a mother would creep into her mind.

Eventually, she would find a way to repress it, but the girl's pretty face kept invading her thoughts.

Mila shook her head and zoned back out. It was too much on her plate. She had to find a way to get shit back to normal.

Mila's idea of normal was something far different than most people. She was hungry to find a throne and instead of creating one for herself. She would choose to take one.

Mila hopped in the ride and backed out of the drive way. She felt so lost, she didn't even have a home anymore, and the only place that she could go besides a hotel was Troy's house. She knew without a doubt that he would be pissed at her but she had a few thousand dollars in her pocket to cheer him up with.

When Mila turned onto Troy's street she could see the thick cloud of smoke in the air and see the lights of the fire trucks.

"What the fuck!" she said.

Mila parked her car as close as she could get, the street was lit up with activity. People were standing outside in their pajamas talking to the news reporters lining the street.

"Yeah!" Mila could hear an older lady say to the reporter.

"I heard a bunch of commotion. I came outside to see what in the sam hell was going on around her. I saw a lady run that cher fella down with her car. I could not believe my eyes!" the lady said.

"So," the reporter said turning the Mic back to her lips, "You witnessed someone being ran over by a car?"

"Does a bear shit in the woods and wipe its ass with a rabbit?" she asked.

Mila's heart dropped down to her shoe. Please no, please no! She rushed toward the yellow tape that surrounded Troy's apartment building. The fire was still smoldering but for the most part it had been put out.

"Troy!" Mila yelled into the crowd of people.

No one responded. She didn't even expect them to. From the moment she heard that lady speaking she knew that Troy was being run down by her mother. Who else would do something like that? On the other hand, she was hoping with everything in her that she was wrong.

Dam, I am about to start crying?

Mila knew crime scenes very well. She ran up to the first of the three ambulances parked in the middle of the street. It was not until she got to the last one where she finally caught a glimpse of Troy's face.

He sat on a stretcher, with his head bandaged up, but otherwise he looked fine.

His eyes shot daggers right through Mila. He straight up ignored her.

"Troy?" she said.

No response.

"Troy, what happened?" she pushed.

No response.

Troy crossed his arms over his chest and continued to ignore Mila. He was pissed right now there was nothing that she could say to him. *Trust and believe I want my fucking money for my belongings but other than that bitch bye. I been friends with you forever through all of your bullshit.* His mind was reeling. There was so much that he wanted to say to her but now was not the place or the time.

"Sir, can we please pull off. Close that door. That girl out there is getting on my last nerves and I have a headache." he said to the EMT, rolling his eyes.

In twenty-four hours she had come in and literally reduced this shit to rubble. Shaking my damn head, he thought.

As the EMT's closed the doors to the ambulance preparing to pull off, he almost thought that he saw a tears streaming down Mila's face.

Chapter 79

KNOCK! KNOCK!

"I will be right there," a sweet voice said.

Dred's mother, Mahogany, was as sweet as they come. She always went out of her way to help other people.

Mahogany stood about 5'4", and she prided herself on being fit and in shape. She usually rocked a fresh doobie wrap. Her teeth were so white it was hard not to notice them. They completed her rich chocolate skin tone. In her day, people used to say she resembled Diana Ross, although she never cared for big hair. The nickname Mahogany actually came from a movie starring her doppelganger Diana Ross.

Mahogany was very classy. She came from humble beginnings, but she worked hard to retire as principal of one of the local high schools.

Mahogany walked almost if she was floating, with her long dress billowing behind her. Looking through the peep hole she grabbed her chest and immediately pressed her life alert button.

Did Mila's mother actually have the audacity to waltz right up to my door? She crept back and grabbed her cell phone off the counter. She tried to keep her regal composure as she pressed the speed dial for her son.

"Ma?" Dred said, answering the phone quickly. He loved to talk to his mom, so it was a pleasure.

"Lola, is knocking on my door!" she whispered in the phone as Lola knocked again.

Mahogany took the phone away from her mouth and said loudly, "Just a second, I am getting decent!"

"Ma, don't answer that! Go get the gun I gave you now!" he told her.

Dred's breathing was labored. This was his worst fear. He made a mistake. He took great care in making sure no one knew where his mom lived. A man of his stature was sure to have enemies. He always took precautions. Everything had happened so fast. Never did he think the inside of his home would be penetrated by an enemy.

****

Out in the hallway Lola was getting impatient. She knew something was up.

"This fake ass Aunt Viv bitch ain't fooling nobody." Lola said.

"Excuse me Ma'am," said a man.

Lola turned around to see two large securities guards approaching her.

"How can I help you?" she said, attempting to sound normal.

"We need to escort you off the premises." One of the armed guards said.

Mahogany stood with her ear against the door, smiling her graceful smile, "Not today!"

Chapter 80

Tony and his men stepped off the tarmac and into the waiting limousines. He had three well known killers with him. These niggas were the best of the best.

Tony was still sick to his stomach about the altercation he had with Dred outside of the Hotel. *This nigga disrespected me to the fullest, now I get the last laugh,* he thought.

You don't fuck with a man like me, I got power too. Tony coached and hyped himself up. He felt like a lame and he knew that he would continue to feel like a lame until Dred took his last breath.

"You can't punk just anybody," Tony said, "I was gonna let bygones be bygones. He forced my hand. He had to keep fucking with me."

Tony paid good money to find out where Dred ran off to. He felt like catching him on vacation was the perfect plan. He was not expecting niggas to come gunning for him there. Tony was sure that he would be catching him completely off guard. This time he did not want to waste any time, no talking, no nothing. That's how nigga's get fucked up these days, wanting to prove a point first.

"Not me." Tony said. He was thinking so hard he actually said that shit out loud.

"Huh," one of the hitmen said, looking at Tony like he was off. "This nigga over there talking to himself. Ha, this shit crazy."

"Oh na, I was just thinking out loud," Tony replied, relieved to see the beach front estate Dred and his people were coming into view.

"Alright, park here." one of the men said.

****

"I would like to get to know if I could be the kind of girl that you could be down for." Asha sung to Rocko as they cuddled under the covers.

"Hell yeah you can!" he said rubbing her firm ass.

"Mm, kiss me bay," she said, wrapping her arms around him.

Rocko wanted to make sure he did not put the moves on her too smooth. This trip was going to be a few nights to remember but he still wanted to make sure she knew that he had other hoes back home. She was a fucking winner but Rocko was indecisive and he felt like he would be doing the women of the world a disservice if he locked his dick down to just one girl. He knew his shit was good.

He could not play her short though. Shit, you never know what could happen. Her pussy was not the best, but it was definitely in the top five and that was saying a lot.

Her soft lips meshed with his as their tongues danced inside of each other's mouth. Asha was in ecstasy. She was trying her hardest not to let this man get her sprung, but the forecast was looking cloudy with a chance of dick. She knew that this was one of those for life fuck buddies. Maybe one day it could be something more, but in this moment she knew exactly what kind of man he was. It was a shame, but it was true. He was a hoe.

"Can you believe we have this whole house to ourselves?" she said excitedly through the kisses.

"Man this shit is the life!" he said, stretching out on the fluffy down covers.

They planned to run around the beach and this house butt naked all day. *Shit why not?* he thought, *we look good as fuck.*

****

The assassins tossed their backpacks over the back fence then climbed over. They walked over to the sliding back door that was connected to the elaborate patio.

They wanted to get in and out. Tony was in the car waiting for them.

Once inside, they closed the door behind them and pointed their automatic assault rifles in front of them. They were ready to blast on anyone they came across.

Silently they crept straight toward the master suite, Tony wanted Dred killed first. No beating around or bullshitting, he had to go.

The men stood outside of the door to the bed room, they could hear muffled laugher. They didn't want the other people in the house to know they were there yet so they pulled out their pistols equipped with silencers.

Without warning they turned the corner and open fire on the bed. All three men unloaded their clips as they watched the sheets turn from white to red.

****

Asha threw the covers off of her. Her body was on fire and her head was spinning. She looked over. She and Rocko's eyes met as she reached over and grabbed his hand. Rocko tried to speak, but the only thing that came out of his mouth was blood. Knowing that it was the end they both silently took their last breath together as tears dropped from their eyes.

Chapter 81

Dred's blood was boiling. She tried to touch his mama though. Muthafuckas were losing their mind.

"Yeah! I got y'all. Hold her until I get there!" Dred said into the phone. The guards knew Dred very well. He paid them extra to pay very close attention to his mother. They had Lola and they told her they needed to keep her for questioning before grabbing her arms and pulling her into an empty apartment on the same floor as Dred's mother.

He was starting to relax. He almost felt his mother was safe, but he still had to get there as soon as he touched down. Lola was dangerous. He told the men that, and hopefully their asses listened.

About an hour passed before the jet started to descend. He and Tessa talked about Lola between each other. They didn't feel the need to disturb Tina and Souped just yet. From the sounds of it though, there was not much going on in there.

****

Lola sat in the room with the security guards pissed.

"Rappppeeee!!!" Lola screamed in the empty apartment, "Rappeeee, hellppp!"

She smiled at the men as she sat there and calmly screamed.

"Yo, Dog, what the fuck is she doing? Nobody's touching her!" one of the guards said to the other.

"You two are going to jail! RRAAAPEE!!" Lola screamed, projecting her voice and far as she could.

They peeped out the window to see people starting to walk toward the building, looking up to see where the screams were coming from. *Hell nah,* one of them thought, *I am not gonna go to fucking jail over a few dollars.* He did not know what to do. He was leaning towards the fact that they needed to get the fuck out of dodge.

"Man, this jig is up. I think the best thing we can do is go guard his mom. If anything happens to her, our ass is dead!" he said, starting to sweat bullets just thinking of having to face Dred.

"Shit, I agree, we just gotta make sure his ma straight, I would rather go to fucking jail than cross that nigga!" the other men said.

The men left Lola where she stood as she continued to scream her lungs out. They dashed down the hallway towards Mahogany's door hoping not to be seen by anyone.

****

As they filed off the plane Dred was hesitant to tell Souped and Tina that Lola had went after their Mama. Souped looked like he was coming down with something. He had made an executive decision that his ill brother did not need the stress. He needed to get that wound checked out.

"Nigga, what's up man, what you hiding?" Tina said, looking at Dred intently. She had just watched his face go through a range of emotions as they walked to the limo.

"Something is fucking up!" Tina said. She did not want him to get used to keeping her out of the loop. She had claimed her spot as second in command and she needed him to treat her as such. To her that meant there would be no secrets between the two of them.

"T, not now, let me think shit out!" Dred said, getting frustrated. His mama's crib was thirty minutes away from where they were. He knew that he needed to get to her ASAP. Lola ass was DOA!

"What you mean, not now?" she said as they sat in the back of the limo. She was pissed and she wanted to know what the fuck was up.

"What y'all hiding?" Dred asked Tina as she looked away. He had every intention of telling her what was going on. The only person he wanted to keep out of the loop was Souped. He told her a few times already that Souped was not about this life.

Dred was still trying to forgive himself for what had happened at the concert. Mila was his exbitch. He felt responsible for everything that happened.

"I ain't hiding shit, that shit is obvious, he need a doctor. Look at him!" Tina said, whipping the sweat off his forehead with the sleeve of her shirt. Tina had to admit to herself she was frustrated. She was taking her anger towards Mila out on Dred and that shit was not right. *I feel bad and all but I still wanna know what the fuck going on*, she thought.

"Man, I need to be dropped off at home. I got a private doctor coming." Souped said, interjecting. "You can stay with them and see what's up." he said, looking at Tina.

Truthfully Souped wanted them to take care of this shit too. He was fed the fuck up from of all of this bullshit. He personally told Tina that he could not wait until she merked her ass.

He was losing money and everything. He was supposed to be doing shows, and his phone had been ringing off the hook the whole time they were there. The stress was starting to build and when it was combined with the pain he was experiencing he was reaching his limit. *Something gotta fucking shake right the fuck now! Mila goofy ass not gonna run me out of my fucking city.*

Souped was even more worried for his brother. *Shit, she touched me,* he thought, having flash backs from his concert. He knew that he did not have to focus on that. *In Dred's line of business there would always be people out to get him,* he reasoned. This was not the first time a muthafucka had come for his brother and it would not be the last.

Chapter 82

NoNo and the five guys he brought with him trashed Tessa's crib, looking for information on who fucked with his daughter. They already had Tessa's name off the mail in her mail box.

NoNo calmly walked around her apartment as his men filled a couple bags with some of Tessa's personal documents. The pictures on the mantel caught his eye as he walked over to see who this "Tessa" person was.

Looking at the first picture of her he could not say that he ever saw her in his life. She didn't look to be the typed to do something like this he observed, but at this level of the game he did not put shit past anyone.

NoNo grabbed a small photo album off of her coffee table and flicked through the pictures. When he stumbled upon a picture of Dred and Tessa together, that made him throw the book as hard as he could into the wall.

"Dred?" he asked out loud, "He really fucked with my family!" he said as his men gathered around him.

"Wooow!" one of the men said, they already knew what this meant. Shit was about to hit the fan; this was not just any regular beef. This was a hood world war. A lot of people were getting ready to lose their lives behind this shit. One thing they all knew for certain is you didn't fuck with NoNo.

On the same hand, Dred was no hoe either.

****

Lola dashed out the back door of Dred's mother's building and took her heels off as she headed straight for her car.

Rushing across the parking lot she almost got hit by a car that just turned into the community.

"Bitch!" Lola yelled, stomping her feet and staring down the car. She knew about road rage. She did it all the time. She didn't realize she had walk rage too, she laughed to herself.

Lola felt untouchable. She got out of every situation she was put into. She cockily continued towards her car when she heard the door of the car she had just yelled at open.

"You tired as bitch!" Tessa said, hoping out the back seat of the whip they had borrowed from Souped when they dropped him off.

Lola's eyes popped out of her head as she chanced it and dipped toward her car.

Chapter 83

Mila felt lost, and in despair. She decided that she would head back to Dred's crib. *Fuck NoNo*, she reasoned. She would have to go ahead and take care of this shit herself. *I am tired of fucking waiting around. I want my fucking house back.*

Mila had been driving around for hours thinking of Troy and feeling like she was not welcome at the hospital. *Knowing Troy, he probably put me on the do not allow list.* She honestly could not blame him this time. Mila did not usually give a fuck but her soft spot for Troy had grown over the years.

No matter what she had put him through, he always remained someone constant in her life. She knew that if she had no one else she had him.

Mila laughed, reminiscing on the first time they met. A few tears slipped from her eyes and she quickly wiped them away.

"Pull it together!" she said checking herself, "There is no room for weakness, fuck love!" she said to herself.

Mila shuddered when she came to the realization that she sounded just like her mother. When she was child she remembered never wanting to be like her. Now she knew for a fact that she was a mirror image.

She had not only given up her baby but she put it in a fucking trash can. The tears rolled down her cheeks as she cried.

Pulling her car into to the house that she shared with Dred, she noticed there were packages sitting on the door step. "Is the door cracked?" she asked herself. It appeared to be open.

Mila could not believe her luck, she needed a few supplies. Inside this house was an arsenal of weapons, she would be able to pick what she needed, get clothes and choose another whip to drive.

Even though she felt a moment of weakness, Mila was who she was. "I can't change," she said. "I don't even know if I want to."

Chapter 84

Monty and Maybelle sat on her couch in the living room for hours having conversations about everything under the sun. She felt blessed that she ran into him at the hospital. Something was telling her that he was a good guy.

They planned and strategized on how they were going to get custody of baby Heaven. First thing in the morning they planned to visit her in the hospital. They even discussed the possibility of sharing custody of her.

Maybelle helped him to see how much of a gift she was. He could not deny he was already starting to look at her as a daddy's girl. Heaven was a gorgeous child.

"I love the name you chose." Monty said, complementing Maybelle.

"Aww thanks," she said, looking away.

"I love everything about you." He said, hoping she would accept his statement as fact.

Maybelle had just thrown down in the kitchen. She cooked him a four course meal that was everything that he thought it would be. He went back for thirds and was now stuffed to the brim.

Monty was disappointed that Belle didn't respond to his remark. He also could tell that herself esteem was on the low side. Monty welcomed the chance to help her blossom. Her potential was out of this world. There was something about her. He felt drawn to her almost as if there was an invisible string connected from his body to hers. He wished that he was closer to her age, but there would never be anything that he could do about that.

Maybelle looked up at her ceiling wondering what GOD was up to. She knew better than to question His Will.

Looking down, she would never forget the sight of the heavenly gates. Maybelle knew that some people would tell her that she imagined it all. The only word she had to believe was the LORD'S and he had said to her that her work was not done. What he meant by that she did not know, but she prayed for wisdom, patience, peace and power in the long journey ahead.

"Well, I think I will head off to bed," Maybelle said, yawning.

Monty looked away. He could feel himself getting turned on by the rise of her breasts.

"Ok, well, may I walk you to your door?" Monty said in his best southern gentleman accent.

"Why, sure you can." Maybelle said, taking his outstretched hand.

Giggling, they walked over a few feet to Maybelle's bedroom door.

"Goodnight," Monty said, releasing her hand.

Once Maybelle entered her bedroom and closed the door, she was not able to contain her excitement. She did the cabbage patch all the way to her bed.

Belle didn't close the door all the way and a gentle breeze cracked it just enough for Monty to see Maybelle dancing. He laughed silently as he headed back to his comfy spot on the couch.

Chapter 85

"You bitch!" Lola said, while she tried to run with that tight ass dress on.

"You damn right I am that bitch!" Tina said, running towards her ass.

Tessa had gotten out of the car as well and was running to her sister's side, her own pistol pointed straight at Lola.

Tina picked up speed and grabbed Lola by her hair, yanking her back towards her. Lola knew she was a sitting duck there was nothing that she could do. The security guards still had her purse from when they snatched her ass up. Without a weapon, Lola was no match for Tina and Tessa.

Tessa sucker punched Lola while Tina held her hair.

"Oh, this some straight up punk shit!" Lola said, feeling her lip go numb.

"Oh, you talking shit and you killed yo baby daddy, bitch!" Tina said.

"Fuck this bum!" Tessa said, cracking her knuckles. "Let's get her in the car."

"Yeah! We got plenty of time to beat that ass!" Tina said.

Dred got out of his car to help them drag her inside the car. She kicked and screamed the whole way.

Once they got her ass in that car, Tina and Tessa held her ass down as Souped's driver speed out of the parking lot heading straight to Dred's house.

When Lola spit in Tessa's face she lost her damn mind. She uppercut the shit out of Lola. Her blood hit the roof of the car.

"Ughhh!!" Tina and Dred screamed at the same time, grossed the fuck out!

"Nah, man. Nah!" Tina said, laughing, "That is E-Fucking-Nuff! We don't know what kind of shit this bitch got in her blood."

Dred stomach felt weak. He retched, rolling down the window to get some fresh air. Tessa just busted Lola's lip to the white meat. With the other arm he tried his best to help Tina hold Lola down.

Lola was moving about looking like a complete lunatic. Tina was mad but that shit was so funny to her. *This bitch brain done went AWOL!*

Dred didn't like to hit women but he was tired of the bullshit. Instead of punching her in her face, he bopped her ass right on the back of her head, knocking her right the fuck out.

"This bitch breath smell like her ass been drinking on some of the old school Wild Irish Rose. Ughhh. Aye, please let's hurry up!" Tina said, covering her nose.

"What the fuck is that" Dred said, covering his nose with his shirt, it was getting funky as hell in that car!

Bloop Bloop!

"AWWWW fuck!" he said.

"EWWW! EEEWWW!" Tina said.

"Phew fucking WEE!!" Tessa said.

Dred had hit Lola so hard that she had lost her fucking bowels in the back seat of the car.

Tina lost it. She was grossed out and weak as fuck at the same time. She didn't even wanna open her mouth. She was trying to laugh with it closed.

"This bitch got on a dress too! Hell nah!" Tina cried. "This Real Housewives of Shitlanta ass bitch!"

Dred didn't want to laugh, but he could feel it building up. *Tina ass is my fucking nigga,* he thought.

Chapter 86

Mila lay in the bed her and Dred used to share. It was so fucking comfortable. Over the last few days she missed the lavish life she had before. She knew that everything was different now. She would have it back, she promised herself. With Dred out of the way shit was hers for the taking.

All she had to do was pay the right people off and she would have no problem taking over all of Dred's assets. She figured that she could start her own shit with the money in a whole new city. Fuck Dred's goofy ass workers.

She laid there planning his downfall and her come up. Mila had no clue were Dred was. She got up to look around the house for clues.

****

When they pulled up to Dred's house he could immediately tell shit was off. For one, he had a maid so there was no way that there should be packages piled up outside.

Looking over at Lola, it didn't take him long to piece together that the new maid probably was dead as a fucking doornail. How else would Lola have been able to get in his shit!

Dred felt a pang of guilt. That woman had kids. He hired her to help her family and in return had done the exact opposite. He promised that he would take care of her kids if what he was thinking was true.

"Cut the engine off!" Dred instructed the driver. "Don't slam y'all door. We don't know what the fuck is going on here yet!"

They all got out of the car leaving the doors open.

"Who gonna put bring her in," Tina asked.

"Shit, the driver, I will pay him." Dred said, walking toward his window.

"Yo, my man. You carry her up to the living room and I will give you a stack." Dred said, pulling out a roll of fresh one-hundred-dollar bills.

"Deal!" Souped's driver said, getting out the car, collecting his money. He scooped Lola up with no shame and followed them as they went into the house.

"Damn, the door open!" Dred said, He was mad as fuck. There is no way his house should just be wide open like this. He felt like he had allowed Mila to pull him way out of character. He was fucking slipping.

Inside the house that was once alive and beautiful, now felt like a tomb. He prayed that it would not be his.

Chapter 87

Mila walked out of the bedroom, her head pounding. She could not believe how everything turned out. Without Troy she truly felt alone. Her mother didn't love her.

No one did.

Maybe her mother was right. Maybe she was unlovable. Maybe there was no such thing as love. Mila didn't want to figure it out all she wanted was Dred's head on a platter. Somehow she associated his death as being the quick fix to all of her problems.

She stepped out the bedroom and in the corner of her eye she saw that the front door was wide open. She hoped with all of her might that what she was seeing was a mirage.

****

As soon as Tina, who was in front of the pack, caught a glimpse of Mila stepping out into the hallway, she could not believe her luck.

It was almost like time had slowed down and everything was going in slow motion. Tina reached in her waist and pulled out her pistol. As she brought it up she heard Tessa scream, "Aim for her legs," but Tina ignored her.

Tina unloaded her clip in Mila's direction.

***

Dred and Tessa ran over to where Mila lay. It had to be a fucking miracle, she was hit but she was still alive.

"She don't deserve a quick death!" Tessa said, looking up at Dred. "For what she did to me! Everything that fucking happened to me!"

Tessa started crying uncontrollably, seeing that bitch laying there made her so happy. She was finally able to release everything that she had been holding inside. *Now I can finally move on with my life*, she thought.

Dred held Tessa as she looked down at Mila, remembering the promise that she made to her.

"I told your ass!! I told you, you had it coming." Tessa said.

Tina, crying, came over and hugged her sister. She spazzed out on Mila, but once she snapped back she could not wait to fuck both of these bitches up!

"Get the rope!" Tessa yelled, "Let's do this shit!"

****

NoNo sat at a round table in his house with his most trusted staff. There were pictures of Dred and everyone associated with him tacked to the wall.

NoNo beat his fist on the marble table, "Nobody fucks with my family! Dred gonna regret the day he touched my daughter"